GOING TO JERUSALEM

A NOVEL BY

JUDITH BRUDER

ILLUSTRATIONS BY CHARLES WALLER

SIMON AND SCHUSTER | NEW YORK

Copyright © 1979 by Judith Bruder
All rights reserved
including the right of reproduction
in whole or in part in any form
Published by Simon and Schuster
A Division of Gulf & Western Corporation
Simon & Schuster Building
Rockefeller Center
1230 Avenue of the Americas
New York, New York 10020
Designed by Edith Fowler
Manufactured in the United States of America

1 2 3 4 5 6 7 8 9 10

Library of Congress Cataloging in Publication Data

Bruder, Judith, date.
    Going to Jerusalem.

    1. Tales, Jewish. I. Title.
PZ4.B8888Go [PS3552.R795] 813'.54 79-12828
ISBN 0-671-24599-6

For Jane and John,
because it is their birthright

CONTENTS

PROLOGUE

WHEN the winter is past, and the snows are melted and gone, and the flowers have sprung from the earth, and the robins appear on the lawns, and the voice of the power mower is heard in the land; when the garden centers are opened, and the first baseball is thrown out, and the taxes are paid for another year, and the Passover displays blossom in the supermarket; then people feel the urge to travel. You might say it's the need for an Exodus.

So it was raining outside, a warm spring rain, and I was alone in the El Al Lounge at Kennedy Airport, my nose in a guidebook, waiting for my flight to Israel, when a group of tourists wandered in. By some strange quirk of chance, each displayed the little plastic nameplate that read "Promises, Promises," which was the tour that I was on, so they were to be my fellow pilgrims, not just for the flight, but beyond. We were so many that we overflowed the couches and chairs, which made for a necessary amount of friendliness to begin with. And when I tell you that El Al Flight 18 was delayed for over three hours, you'll understand how, by the time we had finally boarded our plane, I could tell you each one's life story: who they were, where they came from, what they did, and what they counted for in their community.

But first you may want to know whether these tourists are real or not. How can I say whether the pilgrims I am going to tell you about are real? They're Jews, after all, and to some extent all Jews are fictional. God has been rearranging them in His novel for over four thousand years already. His beginning, we all agree, was very well organized and clearly laid out. But His plot has become more confused since then, and the keenest minds of the ages haven't been able to see even one chapter ahead. And as for the ending—

How will our story end? God knows.

So let me just say that these passengers to Israel on El Al Flight 18 on a rainy Thursday in April, a week before Passover, were as real (or as fictional) as anybody else who's Jewish.

Now that that point's straightened out, let me introduce you.

An ART DEALER was there, a Temple President,
from a fine family, an old Sephardic family who
traced their lineage back to medieval Spain before the expulsion in 1492. He was American-born,
but he had a slight accent from having grown up
speaking four languages at home. His appearance
was very distinguished, up to the pepper-and-salt
sprinkling his sideburns, and his manners were
perfect. He had good taste in everything he did;
it wasn't confined just to his art gallery, although
his was one of the finest on Fifty-seventh Street.
He carried only recognized old masters, and of
those only the finest pieces. He was very rich, of
course, and he lived on a fifteen-acre estate in
Westchester. But he and his wife were quiet-living
people, and his children went to public school
"just like everyone else." The children were raised
that way, to feel that they were "just like everyone
else," and that to boast of material possessions or
lineage was a sin, and besides, it was in very bad
taste. His search for fine art carried him all over
the world, to Brussels and to Bruges, to Vaux, Ge-
neva, and Lausanne, to Munich and Vienna and
Leningrad. Whenever he was at home, he and his
wife would sit in the third row at temple, quietly
enjoying Friday night services, just like everyone
else. He would never contribute to the temple
without the rabbi's personal assurance that his
contribution would be anonymous. (So it really
was a miracle that everyone knew exactly what
a large gift he had given.) He loved beautiful
things. In his gallery he specialized in paintings,
but in his home he kept the decorative art objects
he himself preferred. He had an exquisite illuminated Flemish Book of Hours, a rare Byzantine

icon ablaze with gold and jewels, and a delicate thirteenth-century ivory madonna that was a miracle of human artistry. All his possessions were like that, in perfect taste, never gaudy or excessive. In everything he did, he was indeed a very worthy, perfect gentleman.

With him there was his son, a COLLEGE DROP-OUT. He was about eighteen, good-looking, shorter than his father and of slender build. His red hair he wore in a blazing curly halo, and his loose embroidered shirt bloomed with gaudy red, yellow, orange, and purple flowers. He carried a guitar, and the songs he played on it and sang in a sweet high tenor voice were all about the land, especially the holy, sacred land of Israel. For he was going to Israel not as a pilgrim, but as an immigrant, a settler, a worker, to live on a kibbutz on the holy soil, to till it and to guard it, and to labor. He had always admired the laborer, he explained, the *am haarez*, the man of the land. Cities and intellectuals and luxury were not for him: so he had told the pretty seventeen-year-old sabra from the kibbutz who had been an exchange student at his Westchester high school last year. When he was a little boy and his father had the chauffeur drive him to the school bus stop, he would bribe the man to stop the limousine far enough away so he could get out and walk and no one would see. And he spent his time singing sweet songs on his guitar, just like David the shepherd boy had sung to his harp. He had taken the Twenty-fourth Psalm, "The earth is the Lord's and the fullness thereof, the world and they that dwell in it," and given it a hard-driving folk-rock

arrangement that was much praised. He was very
polite and soft-spoken in his manner, and had ——
beautifully shaped hands, soft and smooth, that
moved gracefully and easily on his guitar. Sometimes he would paint, mostly in the hard-edge
or Op Art styles, but his paintings were kept in a
locked closet, and he showed them to no one.

The wife of the Art Dealer sat beside her husband and her son. She wore an elegant green suit
cut by a master tailor from some expensive fabric.
On her lapel perched a golden peacock, intri-
cately enameled in blue and green, its tail flashing
myriad diamond eyes, a gift from her husband,
and around her neck was a simple silver *Chai*, the
symbol of life. Her hair was black and sleek like
the feathers of a crow. She headed a staff of six
at home, and never asked them to do anything she
couldn't do herself as well or better. In the early
years (although her husband's family had lots of
money) she had ironed her husband's socks and
shorts with her own hands. She still made sure that
the cook prepared the food exactly as her husband
and her son wanted it. If her husband wanted his
steak overdone and her son wanted his raw, then
that's how each would get his steak, and she would
make do with a little slice from the end of each.

THE CHAIRPERSON OF THE MASSACHUSETTS, CON-
NECTICUT, AND RHODE ISLAND TRI-STATE AREA OF
INTERFAITH COUNCILS was traveling with us also.
She was a very good-natured woman, pleasant
to everyone, and she prided herself on appearing
cheerful all the time no matter how terrible she,
personally, might feel; and on being tolerant. For
example, even though she herself never touched

anything more than a drop of Israeli white wine, she refused to condemn others, the Irish, say, for their drinking habits. She would explain, "Everyone knows *Shikker ve a goy*, drunk like Gentiles (not that they all drink, but still), so you can't *blame* them." In general she tried always to be dignified and worthy of her heavy office. What, after all, could be more important than Interfaith —that the Gentiles should understand the Jews? Educating people, stimulating them, enlightening them: these were her goals in life. Her only impatience with her married daughter was because she hadn't yet had children. She couldn't wait to educate those grandchildren! (But of course then her daughter would have to get rid of the cat because it would jump into the crib and suck out the baby's breath.) At services she followed all the prayers from memory and from those helpful little transliterations, and she had taken every course in her local adult education program that had any connection with Judaism. She had strong feelings on the need for personal integrity and ethics in politics, and she always voted the straight Jewish ticket, although she realized you can get fooled that way, with a Schwarz or a Myers. She was a small, round, fluffy woman, very pretty, with beautiful unwrinkled skin. Her cheeks were rosy, her mouth was small and red, and a perfect Cupid's bow in shape. She had pretty light-blue eyes, and no one ever saw her when her blond hair wasn't *just so*. She wore pretty pastel clothes in soft materials, and to each Tri-State Area Interfaith Council meeting she remembered to wear a gold bracelet with her good-luck *mezuzah* jeweled with

coral and emerald beads. She still had a little trouble sorting out the Ascension from the Assumption, but she reassured herself that it didn't really
matter anyhow, her heart was in the right place.
She was, above all, compassionate; and she loved
children. Which was why she was pained at so
much of what went on in the world today, the
violence and pornography and *ugly* language and
jokes about S–E–X right out in the open, in front
of the children. She was so tenderhearted that
when her children were young she would weep
when she probed their little hands or feet with a
sterilized needle to get out a splinter, and her
tears would splash, and her children forever after
associated splinters with the sting of Mother's salt
upon their wounds.

And with the Chairperson of the Massachusetts,
Connecticut, and Rhode Island Tri-State Area of
Interfaith Councils was her HUSBAND. He was a
very quiet, patient man.

With her also was one of her lieutenants, a
woman with five grandchildren all possessed of
the trinitarian virtues, the three B's: they were
Beautiful, Brilliant, and Blond, and she had a
sheaf of pictures to prove it, at least the beautiful
and blond. Whereas the forte of her chief, the
Chairperson, was tact and diplomacy, the INTER-
FAITH LIEUTENANT prided herself on plain speaking, so that she spoke her mind on what she
thought was right, no matter where the chips
might fall or whom the waves she made might
overwhelm. It was so clear to her that right is right
that she could never understand what had gone
wrong at that momentous Interfaith Council meet-

ing when she suggested that the Holy Trinity be expanded by one, by Mary, the Blessed Mother, because, she explained, what could better express the sacred concept of Motherhood than this Jewish Mother, this Mary, whose relation with her Son provided a metaphor for the relation between a person and God in which we could *all*, Jew and Christian alike, come together in belief. "Isn't that," she said passionately, "what Interfaith is all about, to bring us together and show us what glimpses we can share, from our different perspectives, of the single Truth?" Well, the uproar was terrific! And after the meeting the priest gently explained that, while what she had said was a lovely sentiment, she perhaps needed some clarification on the theological implications of the conditions of deity, while her rabbi took her aside and said, "Interfaith is of course extremely important and enriching, but it isn't necessary to be a fanatic."

Next was a HASID, whose workaday vocation was trading in diamonds, but whose spiritual life was with G–d and his miracle teacher, the awe-inspiring Sieniawer *Rebbe*. Even the crumbs that dropped from the *Rebbe's* beard when he ate were holy, and were fought for by his disciples. Not for the Hasidim the cold and austere pleasures of the Talmud scholars, still less the rational pursuits of the Enlightenment. Man's soul walks with G–d, singing and dancing, eating and drinking, says the *Rebbe;* the brain limps behind painfully trying to understand what the soul spontaneously knows. Denial of such senses, which were given to us by G–d, is denial of Him, and therefore a sin.

G–d gave us this world to enjoy, and enjoy it the diamond trader did. He was a *mensh*, a fine manly man, tall and broad, with curly black earlocks and a carefully groomed and glossy beard like heavy black silk. At business he was shrewd, and as hard as the diamonds he carried in paper twists in the pockets of his plain black weekday coat, diamonds that blazed, when unwrapped, with blue-white cold fire. But the holy days in the diamond trader's life were warmth and fiery light. On Sabbath eve and Sabbath day he was a king in his finely tailored, heavy black gabardine caftan and his broadbrimmed beaver felt hat lavishly trimmed with sable fur. In his home he sat on Friday night, a king, with a velvet *yarmelke* embroidered with golden threads crowning his bald head. And he blessed the sweet deep purple sacramental wine in the gold cup, and he blessed the fine plump braided *challahs* his wife had baked that morning, and he knew that G–d sat beside him. He knew that G–d is everywhere, in the streets trading diamonds and in the *Rebbe* and in the Ark at *shul*, but especially G–d was here, in the golden coins which miraculously floated on top of the chicken soup instead of sinking to the bottom of the bowl. And another miracle! In the steaming soup were snowballs, *knaydlach*, matzo balls as white as snow, and tender and melting only in the warmth of a Sabbath mouth. There was a plump roast chicken, its golden-brown skin crinkling deliciously under the knife, and a fiery orange *tzimmis*, sweet and unctuous, of honeyed carrots, and there were apples and grapes and almonds and walnuts and plump

golden raisins. And before him sat his wife, a
Sabbath queen, a fine woman with plenty of meat
on her bones, the way a woman should be, her
crowning glory, her *sheitel*, her imported wig,
gleaming gold in the candlelight, her eyes properly
downcast and submissive. And by her were four
healthy children, demure girls, and the only
thing he was lacking was a son, a plump little
boy to sit up straight beside him, his young eyes
shining at the sight of the Sabbath table, needing
only the beard and a certain inflation to be his father born again, a son, the visible symbol of Jewish
immortality. But he didn't despair. He had faith.
The son, too, G–d would provide. And G–d didn't
remain at the Sabbath table, but went to the
Hasid's bedroom with him, where was recreated
the vanished paradise of the *shtetl*-that-never-was,
the plump pillows stuffed with goose feathers,
and the *yarmelke* thrown by his wife on the crisp
ironed white sheets to aver that she was clean
and ready to be fruitful and to multiply. Let sterile scholars study Torah texts night and day; they
miss the whole point, said the Hasid. G–d gave us
the world to enjoy. And He put women in it, didn't
he? So—enjoy! (And God knows he's right.)

There was also a FUNDRAISER, and he was a
truly remarkable man, a man for all moods and
all sorts and all seasons. He carried three skullcaps
in his pocket at all times. One was a thin, worn
black rayon *yarmelke* that he wore when he was
appealing to older, more austere, sober-minded
patriarchs. Then he carried a blue velvet *yarmelke*
embroidered in gold and silver thread for meeting
with opulent businessmen whose creed was that

money belongs where money already is. And for

the few eccentrics who prided themselves on being modern and up-to-date, but still gave money for traditional charitable purposes and liked their locker-room jokes sprinkled with Yiddishisms, he carried a plaid skullcap. (It was the Macfarlane tartan.) And in his mouth there were speeches to match. He was a wandering minstrel who offered jokes and piety and a pocketful of honor for the taking, an expert on the tax laws, and a better psychologist than many a man who has the degree. If his record of administrative expenses had not been consistently far above the national average for fundraisers, he would have been even more in demand by yeshivas and other worthy institutions than he was. His approaches were the velvet glove, the iron hand, the carrot, the stick, and the hammerlock, or no-holds-barred, and he did most handsomely before Yom Kippur, the Day of Atonement. And he was always courteous and deferential with the rich, which pleased them; and he could hold any liquor in any amount, but he preferred a cordial glass of Amaretto di Saronno, savored slowly, with wealthy widows of a certain age. He was a bachelor, with a bright eye for the ladies. But he never forgot the main purpose of his life, the relief of the deserving poor; and his couplings were always sanctified by an ample donation from his partner, who found her generosity doubly rewarded, measure for measure, doubly blessed, by God and by our fundraiser.

A RETIRED MERCHANT was sitting next to him. He had owned a general store in Harrisburg, Pennsylvania, for forty years, and he wasn't rich, but he

made a nice dollar, and he was a Rotarian and a
Lion and a Mason and past second vice-president
of the Chamber of Commerce. And every day
his lapel boasted a different insignia. When his
wife died—it was the winter of the big snows—he
sold the store and moved to Miami, where he became a familiar face in several brokerage board-
rooms, and he had a standing order for *The Wall
Street Journal* every day and *Barrons Weekly*. He
was a careful man with a dollar, who recounted
how he had made his money in the solemn style
befitting serious matters like business and the stock
market. And he was very well informed on eco-
nomic theory and politics, and he could talk
for hours on the importance of government regula-
tion of labor and the importance of laissez-faire
capitalism (the real thing, not that watery social-
ism all those government spendthrifts keep push-
ing down our throats) to the smaller merchants
who, as everyone knows, are the solid middle
class upon which our whole American system of
free enterprise and well-being rests. He had substantial investments in the market, but he never
got stung by whiz-kid fund fads or get-rich-quick
underwritings. He kept the size of his margin balance strictly between him and his broker, and he
told everybody how he'd bought EZI at 24½ two
years ago, and it went to 48 in six months, but he
told nobody when he sold it and for what price.
He had remarried, a youngish widow, when he
was in Miami, and they had recently moved to
New York, to the East Side, and the cost of living there and the charge accounts in the Fifth Avenue stores and the condominium maintenance

were eating him up, not like it was in Miami, or
in Harrisburg, Pennsylvania.

In a corner quietly sat a SCRIBE, a *sofer,* a young
man whose piety and exquisite calligraphy created gloriously lettered and illuminated *ketubot,*
marriage contracts, and sparkling Torah scrolls,
bright black letters dancing across the parchment,
but who had to eke out a living for his family by
teaching little boys their *Alef Bet* in a tiny Hebrew school in Far Rockaway. He was slender and
blond, and looked scarcely more than a boy himself. He had received his M.A. in Fine Arts from
Princeton, then set out for the Vermont woods
with a natural beard and a barefoot young wife
who constructed their organic clothing on a sew-
ing machine powered by a foot treadle. She has
since traded her beaded headband for a ritual wig,
dark stockings, and long-sleeved dresses. He had a
beard then, and he has a beard now, but somehow,
it's not the same beard. For he had changed direction once again, this time looking for his True
North in a wonder rabbi in Far Rockaway, and he'd
begun his studies all over again, with Torah and
Mishnah and *Gemara.* He would rather study his
well-thumbed books, bound in black or dull red
leather, than eat or sleep or anything else, except
perhaps pray. For he offered up all the appropriate
blessings for every day, a prayer on rising up and
on lying down, on binding his phylacteries for
further prayer, on every morsel of food, on cutting
his fingernails, on seeing a rainbow. He offered up
at least one hundred blessings every day, and formal prayers he offered three times daily, four times
on Sabbaths, New Moons, and major festivals, and

five times on the Day of Atonement. With all his piety, he had a very small balance in the bank, and whatever his *ketubot* brought in, it was spent first on Hebrew books. He spoke no more than was needed, and that little he said with respect and for its lofty moral meaning, while his eyes shone with the love of Torah. Moral virtue was always the substance of his conversation, and he was happy studying, and he would have been happy teaching if only his pupils had wanted to hear what he must teach. Because he wasn't worldly enough to deal with establishment jobs, his clothes were often threadbare, although they were always spotless. His wife and his three small children, none over five years old, were also always immaculately clean. But their clothes, while plain, were of the highest quality, because while his mother admired piety and sanctity as much as the next one, for her grandchildren and her daughter-in-law too far was too far, and enough was enough.

A LAWYER was with us, an urbane man of wit and charm. He had a silken tongue whose edge was razor-sharp; so smoothly slashing was his humor that his victims smiled even as their heads were severed. His sleek, round head, somewhat small, topped a tall, thin body, rather like an inverted exclamation point. He was an elegant dresser, always this side of too sharp, and gold-rimmed aviator's sunglasses shielded his eyes at all times. He was a walking law library. He could cite with equal ease precedents for and against any matter. Juries loved him, because his dry legal substance was always salted with wit. His specialty was negligence cases. His compassion was unbounded: he took

for his own the Biblical text Justice, justice shall
you pursue, and such a zealot for justice unfor-
tunate accident victims have rarely seen. And just
imagine! If they didn't have enough money to re-
tain him, he would represent them for nothing and
only charge a contingency fee if he won their case.
He won the highest settlements of any of his fellows, and his clients would rise up and, clutching
their checks minus a substantial percentage, call
him blessed. And he was sharp on his own account: all his fees he invested in shopping centers
and in other tax shelters. In every court he had a
friend who was delighted to see him and delighted
to help him, but who was just a little nervous until
he left. He took delight in puncturing balloons
of pretense or hypocrisy, no matter who was holding them, man, woman, or child, and took no care
at all of any tears that followed. No lawyer was as
busy and in demand as he was, and yet he seemed
even busier than he was; as practical psychology, I
think this was very sound, don't you?

Next to him sat a PHILANTHROPIST and his wife,
pillars and servants of their suburban community.
Between them they served on the boards of four
golf clubs, three tennis clubs, two synagogues,
and a civic association. In addition, he was the
treasurer of the PTA, a school board member (rep-
resenting the low-tax party), and head of the annual Community Fund Drive. He was a bulwark of
United Jewish Appeal fundraising dinners, and
beamed like the sun whenever his pledge (it was
always the biggest) was announced. He was a large
man, and his wife was large, and their home was
filled with generous armchairs and comfortable

sofas to sink into, and carpet that swallowed your
feet, it was so thick. His house was never without
all manner of delicacies of fish and flesh, and all in
abundance. Steak was for every day. In winter on
his table were the reddest, biggest summer straw-
berries, and huge hothouse honeydew melons
whose juice would gush forth at the lightest stroke
of a knife across their smooth frosted sides. In his
house it snowed meat and drink, and the dining-
room table was always set for company. After all,
he said, doesn't Ecclesiastes tell us that a man has
no better thing under the sun than to eat and to
drink, and to be merry? Their daughter's wedding was a legend: it lasted from one morning until the next, with two bands pouring forth music
continuously in a huge tent hung with white and
gold daisies spilling from great gilt tubs, and the
ring of dancers to do the hora swelled as large as
the tent. He knew, he said, that three things expand a man's spirit: a beautiful dwelling, a beautiful wife, and beautiful clothes; and he did his best.
For him, too much was only the beginning. As he
sailed through his years, a wake of bronze plaques
testified to his passage. All these riches flowed
from the family business, because he came from
an old German-Jewish family of immense pres-
tige and wealth. But he didn't only take from the
business; no, he was as excellent a businessman as
he was a philanthropist. When the workers at his
upstate factory struck, he had that strike broken
in four days, and no increase in wages either. A
good name, he always said, is rather to be chosen
than great riches, but both together are best.

A group of BUSINESSMEN and their wives took

up several seats. Some were from Westchester, or

maybe it was Long Island, I forget exactly which,

but it was some New York suburb, and the others

were from Atlanta or some other small Southern
town. The New Yorkers were in toys, or in
plastics or in sweaters, or in discount appliances.
And, allowing for individual variance in height
and weight, they might have been a band of
brothers, snow-white hair (layer-cut) capping
large guileless baby faces lit by shrewd cold eyes
frostily twinkling beyond a cigar-smoke screen.
They were very clean and scoured shiny-pink, and
they smelled of musk oil for men and of Havana
cigars. Each week a blond *shiksa* manicurist
named Muriel (or Dorothy or Alice) carefully removed their diamond rings from their pinky fingers
before plunging plump pink hands into white
sudsy baths. Everything about them was clean
and new: suits (Cardin), shoes (Bally), ties
(Givenchy), shirts (Turnbull & Asser), gold digi-
tal watches (Patek Philippe) that concealed the
time from all except their owners. Oh, yes, and
their money was new. In local delicatessens on
Sunday mornings they shouldered their way,
growling, to the front of the crowded counter.
"Gimme a pound of Novy, the thinnest." "Gimme a
nice whitefish, the fattest." "Gimme a nice piece
sturgeon, the best." And for growling "Gimme,"
they wore Harris tweeds and Allan Solly shirts.
They were all exponents of the new high style:
Speak Yiddish, dress British. Their expensive wives
bore the same family resemblance. They were all
blond, all slim, all tennis players. They all wore
perforated Adidas tennis sneakers (although the

color of the pompoms on their cute little tennis socks varied according to the personality of the wearer). They didn't have to feel guilty about playing tennis in the afternoon, either, because the housekeeper was home for the children. They all drove Mercedes Benzes, and they all wore Cartier watches. I don't think they all went to the same hairdresser, although it looked as if they did, and the closer one's hair style matched another's, the happier they both were. Each was an expert player of "The Name Game." For instance, they all knew that at this time Gucci bags and Pucci prints and Louis Vuitton everything were definitely *out*. The challenge and the gamble lay in being the first to spot who was coming *in*. So they shopped religiously at Bloomingdale's, sunglasses shoved on top of their heads, turning blind eyes to the heavens.

Now the Southern businessmen, they owned dry-goods stores or hardware stores or shoestores. There were quite a few of these Southerners, but you often didn't notice they were there, so quiet and subdued were they, until one would say hello to you in a pleasant voice, and his or her face would wear a pleasant smile, and their Southern drawl would transmute brisk Hebrew words of greeting into something soft and strange and exotic to a Northern ear.

The women were very nicely dressed, often in flowered prints, unremarkable but soothing to the eye. They were of a certain age, most of them, and as often as not they had gray hair and were, if not plump, then ample; and the men were also unremarkable. Wherever we went and there was a line, they didn't shove or jostle or look for some-

one to complain to in a loud and angry voice, but
they talked among each other, the women about
their children and their grandchildren and the
sisterhoods and Hadassah groups and civic sym-
phonies they worked for, and the men about
those perennial favorites, business and politics
(they were conservative in both), and it was all
quite ordinary if you overheard it, but somehow,
when it was time to move on again, someone had
to summon the group from conversation, and
they all looked around with a slightly bewildered
air before gathering themselves together and re-
joining our world.

And they were all very polite and friendly to the
others on our tour, with one exception. It was a
strange thing, but the businessmen and their wives
from New York and the businessmen and their
wives from Atlanta never seemed to mix, although
I would have thought they'd have a lot in common, but they never spoke to one another and
never mingled, but always stayed separate, like oil
and water.

A little apart there sat a short-order COOK, a
brawny, beefy man, sweating even in our air-
conditioned lounge. He was the fastest and the
best short-order cook in the entire Cleveland area,
and he could prepare perfect eggs whether
scrambled, poached, boiled, coddled, fried up or
easy over. And he could make a malted while
flipping pancakes and never miss a beat. When he
leaned over the fire to tend his hamburgers, the
sweat would drip from his shiny bald head, and
the flames would sputter and spit. His rice pudding was the creamiest to be found. He seldom

smiled and seldom spoke, and then mostly in the language of luncheonettes: "Draw one," "Burn one," "A side of down." But the corners of his mouth sometimes twitched a little at an order of poached eggs on toast: "Adam and Eve on a raft." He smelled of alcohol, and even though he swigged at frequent intervals from a bottle he kept by the grill, his hand never lost its cunning with the waffles or the hash browns. So hairy were his forearms that not even the regulars could easily spot the number tattooed above his left wrist, a souvenir from Auschwitz.

An ENGLISH PROFESSOR was with us, too, in leather sandals and faded jeans, his sport shirt of many colors unbuttoned far enough down to let the pieces of his silver conch necklace gleam against his curly graying chest hairs, where a peace sign used to hang. He was one of the original long-haired radicals of the sixties. He'd marched for the blacks and against the Vietnam war, and fasted for Biafra (although never for Yom Kippur). He was proud when rednecks called him a bleeding-heart liberal, although he never found a single drop to spare for any Jewish cause. The Holocaust? Someone else's bad dream. On the commune where he had briefly lived, he had violent arguments with deluded fellow members who compared it to a kibbutz. A black college student, a classmate at Dartmouth, had rejected his help during a demonstration of Black-Arab solidarity, and had told him, "We don't trust you. You turn away from your own brothers today, you turn away from us tomorrow." He had gone back to his room and cried, and cursed the fate that had borne him to a

Jewish mother. But now his pioneering moustache
and beard were graying; he was an establishment
Marxist, a firebrand whose embers had burned
down to glowing ashes. They gave off a comfortable warmth as he cruised the academic conference circuit, weighing anchor at congenial ports like the Universities of Hawaii and Texas and Florida, and Sarah Lawrence and Bennington and Vassar, and now Tel Aviv. His companion was a twenty-one-year-old undergraduate, a beautiful blond Presbyterian from Phoenix, Arizona, who, before discovering the halls of Academe, had been a blue-ribbon winner in regional horse shows. He had been born Shimon Cohen, but had long ago gone to court to change all that, and she knew him only as Simon Priest, Professor of English Literature.

There was a PLASTIC SURGEON, the biggest man in his field, devoutly confirmed in his calling, which he saw as completing and improving God's handiwork, at an appropriate price. He stood six feet, three and one-half inches, and had massive hands, with fingers like sausages. But with them he worked magic. He could take in or let out noses and chins. The track of crow's-feet he could wipe away, and eliminate the sag in eye pouches, jowls, breasts, bellies, and buttocks. He was a very perfect practitioner, and perfection was his goal. Orthodontists and dermatologists? Mere cosmeticians, he confided. His art went to the root of the matter. He knew—who better?—that beauty is indeed skin-deep: who doesn't judge a book by its cover? His patients, looking in their full-length mirrors, blessed their Re-Creator. And he worked closely with his friend, the administrator of a private hospital (in which our plastic surgeon had a one-third interest), so that his ladies could be comfortable while their black-and-blue faded and their swellings subsided. His office was on the ground floor of a fine building on Fifth Avenue; he lived with his wife in a penthouse twenty stories above, over the office. He had surely been destined to his profession, for he had been born under the influence of the planet Mars, and a friend had told him that anyone born under Mars was sure to be a shedder of blood—a surgeon, a thief, or a slaughterer. He had gone to Hebrew school under protest until he was thirteen and a Bar Mitzvah, and he hadn't set foot in a synagogue from that day to this. In all conscience, he said, he could not, as a man of science, send his children to Hebrew school to study mumbo jumbo and superstitition. But he flew to Israel during the Six Day War at his own expense and spent three almost-sleepless weeks standing over an operating table putting faces back on soldiers. The soldiers mostly were Israelis, but sometimes they were Arabs, and they went on the operating table, too, and no questions were asked. And lo! he had cast his bread upon the waters and it had come back buttered. For it was truly providential that the newspapers here picked up the nickname the soldiers had given him, "Balm in Gilead," and the resulting publicity brought in a great sea of new patients that nearly flooded his office, and he had had to open a second office and divide the sea.

A WIDOW there was, from Bridgeport, where she owned a knitting store, and carried only the finest,

softest, brightest yarns. And her fingers were so
clever! Golden hands she had, and she could
stitch and shape and block to every woman's perfect measure, and so her knitting store flourished.
In her own home town synagogue she was the un-
official "greeter" at Friday-night services; she stood
by the door and smiled and kissed and shook
hands with everyone. But woe to the unwary Sis-
terhood member (it could only be a new one, the
old ones all knew) who tried to pour from the big
coffee urn unless our Eva was away that night, or
had graciously granted a special dispensation, to a
first-time grandmother, say, or the mother of a
bride-to-be. She had red hair, and a high color,
and green eyes, and she spoke her mind as she felt
it, as it is said, "What's on the tongue is on the
lung." Her figure was good and ample, and she was
her own best advertisement for the lure of hand-
knit clothes. She was a little deaf, but she knew
how to turn a good ear, and she never let it hold
her back from the center of a conversation. Although she often sighed for the days of the
patriarchs and reflected that men aren't what they
used to be, she always added briskly, "But then
again, what is?" And so she was always "looking."
Three husbands she'd stood up with under the
chuppa, the marriage canopy, so far, and she
knew more of men than anyone, and still she was
ready to try again because, as it is said, "It is better to live in companionship than in widowhood,"
and, it is also said, "He who has no wife lives without goods or help or joy or blessing or atonement,
and it's a pity on him." She was a well-traveled
woman, and had stood with tour groups on the

slopes of volcanoes in Hawaii and Italy and on lines at both Disneylands, East and West. She had attended Sabbath services in Rome, London, Paris, Tokyo, and Kowloon. She kept a large round orange felt hat rolled up in the corner of her suit-case to wear to synagogue, and the hat shone like the sun to mark her presence well up toward the front of the women's balcony. And if her voice was heard she was not ashamed, because she could pray as well as any man.

A good religious man there was, a poor RABBI of an inner-city backwater, but he was rich in holy thoughts and works. He was a learned man who liked to preach and teach, but, he said, he had learned the answer to only four questions. Who is wise? He who learns from all men. Who is strong? He who controls his inclinations. Who is wealthy? He who is content in his portion. Who is hon-ored? He who honors others. He recognized that his answers might be eccentric, but he was happy with them; and other questions, such as how to ex-plain the good fortune of the wicked or the suffer-ings of the righteous, he said he had to leave to God to answer. His congregation had dwindled sadly, and their homes were far-flung in run-down, even dangerous, areas. But he never hesitated, even at night, to visit the sick, and he truly believed in the face of all worldly wisdom that it is better to visit the house of mourning than the house of rejoicing. He said, when asked why he didn't seek pleasanter, more lucrative pastures elsewhere, that it was a sorry shepherd who ran from his flock when the wolves were prowling around them, and so he stayed with those the suburban Exodus had left

behind, the old, the sick, the poor. In a time when
the community is in anguish, he said, one should
not say, "I will go home, eat and drink, and rest
content." Rather, it was a *mitzvah* for a man to
share in the community's anguish. The blessing of
his infancy had been the same as any Jewish
child's: May he enter into Torah, into marriage,
and into good deeds. But the spirit of his blessing
remained with him after the sound of the words
had died away, and so he grew up. He was a
good husband to his wife and a good father to his
children; he fled from honor, but ran to do good
deeds; and he not only preached and taught the
Torah, but first he lived it, so that he entered into
it, and indeed his life *became* Torah. His sermons,
however, were another matter. In one of his rare
ventures into modern slang, he prided himself in
his sermons on "winging it," because, he said, it
made him think of angels and heavenly inspiration. (His wife knew it was because he hated to
sit down and prepare and polish and edit a sermon, but she had long since stopped nagging
him.) He didn't despise sinners, either, but spoke
to them with patience and mild words. But the
person who was obstinate or unrepentant or com-
placent, that person the Rabbi would sternly repri-
mand. He would comfort the disturbed, yes; but he
would also disturb the comfortable. He was an
ugly man, but when he spoke, his voice sounded
with sweet, solemn music, and when he smiled, the
darkest corners filled with radiance; and his name
was Abraham.

With him was the RABBI'S WIFE, the *Rebbitzen*.
She came from Texas, and in all her years in the

city she felt a sweet sadness when she pictured
the rambling frame house on the fringe of the oil
fields where her immigrant parents had lived. Like
flipping the pages of a photograph album she
could turn the scenes in the back of her mind: her
Mamma driving a buggy, milking a cow, feeding
the chickens, nursing six children. She remembered the excitement during the year when the
ritual slaughterer came all the way from Galves-
ton at the expense of the six Jewish families in
their outpost town, and slaughtered enough so
that each family might taste meat, kosher meat,
one time a week. She respected her husband's wisdom, and didn't claim any but some plain down-
to-earth knowledge for her own. For instance,
she would say, "If you have to sew something
while you're wearing it, chew a piece of thread so
you don't sew up your brains." Her sayings were
inelegant, but to the point; and when she said
of someone, "If I could buy him for what he's
worth and sell him for what he thinks he's worth,
I'd be a millionaire," her husband knew it would
be wise to listen to that man's case with extra cau-
tion. And it was she who, after the Rabbi had
counseled a young couple on the solemnity
of marriage, would offer them blackberry brandy
and honey cake and tell them to remember just
two things: That when love is strong, a bed thin
as the edge of a razor blade is enough, but when
love grows weak, the biggest bed won't be big
enough; and also that any love which depends on
a reason, if the reason goes away, the love goes
away, but a love that doesn't depend on a reason
will never go away. She worried about the Rabbi

in his comings and in his goings, but she smiled
and kissed him goodbye all the same, and never
told him not to go, not even late at night in winter, when she'd have to bite her lip to keep the
words back. And she was healthy always, and she
knew why. It was because she always followed
the saying of her mamma, she should rest in peace,
to eat a third, drink a third, and leave a third of
your stomach empty, so that if you become angry,
your stomach will have room to boil. There had
been troubles and sorrows in her life—in whose life
aren't there troubles and sorrows?—but she understood that it's part of the bargain that you love
God with a whole heart and bless Him in bad times
the same way that you do in good. And she had
taken for her own the saying from Micah, "It hath
been told thee, O woman, what is good, and what
the Lord doth require of thee: only to do justly,
and to love mercy, and to walk humbly with thy
God."

A CABDRIVER was on our tour, thick-necked,
broad-shouldered, loud-voiced, a bull of a man.
He was bald on his head, but hairy everywhere
else. Stiff red hair, like the bristles of a sow's ear,
sprouted from his ears and nostrils. Curly red fur
matted his forearms, his chest, the back of his
neck and his hands. He was the finest cabby in the
city, and he knew the best and quickest routes
to any destination. (Whether he always took them
or not, I don't know.) And the way he drove! Like
a champion he was. Sometimes he sent his cab
skimming lightly through traffic, like a gull or an
Olympic figure skater. Sometimes he plowed
straight ahead, a fullback bulling across the five-

yard line and goal to go. Sometimes he would slalom down Fifth Avenue and scatter pedestrians, like flocks of chickens, before him. (His favorite television program was the Saturday *Wide World of Sports*.) His wife was traveling with him. She was a small woman, but she had a truly monumental rear end, of which he was very proud. "She's built," he'd say, and wink, "like the back end of a brick you-know-what." That is, if his daughter was around, because it isn't nice to use words like shithouse in front of the children. She was a child, at least she was still only fifteen, but she was really built, just like her mother, and she looked like twenty-five, and don't think he didn't worry about her plenty. They were bossy females, both of them, and sometimes they'd screech at him, shrill as barnyard fowl, but he'd bellow back at them and they'd shut up. He was cock of his own walk. This was a business trip, in a way, for him, because isn't the land of Israel the Paradise of cabdrivers? There drivers drive faster, follow closer, and honk louder than anywhere else in the world. He was proud of being a cabby, even in this day and age where every little *pisher* had to get a college degree and then didn't want to dirty his hands with work. And maybe there hadn't been enough money for him to go to college, or finish high school for that matter. But don't think he was stupid. He couldn't read Hebrew, but he'd managed to study the Bible. And he would say to himself the verse he'd found in 2 Kings IX, "Thy driving is like the driving of Jehu the son of Nimshi; for he driveth furiously"; and he would think of himself as Jehu, the charioteer, who warred

against the offspring of Jezebel, bastards and
sons of bitches just like the wanton and malicious
and incompetent drivers and pedestrians he bat-
tled daily. And he cursed them to the same fate,
that they shall be eaten by dogs in the streets of
Jezreel, which must be like the South Bronx. At the
evening hour he would recite this prayer that
he'd made up himself, while he steered through
the crowded streets: "Lord of the World, if you
needed a cab, you know that mine would be
ready and available to you at all times, even on
Fridays and rainy afternoons at rush hour, and I
would keep the flag down, even though I make my
living driving my cab, special for You."

The EXECUTIVE DIRECTOR of a large suburban
temple was along also. He was a tall, thin man
with a sour stomach and a sour smile, and he
gulped down Tums by the handful from the rolls
in his desk drawer, all day long. He had over thirty
bosses, experts on all temple affairs, who were the
board of trustees, at least a dozen of whom knew
what they were doing, all with college degrees and
several with master's. And yet the Director, with
his business-school certificate, ran the temple show.
He kept the books in perfect order; he sched-
uled all Bar Mitzvahs, meetings, services. You
couldn't get married in the temple without his
okay, and it was a good idea to check with him before dying, if possible. He hired and fired; he dealt
with caterers, musicians, garbage men, suppliers,
building inspectors, tax auditors, and irate congre-
gants. He it was who decided at what time the
temple doors opened, and at what time they
closed. You might say he had a finger in every

knish. He was an administrator without portfolio, a manager of other people's affairs. And the rabbi and everyone on the board of trustees were perfectly content to let him take on everyone else's function, except their own. Ten years ago, his congregation, had never heard of such an animal as an Executive Director. But the congregation was now too big to congregate under its own power. When it had grown, you should excuse the expression, from a parish to a diocese, up he had sprung like a mushroom, spawned by necessity.

There was also a CATERER, a man who'd spent his whole life in the business. He'd started as a young busboy in the fancy catering halls of Brooklyn's Eastern Parkway, and now he was old, a dried-up stick of a man in a tweed jacket, the sides of his mouth creased in a deep parenthesis from constant smiling, and no one was more experienced than he was. He knew every trick of provisioners and waiters and cooks and busboys; and who to gift at Purim time to get his firm an exclusive, or a semi-exclusive, on a synagogue's "acceptable" list. But more important, he was a genius at pleasing customers. His wedding cakes were famous, and his bridal matzo-ball soup. But he worked his finest magic on Bar Mitzvahs, which had become legends in his own time. Wave your checkbook and name your fantasy: this wizard could make it come to life whether it was a space odyssey, a pirate expedition, or a jungle safari complete with diapered chimpanzee to shake hands with arriving guests. Each affair had his personal attendance and his personal touch: he could provide a bust of the Bar Mitzvah boy in chopped

liver or in ice of purest spring water. And his magical Midas touch worked the modern alchemy: he
turned halves of spring chicken and circles of
stuffed derma into gold, because he was as expert
at cost accounting as he was at pleasing customers.
He'd seen all the fads come and go, the ice-cream
bars, the made-to-order omelets, the crepes filled
and rolled before your very eyes. The Internal
Revenue Service had audited him time and again,
and never found any fiddles, yet his profits soared
more than any other caterer's, and that too was
magical. He knew his cold cuts and his smoked
fish, his (strictly kosher) seafood crepes and his
(strictly kosher) Chinese egg rolls down to the
last eighth of an ounce of slivered celery. Most of
all, he knew the importance of good-looking, fresh-
faced young boys and girls in evening clothes and
fresh white gloves to serve the guests with a smile
and a clean starched napkin every time they got
up from a table to gossip or to dance. The young
servers were allowed to eat dinner after the affair
was over, but woe to him or her caught sneaking
a double portion. They were afraid to sit down for
even a moment while an affair was in progress because the caterer had the eye of a hawk or an
eagle; he was everywhere, hovering like a vulture.
He sneaked around his help like the Angel of
Death, and he pounced without warning. But most
of all the young girls hated when the long-time
widower would pat or stroke them unawares,
for his hands were cold and dry as the hands of
a corpse, and his smile never reached as high as
his cold, dead eyes. He sat somewhat apart in the
lounge, and fixed us all with an unblinking owlish

stare, and on his sparse white hair he wore a black velvet skullcap.

Near him was a MASHGIACH, a religious official properly trained and qualified to examine and certify the *kashruth*, the ritual cleanliness, of any product and any place, for an appropriate fee. Even though he sold his name, and not the observations of his eyes, he wasn't exactly fraudulent. After all, why should we blame him? His name on the little seal with Hebrew letters was what people were buying, and they weren't concerned with how or why it got there, or what it stood for. A little too pragmatic he was, maybe. But he had precedent: wasn't there the well-known story of the *mashgiach*, dead for years, who went on miraculously certifying the purity of a major dairy's kosher milk? He claimed to be a rabbi, and if no one asked, why did he need to produce his certificate of ordination? He was a jovial man with a red face. Rivers of veins ran down his nose. His narrow eyes were overhung by deep ledges of bushy eyebrows, and he had a full head of graying hair. "Snow on the chimney, fire within," he'd say, and laugh his booming laugh, for he liked women at least half as much as he liked food, and he was no stricter to certify the cleaniness of one than the other. He loved a shot or two of *schnapps*, and when he'd had enough he'd reel off ritual terms in Hebrew, and Shibboleth would turn to Sibboleth, as it did in the mouths of the Ephraimites in Gilead long ago. He was a good fellow who didn't want to put anybody out of work, and didn't want the wails of a poor tradesman's hungry children on his con-

science, so he'd let a small lapse go by for nothing
more than a fifth of twenty-five-year-old-Scotch.

And finally, there was an ADULT BOOKSTORE
OWNER, and his traveling companion, a boy of
blank good looks and no words at all. But the bookstore owner was sociable enough for two. He wore
a belted leather coat, and his curly hair splayed
in a thinning halo around his aging baby face,
lined and grooved like a tree trunk that adds a
ring each year, and his face counted to the wrong
side of thirty. He lived high above the East River
in a penthouse with a succession of smooth-
skinned, baby-faced Gentile chorus boys with
whom he listened to old Judy Garland records and
wept. When he went to his parents' apartment his
mother still stuffed him with potato pancakes
heavy like lead and his father asked him, "So,
nu, when are you going to bring a nice girl around
to me, you'll get married?" His father had never
been there, but he figured his son's bookstore was
for adults because it didn't stock comics, and he
had a vague vision of expensive imported art
books, Michelangelo and Van Gogh, lying heaped
on counters. In fact, the bookstore was one of the
biggest of its kind, clean and bright and well lit,
a palace of pleasures, and there was nothing new
and up-to-the-minute in the world of pleasure that
its owner didn't stock. There were magazines for
enthusiasts of every taste and quirk, for fanciers of
straight sex, oral and anal sex, the leather and rubber crowd, and the fans of whips and chains, but
they were all sealed in shiny Cellophane so you
were assured of clean new copies, unsoiled by
greasy fingerprints. At his store there were manuals

for transvestites, and there were magazines for gays and lesbians, and him-and-her, her-and-her, him-and-her-and-him, her-and-it, and every other possible combination. Bestiality was big this year, with standard white poodles slightly outnumbering Dobermans and Irish wolfhounds on glossy covers. There were twenty private viewing cubicles where, for a quarter a minute, you could see everything new under the sun. And he had 16 mm. movies for rent or sale. Some featured water sports, for those who get their kicks from peeing on each other. You could buy the "Golden Showers" feature, or the heavier "Brown Showers." He thought of his store as an educational institution, to expand the narrow horizons of the repressed and insecure, because he believed that you take your pleasure where you find it, and he wholeheartedly subscribed to the scriptural adage "Judge not, lest ye be judged." He had booths displaying a wide range of interesting objects, such as dildoes, penises and vaginas in the best quality synthetics, and the finest rubber bags and other accessories for those addicted to enemas. But his prize item was a full-length inflatable woman, with a real working vagina, anus, and mouth. And he was very ethical; he was so scrupulous that he would fire on the spot any employee he ever found selling merchandise to a minor.

So now I've told you all I know about our assembly of pilgrims, and I'll be glad to go on and tell you, if you're still with me, about the rest of our trip, and the contest and all, but before I do, I have a confession to make. It's about me.

You probably think, because I'm writing this, 43 that I'm a writer. You know, a *real* writer, a professional writer, like William Faulkner, or like Harold Robbins or Jacqueline Susann. But you have to understand, I'm just a small-letter-*w* writer, not a WRITER, if you follow me. What happened was this: El Al, the airline of Israel, ran a contest for a new advertising campaign. The winning slogan would receive an all-expenses-paid trip to Israel. So I submitted my slogan, and I was more surprised than anyone else when it won. (What was it? "Promise her anything, but give her Israel. Come to the Promised Land!" So now you know why our tour was called "Promises, Promises.") And *that*, you understand, makes me a writer. Of course, I'm a writer like the captain in the joke. Maybe you know it. A man comes to see his old mamma wearing a brand-new, gold-buttoned navy blazer, white flannel slacks, and a gold-braided yachting cap.

"So, *nu*, son, what is this get-up?" she says to him.

"Ma," he says, "this is what a captain wears."

"So who's a captain?" says his mother.

"I'm a captain. You know, my boat is 80 feet long, and it sleeps eight, and I'm the captain."

"This makes you a captain?" says his mother.

"Yes," he says, angry.

"All right, all right, son," says his mother. "You're a captain."

He beams. But she's not finished.

"Look, son, by me you're a captain and by you you're a captain. But by a *captain*—you're no captain."

So, you see, by El Al I'm a writer and by my husband and my children and my neighbors I'm a writer, but I have to tell you the truth because you'll find it out anyway, by a writer I'm no writer. So forgive me if I don't do justice to these people or transcribe them faithfully. I'm doing the best I can, I give you my word, and after all, I'm really just an ignorant housewife and a woman.

Well, the plane flight was just like every other plane flight, except for the El Al security guards riding shotgun like in the Old West, all tanned, tight-lipped, good-looking, and laconic, like Jewish John Waynes, or what James Bond would look like if James Bond were in his early twenties, and happened to be Jewish.

But generally shorter.

And our arrival at Ben-Gurion Airport was just like every other arrival except, of course, this was Israel and even the *policemen* are Jewish, imagine that; and then we went to sleep or bathe or un-pack, according to our inclinations. So it wasn't until the next morning at a meeting in the lobby of our hotel in Tel Aviv that we met our guide, Harry Bailley. He was a big man, black-haired, black-bearded, ruddy-faced, sporting a cowboy hat of woven straw, and energy seemed to shoot out of him like arrows, and he went around like a diplo-mat or an official city greeter, smiling at every-body, shaking hands with this one, and embracing that one's shoulders. He carried a tall staff, which he raised high overhead, so we could find and fol-low him in the thickest crowd, and when he spoke his voice could boom like waves crashing on a

shore, so we could hear him above any other guide
or any other group, but he could coo as gently as
a dove when he had to, when one of his lambs
needed comforting, and indeed, once, when I exclaimed at the great range of his knowledge, he
said to me, "You know, the job of a guide is less to
know things than to wipe people's noses and take
them to the bathroom, to find Kleenex, Lomotil,
lost sheep, and fresh orange-juice stands." And of
course he was right. He was, he explained, our
host, our tour guide, our wish was his command,
and he complimented our fine appearance.

"You are," he said, "the highest-class, most congenial bunch I've seen in a long time. We're gonna
have fun and pass the long hours on the bus we're
taking to Jerusalem. Now we're going to see the
Holy Land, God willing, and a lot of time will be
wonderful, at shrines and ruins and all, but a lot
of time is gonna be bumping along on the bus,
and it's no fun to sit like stones and not say anything the whole trip. So if you want—and you'll
let me be the MC—I swear by my father, may he
rest in peace, that we'll have a terrific time. All in
favor, hold up your hands and say Aye."

And we all did, some slower than others, but we
all did, and told him to plan his program. He said,
"Not to beat around the bush and to make a long
story short I'll cut the gab and get to the point. It's
story time!"

There was a kind of quiet drawn-out sigh, an
"Oy vay," that rustled through the group, but he
went right on, happily unheeding. "How long is it
since you told a story? A real story, not a joke or
a piece of gossip. How long even since you heard

one? A lot of years, right? Okay, what else are you doing now but traveling back to find your roots in time, to Abraham, Isaac, and Jacob, to Sarah, Leah, Rachel, and Rebecca? Well, what I'm telling you is gonna be a practice run. We'll get you back to when you were a little boy. Unless, of course, you were a little girl, in which case you'll go back in *that* direction. Look, you can laugh, I don't charge extra. Now, this is what you'll each do. A story, any story, that you've heard or that happened to you or even that you've made up, if you got a talent that way. But it should be a good story, something we'll enjoy listening to, that'll entertain us, pass the time on the bus, we shouldn't begin to squirm and itch. And the best story will, let's see, it'll get a free dinner, you'll all chip in, at the King David Hotel when we get to Jerusalem, and anybody who thinks a different story is better than the one I pick, the check will be on him! I'm a man of few words, so, if you like the idea, say Aye! So. Done, as sure as my name is Harry Bailley. And so you shouldn't ask, before we changed it, it was Bialystoker, but who can spell Bialystoker?"

And so we gave him the authority to judge our stories and pick the winner; and from somewhere he produced some bottles of extra-thick, extra-sweet sacramental grape wine and some plastic cups, and the wine was poured and passed around, and we all drank to our stories, and to our tour, and to Jerusalem.

THE ART DEALER: A HEBREW ROMANCE

TEL AVIV had been our first introduction to Israel, and an easy, gradual introduction it was. We marveled at how comfortable we all felt. Its middle-class apartment buildings, except that they were shorter and newer, brought to mind residential sections of Copenhagen or Amsterdam or, for that matter, Forest Hills, that you can glimpse from a bus on the way in from an airport. But Tel Aviv had palm trees. Its bustling commercial streets boasted lots of cafés and patisseries, 47 camera stores and fancy boutiques. All kinds of international wares were for sale, such as Seiko watches, Puma sneakers, Levi jeans, Kodak film, Coca-Cola, everything so you didn't even have to feel like you'd left home.

Some of us went shopping, and some of us penetrated to the beach beyond the rows of new hotels lining the shore like at Miami Beach or San Juan, Puerto Rico, to the blue Mediterranean, and joined the scores of men, women, children, even a few brave pet dogs, splashing in the gentle waves tamed by stone breakwaters. I set off to find *felafel* on Dizengoff Street. Now *felafel,* which is fried chickpea balls stuffed into half-circles of flat *pita* bread, with salad, and *tahine* dressing poured over it all, and a hot pepper sauce for the iron-stomached, is supposed to be the national dish of Israel, like hot dogs in America. But as I strolled up and down, I was confronted by pizza stands and pancake houses, cheek by jowl, and all the length of Dizengoff I could find only two *felafel* stands, lonely and somehow slightly out of place.

And when the hot and humid air became too oppressive I could refresh myself with *mitz,* which is juice, at the fruit-juice bars that seemed to spring up every few feet to tempt me, heaped high with the oranges of Israel, and grapefruits, and coconuts and bananas and grapes and every kind of fruit that could possibly be squeezed into a glass. So I could feast to my heart's content on pizza and pancakes and orange juice, just like home.

And that was Tel Aviv.

The next morning we boarded our big shiny

red-and-white air-conditioned tour bus, with the
big sign that read "Promises, Promises" on the
front, and pulled away from our hotel through the
crowded streets of Tel Aviv, a big placid fish swimming out through shoals of excitable smaller fish
that were the taxis that darted and flashed around
us, using their horns instead of their brakes and
bringing an exultant grin to the face of our cabdriver, and then we were out on the road heading
north along the Mediterranean coast.

Constant traffic whizzed around us, big con-
struction trucks, not shiny like at home, but shabby
and worn, and little passenger cars all riding on
horn power, or so it seemed from the relentless
noise, and army trucks and jeeps and old green
buses and blue-and-white buses marked in Hebrew
and Arabic characters, and other red-and-white
tour buses, but none quite so new or red or shining
as ours was. And it was then, speeding toward
Caesarea to see such items of Jewish interest as
Roman antiquities and Crusader forts, that Harry
Bailley returned to the subject of our storytelling
contest.

"Attention, all you Goldbergs and Shapiros
and Levys and Cohens (and even an O'Reilley, if
we should happen to have one on board)! The
time has come for all of you to dip into the ware-
house of your memory and come up with a story
to entertain us on our way. Remember, for the best
storyteller there'll be a free dinner at the King
David Hotel in Jerusalem—and the rest of you? At
least you can enjoy the sound of your own voices
for a while! Now in this bag you see in my hand
are lots, like on Purim, chances, and the one who

picks the black dot, they'll be the first. So don't be shy, don't hide your face, take a paper, and we'll begin."

He went up and down the aisle, and we each dipped into the bag, and whether it was merest chance or destiny or some sleight-of-hand by Harry Bailley, I don't know, but the lot fell to that perfect gentleman, the Art Dealer, who looked somewhat taken aback and fingered his salt-and- pepper moustache, but then decided to go along with a good grace and said, "Since it's God's will that I begin, then I will begin."

THE ART DEALER'S STORY

FIRST, let me give you the provenance of my story. Once, when I had been called in as a consultant to an Italian cathedral's library, I came across a curious volume. The book was bound in leather, a fifteenth-century binding, adorned with metal-gilt cleverly worked into a filigree tree, and on the tree hung a jeweled apple, lustrous red enamel shining among green enamel leaves, and the apple was dimpled with tiny dewdrops of diamonds and pearls. Underneath the filigree work, tooled into the leather in gold leaf long since tarnished and worn, were the words *Melech Artus*, that is, King Arthur, in Hebrew characters. As an example of the binder's art, the book was a beautiful thing.

I was intrigued, and I opened the book. Inside, on vellum leaves, finer than ordinary parchment, I found one of the most extraordinary manuscripts

it has been my privilege to examine. In characters as bright and black as the day the scribe had
set them down, thanks to ink of oak gall mixed
with iron, sharp and unfading, I found a thirteenth-century romance telling a story of Sir
Lancelot, the only knight of Jewish descent at King
Arthur's court, at least according to my manu-
script, which began, "These are the generations of
Sir Lancelot. King Bano of Benoic and King Borz
of Gaunes were brothers, and they married two
sisters, descendants of the royal House of David.
King Bano begat a son, and he called his name, as
it is written, Lancelot del Lac."

The story begins. . . .

But just then the Cabdriver, his face very red,
interrupted with a loud laugh.

"Now wait just a minute there, mister. You call
that a story for Jews? All it's about is outsides, what
things look like, bindings and pictures, outsides,
only outsides! It's what *inside* that counts. Insides
are what are important, and inside your beautiful
book is just a phony Jew, a *goy* who's got a Jewish
ancestor. Your story is nothing but an imitation
of the Gentiles, a Jewish knight named Lancelot
at King Arthur's Court, my God! A Jewish man
should tell a Jewish story with a Jewish hero. Let
me tell you such a story, about the Rabbi of Prague
and . . ."

Now the Art Dealer was such a perfect gentleman, he hadn't even said a word through all this.
But our tour guide, Harry Bailley, he'd turned
deep purple like an eggplant, and he waded right
in on the Cabdriver.

THE
CABDRIVER:
A HERO
IS A HERO

"THAT was going to be a fine story, very beautiful," said Harry Bailley in a loud, angry voice. "Little apples with diamond dewdrops and all, beautiful, I'm sure we're very grateful and we'd like to hear the rest."

"Not me," said the Cabdriver, under his breath, not very far under.

But the Art Dealer had already politely but firmly retired from the contest. Harry Bailley, trying to retrieve what was left of his idea, valiantly tried again.

"Then perhaps one of the professional people travel-

ing with us might choose to honor us with something of wisdom or of pleasure."

The caterer spoke up disagreeably, in his dry voice, like sticks breaking. "Did someone die and leave you God, that you decide who's going to talk? What are we? Puppets?"

The Executive Director began to make some soothing, shushing noises, but the Fundraiser spoke up, his forehead wrinkled anxiously. "What are we supposed to tell our stories about anyway? There's everything under the sun to talk about. I myself, it's my profession, after all, I have got a story to match each occasion. But what exactly *is* this occasion? What is it supposed to be?"

And the Interfaith Chairperson chimed in, "Perhaps we need someone to give us a little direction. Now I have had a little experience in this line . . ."

But the Cabdriver was not to be denied.

"Hold your horses!" he bellowed.

"Hold your own horses, Sam," screeched his wife. (I think she was embarrassed for him.)

"Shut up yourself!" he shouted back at her. "I can talk! When God created Adam, did He create him a *professional* man? He maybe gave him a diploma instead of a fig leaf? Let me tell you, Mr.-Tour-Guide-Who-Loves-Professional-Men, you can take your college diplomas and you can—use them instead of a fig leaf, because if you don't do any honest work, where do you think the clothes are gonna come from? It says right there in Genesis, And man shall earn his bread by the sweat of his brow, and how many of you *gentlemen* have worked up an honest sweat? I don't mean on the tennis court. I have, so I can talk!"

Now the Short-Order Cook began, "Hey, mister . . ." and the Widow, the one who owned a knitting store, said, "I'll have you know . . ." and our tour guide got as far as, "If you think *this* isn't work . . ."

But they didn't have a prayer. The Cabdriver was in full torrent.

"Oh, it was a sad day for the Jews," he said, "when the rabbis departed from their ancient ways. The great Rabbi Hillel, he was a woodcutter, and Rabbi Johanan made sandals, and Isaac was a blacksmith, and Joshua the son of Hananiah, he made charcoal, or maybe it was needles. Probably charcoal. Anyway, it's written right in the Talmud or somewhere, A man shouldn't make money from Torah. He needs to know what's it's like to have to make a living, and he studies when he can between times. Like me, I read whenever I can, between fares. Listen, I've read in the Talmud, No labor, however humble, is dishonoring. And it says too, If a man works, he is blessed. So look at me, I'm blessed and not dishonored. So I can talk. In my union they're happy to let me talk. In contract negotiations I can show them where it's written, The right of the working man always comes first. And I quote the great rabbis, what they said to the employers of workmen. This poor guy, they said, climbs up the highest scaffolding, and that poor guy climbs the highest ladder, and for why do they expose themselves to such danger if not to earn a living? Therefore, said those rabbis, therefore be careful you don't oppress them in their wages because it means their very life. And cabdrivers these days, it means their life, too! And we won the raise, so I can talk."

I don't know if he was impressed by the Cabdriver's logic or ground down by his avalanche of
words, but Harry Bailley threw up his hands,
shrugged his shoulders in resignation and said,
"All right already, we believe you. You can talk."

THE CABDRIVER'S STORY

THIS STORY I'm gonna tell you, this *Jewish* story, it
happened long ago, maybe a hundred years ago,
in Prague. That's a city somewhere in the middle of
Europe, maybe in Poland. All right, not in Poland.
Anyway in Prague. What was Prague like all those
years ago? (Now, too, for all I know.) I'll tell you,
if you drove a cab there, you'd have a hard time of
it, dodging little kids and absentminded rabbis and
goats and chickens on narrow, dirty streets without curbs or sidewalks or traffic lights. And there
were piles of garbage everywhere, because there
weren't any garbage men, not even to go on strike.
What you'd be driving would be a cart or a wagon,
and when a nobleman came by on horseback, or a
noblelady in her carriage, why, you'd have trouble, because they could whip you to make you
get out of the way. With the houses built bigger
than the land they stood on, they sort of hung over
the streets, almost touching each other, so that it
was dark. And that's by day. By night it was impossible to drive, not just because of all these things
I told you about, but because there was almost always a curfew on account of some outrage or
other. Remember, there was maybe only a few

oil lamps flickering on the streets here and there, and in winter it gets dark by three-thirty in the afternoon in Prague. Between was darkness. In the houses, darkness, because people went to bed early, there being no TV. The moon could barely squeeze some skinny rays between the hulks of houses. Just a few gleams from the eyes of stray cats, and a few oil lamps, that's it. Well, there weren't even many of those, and all you need is a few troublemakers with stones, every trouble-maker a David, just a few spindly Goliaths, and before you know it, you're in business, troublemaker business. Blackout! There'd be roving gangs of kids, they'd bust the few oil lamps, and in the darkness they'd break any windows around, if there were any, and force the bars across the heavy wooden doors and break open the wooden shutters, and they'd steal and they'd rape and, if they were really in a party mood, they'd set fire to the wooden houses and stores, there'd be a nice blaze and no fire department. So while everybody screamed and ran around in circles like chickens with their heads cut off and dragged their feather beds and their candlesticks to safety, the trouble-makers could stroll on home as easy as can be, laughing all the way. A New Yorker would feel right at home.

Now, if it was like this in the Christian part of town, it was ten times worse in the ghetto, which was the troublemakers' favorite target. The streets of the Jewish quarter were the narrowest and dirti-est and darkest of all, huddled around the ceme-tery, a little way up from the river, the Moldau River. And the gates of the ghetto were supposed

to be locked and guarded by Christian guards
every night, but somehow, more nights than not,
gates and guards didn't stop the stealing and the
raping and the fires. And the Jews had (you should
excuse the expression) another cross to bear. As
soon as Passover was coming, some of the Christians would drag out the old blood charge, you
know, that the Jews would steal Christian children
and murder them and drain their blood to use to
make matzos for the feast of the Passover. Nobody
really believed it (you could tell from tasting
there's nothing stronger in matzo than flour and
water) but it came in handy, any excuse for a pogrom. So the Jews would try and watch at night
when Christians might smuggle in a dead child.
(Children died like flies in those days, Jewish children too, probably the garbage in the streets.) Then
the Christians could show up the next morning
with the police chief, "Look, officer, my darling
murdered child! Off with their heads!" Which
promptly went off, along with arms, legs, testicles,
whatever. So Passover, which celebrates our deliverance from slavery, meant being delivered over
to murder for these poor Jews of Prague. And that
was the way it was until a hero, a real Jewish hero,
came to town. His name was Rabbi Judah the Lion,
and he was the wisest scholar in Europe, but he was
more than just a scholar, he was a scientist and he
did experiments in chemistry before they even
called it chemistry. He had influential friends
among the Gentiles, too; he was a friend of somebody named Tycho Brahe, which evidently was a
big deal. I can't tell you why, I just read it in a
book and it said Tycho Brahe was an intimate

friend of Rabbi Lion, that's what the book said, an
intimate friend. And Rabbi Lion called on all his
influential friends to make peace in the streets, and
for a while things would get better, and then
they'd get worse again. And one year, this year I'm
telling you about, the month before Passover,
things were the worst they'd ever been. And Rabbi
Lion said to himself, "Enough with the influential
friends. I've got to go to the higher-ups." So he sat
down and he prayed for guidance, nonstop for
twenty-four hours he prayed. And a voice from
Heaven said, "Lion, brains can go only so far. You
need some muscle power. Here's what you do, you
create a golem out of clay to fight the enemies of
Israel."

You will ask me, "What is a golem?" And I'll tell
you. A golem is a golem. A golem is a thing, a hulk,
a shapeless bunch of something before it's really
been formed, that's a golem. You might say an
embryo is a kind of a golem. But the rabbi's
golem, you'll see, was different from a human embryo, because all we can develop into is men, and
that's hard enough for some of us. But the rabbi's
golem became a superman. How did he do this?
After all, it is not such an easy thing to create a
man, let alone a superman, all by yourself in one
night. If it were, somebody'd sure be turning out
supermen on an assembly line like Mr. Ford's cars,
a really truly arms race, arms and legs and heads
and bodies, and make a fortune selling them to
those emerging nations, which are kind of like
golems themselves, if you look at it that way.

Anyhow, the rabbi chose two helpers, his son-in-
law and his favorite disciple (I can't remember

their names, I'm sorry), and all three of them spent a whole week praying, except for mealtimes and a little sleep. At four o'clock of the eighth morning, before sunrise, they stole out of the ghetto and went down to the river and found a place where clay was mixed with the earth, and they formed it into the shape of a man about nine feet long, and they made a face and hands and feet. They stood at its feet, facing its face. First the rabbi told his son-in-law to march seven times around the golem in a clockwise direction, while he muttered and prayed his secret prayers. When the seven times were done, the body of the golem glowed red-hot like coals in a fireplace. Then the rabbi told his disciple to walk around seven more times, while he said more prayers. The fireglow died down, and water streamed over the golem's body. Steam rose from it, nails sprang from his fingertips, and hair grew on his head and his face until he was bearded and as hairy as a Hasid. Then the rabbi made the seven turns, and the three of them recited the verse from Genesis: "And he breathed the spirit of life into his nostrils, and man became a living creature." Talk about your kiss of life!

Now what happened next is a problem. You see, one book says the rabbi had ready a strip of parchment with the four secret letters, you know, of God's Unpronounceable Sacred Name, and he put it on the golem's forehead and it stuck there. Another book says he rolled up the parchment and stuck it in the golem's mouth, like a dentist tucking in cotton before he fills a cavity, at least my dentist does. Another book says it was three letters, those that spell the Hebrew word for truth, and *another* book says there wasn't any parchment with any letters, the rabbi blew into the golem's mouth and nose. Me, I don't know, and nobody else does either, or there wouldn't be so many different stories.

Anyway, whatever happened, happened. And the golem opened his eyes. He blinked, and stared at the men like he didn't know who or what or where he was, which he probably didn't. Well, the rabbi commanded him to rise, and he got up to his full nine feet, and the rabbi looked at him, and he saw that he was good. But he was all naked (because he was made of bare earth, bare, you get it?), so they gave him decent clothes to wear, he shouldn't attract attention. And boots they gave him too, like a servant, or a soldier. And there he was, the golem. He was a hulk of a man, broad-shouldered, built like a wrestler, a little flat-faced maybe, but I've seen a lot worse on Forty-second Street hanging around waiting for the dirty movies to open. So he was made of earth? It was good enough for Adam, it's good enough for the golem. Anyway, a monster is in the eyes of the beholder. To a people who went slinking around corners scared of their own shadows, the golem would be beautiful. Strength was what was needed to save the Jews, not prayers or learning or fine white hands or looks like a movie star; and the golem was strong, like a Samson.

Right there on the riverbank, with the sun coming up, the rabbi told the golem his purpose in life, which was to fight for the Jews, and to protect them from sorrows and dangers and Christians.

And he named him Joseph, because he liked the
name, I guess, and he told him he had to obey all
his commands, even if the rabbi told him to stand
on his head or jump out of a high window, or lie
down under the wheels of a carriage. He told the
golem Joseph he was a superman, that fire couldn't
burn him, and knives couldn't cut him, and water
couldn't drown him, so he never had to be afraid
to fight. And so it was that the golem became a
man. He could see and hear and understand orders, but he couldn't talk, he was what you call a
dummy. Not stupid. Dumb. Mute.

Three men went out of the ghetto at four in the
morning, and as the roosters crowed all over town
to greet the first red rays of the sun, four men returned. The rabbi explained to his wife and his
household that he'd found this poor mute wandering down by the river when he'd gone for his
ritual bath, and he was hiring him to be his personal servant. (But we all know there was no
such thing as wages for Joseph.) And so Joseph
served the rabbi. He did what he was told, and he
never thought about *why* at all. There was no *yetzer ra* or *yetzer tov* in him, no evil angel and no
good one either. It never entered his head he
might question the rabbi or understand the reason he did anything, or if it was good or not. No,
he was a good soldier, he just obeyed orders. I'll
show you what I mean.

The rabbi had said that no one should give orders to Joseph except himself. But one day when he
was out, his wife, Pearl, needed water, and she
was too lazy to go down to the well herself, so she
sent Joseph with two big buckets to bring water,

he should fill the water barrels in the house, there being no such thing as plumbing in Prague at that time. Well, Joseph took the buckets to the well and he filled them up and he brought them back and he dumped them into the barrels and he went to get more. And he brought and he filled and he dumped, and by and by the rabbi's wife got busy with her needlepoint or whatever it is that women always seem to get busy with, and she forgot she'd commanded Joseph to fetch water. So he kept on all day, bringing and filling and dumping, and before long, the barrels were filled. But did Joseph stop? Of course not. Nobody told him to stop. So on he went, bringing and filling and dumping and the water spilled on the floor, and into the halls, and pretty soon there was water all over the house. Just in time the rabbi came back, and I don't know what he said to his wife but after that she never gave Joseph any orders any more.

But the rabbi gave Joseph *his* orders, and soon looters and troublemakers found a huge man dropping down from a roof above them and cracking their heads together like eggs, three at a time, and spilling their brains like yolks all over the ground, while the Jewish shopkeepers watched and cheered. Arsonists he'd hold over their own fires like marshmallows until they started to toast, then he'd hurl them all the way into the river and the waters would hiss putting out the fire. And a great shout would go up above the ghetto roofs, like from the bleachers at a ball field. The whole month before Passover he did special sentry duty from evening to dawn, patrolling the ghetto streets. He couldn't talk, that golem Joseph, but he had extra-sharp hearing. He could hear plots being hatched anywhere in the city. So when plotters would steal into the ghetto at night with a bundle over their shoulders or in a cart, he'd be there waiting for them, and he'd examine the bundle, and if it was a dead child, he knew it was a booby trap, and he'd tie the man and the body together and haul them off by the rope to the police chief to be punished. And when Joseph came back to the ghetto, people would clap their hands and bow as he walked by.

Well, by the eve of Passover there was wonderful news for the Jews. All the looters and troublemakers and arsonists and plotters were afraid to go out. The golem Joseph had made the streets safe. The rabbi commanded Joseph to stop his patrolling, and to stay home. That wasn't such wonderful news for Joseph. All of a sudden he's unemployed. He had no brains, you understand, no professional training, nothing. All he had was his strength, and his skill at protecting, and now the Jews didn't need him any more. Remember those veterans who came home, from Korea, from Vietnam, covered with ribbons and medals and found out that nobody gave a damn? Who cared? They risked their lives for their people, and who cared? So what! So this: Before Joseph's a hero, now he's a bum.

They wouldn't let him into the synagogue for services. And the women wouldn't let their daughters go out with him, even though he was bearded like a Hasid and his godfather was the great Rabbi Lion. Nine feet tall, he can't talk, from who-knows-where, no family, a servant, no profession—who needs him? All they would let him do was empty slops every morning down at the river, and light their stoves on Saturday, and chop firewood. And no one bothered to talk to him because he was dumb and couldn't answer. And what kind of a life is that for a man, even if he is a golem?

So he lounged around the streets of the ghetto, and he kicked at stones, and he looked mean at people. Well, that's bad enough with an ordinary man. But when it's a superman nine feet tall who fire can't burn, and knives can't cut, and water can't drown, it makes people very nervous. So they came to the rabbi by ones and twos and threes, whispering to him now he should get rid of Joseph, nobody needed him and he made them nervous and better get rid of him before trouble starts and nobody's safe and it's too late.

What they all forgot was that Joseph had been created with this terrific hearing, and even though they waited till he was down at the river empty-ing the slops, he could hear all the whispers and the threats and the plots.

One evening the rabbi called for Joseph to come to him. "Tonight," said the rabbi, "I don't want you to sleep behind the stove where you usually do. I order you to go up to the attic of the syna-gogue and sleep there." (The rabbi had it in mind that, at the same hour of the morning when he'd created the golem, he'd creep silently up to the attic with his son-in-law and his disciple, and by walking the three times seven around the oppo-site way and saying the prayers backwards, he would undo the golem.)

"Now go!" commanded the rabbi. But the golem didn't move.

"You heard me," said the rabbi. "I order you to go to the attic of the synagogue." But the golem still didn't move. And then, the rabbi couldn't believe it, in a creaking, rusty voice like a gate nobody's used or oiled, the golem spoke.

"I don't want to die," he said.

"How can you die?" said the rabbi. "You were never alive."

"Yes, I am alive," said the golem. "God's breath is in me. All I want is to be a Jew just like everybody else. I want a wife, I want to work, I want to pray in the synagogue. Haven't I done everything you commanded me to do?"

"Yes," said the rabbi.

"Then please let me live. Let me live like everybody else."

"Impossible," said the rabbi. "You weren't born the right way, you're nine feet tall, you're a golem!"

"God made Adam from the earth. And me, I'm made from the earth too."

"But God didn't make you," explained the rabbi. "I did."

"Oh, no," said the golem. "It was God's breath breathing through you."

And he began kicking at the walls and the furniture of the rabbi's house, and it shook like an earthquake. "You are a blasphemer," he called in a great rusty voice, and hurled a chair across the room. "And I've served you and the Jews faithfully and long and now you want to destroy me. I'll destroy you instead. I'll destroy you all!" And he threw an oil lamp.

But the rabbi thundered, "I command you to

stop! By the sacred letters, I command you!" And slowly, the golem turned around and bowed his head before the rabbi. The rabbi marched the golem outside, where all the Jews of the ghetto had rushed to see what was making such a racket. There they stood, and they trembled to see the angry golem and the angry rabbi.

"Jews of Prague," said the rabbi, "I tell you that my servant Joseph is really a golem who I myself brought to life, and now he must be destroyed."

"No," shouted the golem.

"Yes," shouted the rabbi.

He marched forward, but a push from the golem's long arm, and the rabbi fell head over heels, and all the Jews of Prague got ready to run away. But the golem called to them.

"Jews who I fought for! I've protected you and I've saved you, all of you, and will one of you save me now?"

There was silence in the street.

"Just one," begged the golem.

But only silence answered him. And into the silence spoke the rabbi of Prague.

"Every man's hand is against you. Those words on your forehead, you think they're sacred. Well, they are, but they are the sacred mark of Cain. You are Cain, the killer, and see, every man's hand is against you."

The golem looked around him. The ghetto street was almost dark. No one spoke. He pointed to his forehead, and he spoke, and this time his voice wasn't creaking and rusty any more. It was deep and strong and firm.

"Rabbi Lion, I know that this isn't the mark of

Cain. It's the mark of God. It's the Truth, *Emet,*
that you've written on my forehead, just as God
wrote on Adam's forehead when He created
Adam. And when He decided that Adam should
die, He erased one letter, the *E,* from *Emet,* and
Adam was dead, *Met.* So now I ask you to do the
same to me, and I say this to you. Never again
create a man. Come, take away the letter."

But the rabbi stood rooted to the spot, and the
rest of the Jews huddled like sheep around him.
Then, with a kind of a look, I can't describe it to
you, the golem reached up and began slowly pulling the parchment from his forehead. And suddenly the rabbi ran up to him and pulled it all
away. For a few seconds the golem towered
against the evening sky like a mountain. Then, between one blink of an eye and the next, he wasn't
there any more, and in front of the Jews was a
big heap of clay and dirt. That's all.

And that's the end of the story. They dumped
the heap of earth down by the river. No gratitude,
no thanks, no appreciation, no *Kaddish,* not even
a rock for a headstone. Just dumped the earth.
See, the Messiah doesn't come and he doesn't
come, and now you know why. So long as Jews
don't have respect for a person, for the breath of
God in him, for what he can do and how well he
does it, and they look down on him for not doing
what's better in *their* eyes, never mind what God
sees, that's how long the Messiah won't come.
I'll tell you the truth, the real reason the Messiah
doesn't come. Until we learn to see clear, and
see the same all the time, the Messiah knows if he
came, the odds are a hundred to one, with our
eyes, nobody would even recognize him.

THE EXECUTIVE DIRECTOR: THE HOLY SITE

For some time now while the Cabdriver was telling the story of the Rabbi's golem, the Chairperson of the Massachusetts, Connecticut, and Rhode Island Tri-State Area of Interfaith Councils had been bouncing up and down in her seat, bouncing more, I mean, than the springs of our tour bus already had all of us bouncing up and down. Something seemed to be bubbling inside her, and sure enough, the moment he finished she fizzed over with words like a soda bottle someone shook too hard.

"Listen to the man!" she stormed. "Heads break-

ing, beatings up, violence, that's how a man sees
the answer to a problem in interfaith relations.
And everybody knows that Jews wouldn't act that
way, anyway!" Her cheeks glowed with two red
spots, and her blue eyes were burning. "And to
make a fairy tale of such a thing, not a fairy tale
either, a story to scare little children with, that's
what you've made. It doesn't concern you, sir,
it doesn't concern you the probably irreparable, I
repeat, irreparable damage you are doing to what
is, after all, the most important thing there is, the
relationship between *them and us?*" And she
turned to the Gentile girl, the one who was traveling with the English Professor, and she favored
her with a bright smile and said, "Isn't that right,
dear?"

The Cabdriver muttered something under his
breath. It sounded to me like "Balls!" but I certainly wouldn't swear to that, because she was
such a fine and serious-minded lady it's hard to
imagine why he would say such a thing to her. So
"Balls!" is what I heard, but it probably isn't what
he said.

"Tell me," she challenged all of us in the bus.
"Tell me what could be more important than
improving understanding between Gentiles and
Jews." Someone, I think it was the Negligence
Lawyer, he had a kind of a half-smile on his
face, started to say a word, but she had already
gone on.

"Nothing, that's right, nothing, could be more
important. So to invoke the name of the Lord,
blessed be His Holy Name, might certainly prove
to be necessary in some emergency occasion, but

not for violent purposes, no, for improving understanding in the right way only, the way of peace. In my organization, the Massachusetts, Connecticut, and Rhode Island Tri-State Area of Interfaith Councils, we understand the ways of peace and understanding. Those are our goals—peace and understanding and an annual Interfaith Dinner. That is our year-around crusade. We are crusaders for peace and understanding, not like those crusaders from long ago, *feh*, the terrible Gentile ones who murdered and raped and burned the poor Jews all over Europe."

The Cabdriver was starting to puff up like a bullfrog. His eyes were bulging, and his wife had her hand on his arm, and the tension and unpleasantness were building up for all of us when another voice was heard from. It was the efficient, no-nonsense voice of the Executive Director, who rarely spoke, but was generally seen making lengthy pencil notes in a black morocco leather pocket notebook that he carried everywhere.

He seemed every bit as efficient and businesslike on our trip as he did back home in his office in a suburban temple, and it was no wonder that his board of trustees—most of whom were both richer and better educated than he was—were no match for him in making arrangements and conducting affairs. For all that he was somewhat brisk and brusque, you could relax with him, because you knew that in the end all the i's would end up dotted, and all the t's crossed, which might sometimes be intensely irritating, but under the circumstances was very reassuring. Here, you felt, was a man used to resolving squabbles.

"Now, now," he began. And "Now, now" he repeated, until he had everyone's attention.

"It seems to me," he said, "as if you are both
talking about peace and understanding, but you
are approaching from opposite directions, so that
you seem to be disagreeing. Which reminds me
of a story about two brothers. It takes place long
ago, when the elders of Jerusalem wanted to select
a building site for the new Temple, the one Solomon donated the money for. There was a lot of
squabbling and infighting, so much that it looked
for a while like the whole project would be
swamped by politics. So the Lord intervened. He
chose for His instruments two brothers who . . .

"But let me begin at the beginning."

The bus party sighed, tension draining away.
We all leaned back in our seats and settled ourselves to listen.

THE EXECUTIVE DIRECTOR'S STORY

THERE WERE once two brothers in Jerusalem long
ago, as I said, before the building of the Temple,
when there was bitter dispute over the site among
the elders of the city.

These brothers had always been close to each
other, so when one married, it seemed natural for
him to bring his wife home to the house he shared
with his brother, and the three went on living under the same roof. Even as children came along,
first one, then another, somehow the house seemed

to expand to accommodate them, and the brothers remained together, the one a bachelor, the other with his wife and family.

It was a house of love and sharing, never marred by bickering or petty jealousy.

The two brothers were farmers, and they also shared a field in which they grew grain. At harvest time, they reaped and threshed their wheat, and then divided it into two equal piles, one at one end of the field and one at the other. And this had been their normal operating procedure for as long as they could remember.

But this year, one night, instead of sleeping soundly as usual, the brother who was a bachelor found himself lying awake thinking. He said to himself, "My brother has a wife and children to support, and I have only myself. To divide our grain equally, then, is actually unfair to my brother." So he rose and dressed himself, very quietly, went out to the field, and in the darkness moved half of his pile of wheat to the other end of the field, to his brother's pile. Then he smiled to himself, and he returned to the house, undressed, and went back to sleep.

Later that night the other brother awoke, and he lay in his bed thinking to himself. "How much richer I am than my brother. He has no wife to laugh with, no children to rejoice in, as I do. Then to divide our grain equally seems unfair to him, since my portion is already so much larger than his." So he rose and dressed himself, very quietly, went out to the field, and in the darkness moved half of his pile of wheat to the other end of the field, to his brother's pile. Then he smiled to

himself, and he returned to the house, undressed,
and went back to sleep.

Imagine how the two brothers felt the next
morning when they arrived at the field, to discover
that both piles of wheat were exactly the same.
Each was puzzled, but neither, of course, said anything to the other.

That night the same thing happened. Each
brother, one early, one late, got up, went to the
field, and gave half of his own grain to his brother.
And the following morning, the shares of grain
were still equal.

And so it went, the next night, and the next, and
the next. On the sixth night, the bachelor brother
fell asleep, and only woke after a few hours, ready
to go to the field, so that it was actually later than
it was his practice to go. And the married brother
had trouble falling asleep, so that he arose to
go to the field earlier than it was *his* practice
to go.

So it happened, as each was crossing the field
in the darkness, his arms heaped with grain, that
the two brothers bumped into each other in the
middle. And then the puzzle was solved. They embraced each other and laughed together in love
and tenderness.

They treated the story as a big joke, a joke on
them, when they told it to a neighbor. He told it
in turn to another neighbor, and he to another,
and so it arrived at the ears of the elders of Jerusalem, who didn't laugh, but bought the field from
the two brothers for a large sum of gold, and built
the Holy Temple upon it. And the Holy Ark was
placed directly over the spot where the two broth-

ers had met in the darkness, their arms full to overflowing with grain for each other.

The Interfaith Chairperson sighed happily, her blue eyes misty. "Now that was a lovely story," she said, "filled with love and understanding."

"But it grew out of a *misunderstanding*, that is my point," said the Executive Director. "God moves in mysterious ways, you see. But always efficiently. God is a master planner."

"Yes, indeed," said the Philanthropist, in his loud, positive voice. "God is a master planner whose plans often are hidden from us for a long, long time. Take this land we are privileged to be in today. Out of the ashes of the Holocaust has risen the state of Israel, reborn, like the magical bird, and I flatter myself that I, we, all of us here, are helping this miracle of God's grace to flourish through our own small contributions to its safety and well-being. For instance, before we leave this Holy Land, my wife and I will visit our plantations, to sit in the shade of our trees in the forests our contributions have been planting these twenty years together, to see the green leaves against the holy sky, and to marvel that once there was desert, here where the land now blooms."

I thought I overheard the Dropout murmur "Far out!" admiringly, but he spoke so quietly, really to himself, that I can't be sure.

And all around us indeed the land was truly blooming, both blooming and booming, for we had come to the port city of Haifa.

THE PHIL-
ANTHROPIST:
THE TWO
BEGGARS

Now it was in Haifa that the Philanthropist really bloomed. The dust and heat, the noise and litter, the sprawling suburbs and skimpy cement buildings of Tel Aviv had not really been to his liking, although he had oohed and ahed vigorously out of a sense of loyalty. But Haifa was different. It was one of the cleanest places I have ever been in. We drove up and up, on hills like San Francisco's, past rows of white cement houses with pleasant gardens on tree-lined streets, all neat and orderly as befits a town planned and built by German organization and method, and it was much approved by our German-Jewish New Yorker, whose whole life, like his giving, was on a lavish, but always orderly, scale.

While those of us who long ago and far away had donated a few dollars in Sunday school sometimes felt a twinge of curiosity about exactly which tree, or clump, or maybe even grove, we had created, the Philanthropist, as he had said, was radiant at the prospect of his forests, and from the glow of his face at the leafy spreading trees of Haifa and the slim cypresses punctuating the hill of Mount Carmel above it like exclamation points, I suspected he was already seeing them.

From the top of Mount Carmel, on a good day, the city spreads itself pearly white on the shores of the sparkling Mediterranean. That depends, of course, on the density of the smog over the town and the degree of pollution of the sea on any given day. Since the successful development of industry at the harbor, the sparkle is intermittent and occasionally nonexistent. But we were lucky, our tour guide, Harry Bailley, proudly told us, as if he'd arranged it himself. That day the sun shone through clear air on a Mediterranean glinting brilliant aquamarine, just as advertised.

And it was in Haifa that we had the first spiritual experience on our itinerary, a visit to Elijah's Cave, the Jewish Lourdes, atop Mount Carmel. That's the cave where the prophet took refuge from soldiers come to kill him, and for centuries sick Jews have toiled up the hill to be healed. And there is plenty of evidence that the cave *is* a place of healing, for its walls are hung with crutches,

eyeglasses, hearing aids, and other relics, and after all, who would leave them behind except successful pilgrims?

Yes, Haifa was a thoroughly satisfying experience for the Philanthropist, whose large frame expanded visibly before us. The next day, when
we were back on the bus, he returned to his solemn theme.

"The best part of being blessed with wealth,"
he said, "is being able to experience the pleasure
of giving," he said.

"Hear, hear!" exclaimed the Fundraiser. "A Dan-
iel is risen among us."

"The best part of being wealthy is the money,"
said the Caterer dryly. (That caterer was all right,
I guess, but I found him maybe a little cynical.)

"You know a saying I once heard?" said the
Cabdriver. "If the rich could only hire the poor to
die for them, then what a living the poor could
make!" He put back his head and laughed immoderately. Near me the Art Dealer kind of
sighed, and rolled his eyes up to heaven.

"I often wonder," said the Lawyer, stretched
out at ease, his long legs extended across the aisle,
"which is the greater joy for my clients, the giving,
or the corresponding tax deduction."

"And where is it written," protested the Philanthropist, "that good deeds have to hurt? Is it so
terrible if I get pleasure and advantage from my
good deeds? The way I look at it is this: the evidence is that God Himself smiles at me, and my
business (thank God!) shows every year a nice
rate of increase. The more I give, the more I get.

And this is not *my* doing, but the doing of heaven. Listen, somewhere, I don't know exactly the chapter and verse, but somewhere it *is* written, Feasts are made for laughter, and wine makes merry, but money answers all things. And furthermore, I'm not ashamed of my wealth either, and I don't have to be. When blessed King David said to God, 'O Lord of the World, make equality in Your World,' God answered him, 'If I made everyone equal, who then would practice faithfulness and loving kindness?' "

The Lawyer spoke in a dispassionate voice. "Somewhere it is also written that the highest form of charity is to give anonymously."

The Philanthropist looked at him and smiled, a big broad smile like the sun. "And tell me, Counselor," he said good-naturedly, "am I the only person in the world who finds a little recognition is good for the soul?"

The Lawyer raised two fingers in salute.

"And furthermore," said the Philanthropist, "on the Day of Atonement it is written and ordained and sealed, who shall live and who shall die, who shall be rich and who shall be poor. Then who am I to rage against God's decree? Besides, in all modesty, I say in my own defense that I seek to do charity and I don't wait to be asked, that I give with an open hand and not a grudging fist, that I did this when I was young and struggling as well as in my prime, and that I do *not* look for my own advantage, but I leave that to heaven. I'll be frank. I give because I take pleasure in giving, and I am blessed with a wife who feels the same. I think my favorite story in the Bible is about Abraham and the three travelers who suddenly appeared on the track near his tents. And Abraham, by the way, was no pauper, but a man of substance with tents and flocks and servants, and I don't remember him apologizing about it. So Abraham ran out to these travelers, total strangers, all dust-stained, and said, 'Come in, come in, and do me the honor of being my guests. I will bring you a crust of bread and some water, whatever I can.'

"But of course, after sitting them down at ease on some silken cushions, Abraham rushed out to Sarah and told her to prepare loaves of bread from three measures of the finest meal, the best flour and plenty of it, enough for a small army, and he set Ishmael in charge of slaughtering three calves and dressing the meat and he himself went to fetch butter and milk, and when the roast meat and the bread was ready, he spread all this feast before the travelers and they ate."

"Wait a minute!" exclaimed the English Professor. "Bread and milk and butter and meat. Explain that."

The Philanthropist looked blank. "Come again, I didn't get you, explain what?"

"Meat and milk at the same meal. That isn't kosher, by your Jewish standards, but Abraham is the father of the Jews. Explain that."

The Philanthropist, frowning, thought for a moment. Then his face cleared, his sunny smile beamed, and he said, "It is written, hospitality overrides even the *kashruth!*"

"Chapter and verse, please," murmured the Lawyer, but very low, so no one else heard.

"Thought you had me there, didn't you?" The

Philanthropist smiled. "Anyway, the travelers—who, as you all know, were angels and messengers of the Lord—the travelers ate."

"Since when do angels eat?" asked the Adult Bookstore Owner in his soft voice.

The young Scribe said, "Rashi says they only pretended to eat, out of courtesy."

The Hasid, who had been following with interest, absently stroking his glossy black beard, spoke up. "A heavenly fire consumed the angelic portions, so Abraham thought they ate."

The Caterer made his pronouncement quietly but firmly. "Of course they ate. When food is fit for angels, even angels eat. In my years of experience—"

"Gentlemen! Gentlemen!" rebuked the Philanthropist. "It says in the Scriptures, in the Holy Scriptures it says, 'And he took butter and milk and the calves which he had dressed and set it before them, and he stood by them under the trees, and they did eat.'"

"I thought you said they were in the tent," objected the Lawyer.

"Tent, trees," said the Philanthropist, exasperated at last. "The principle is the same. And from his hospitality, what were the benefits? First of all, Abraham felt good, he'd done a good deed, and on top of that the angel Michael, one of the three, announced that Abraham and Sarah would have a son, which was no insignificant reward, since they were both old at the time, as you have heard, and had been trying for decades. A son! For only three calves, and the very best bread. And furthermore, it was the hospitality which Lot had

learned from his uncle Abraham that saved *him* on
the night the angels came to destroy Sodom, so
don't knock it, please, anybody."

"Truly," said the Rabbi, "the giver is blessed
for his gift, no matter why he has given. What does
the poor man care if the donor of his dinner is
honored or flattered for his gift? The poor man
has eaten! And clearly that is better than if he had
starved while a rich man debated about the purity
of his motives in giving charity. Sometimes there
is a lot of nonsense talked about the selfishness of
the rich, who take pleasure in their giving. Why
should they not, so long as the cause to which they
give is worthy? In the case of charity—unlike what
my wife always told my children about birthday
presents—it is the gift, not the thought, which
counts. But lest anyone be mistaken on this point,
charity is not only a source of pleasure, it is an obligation, and one incumbent not only on the rich,
but on anyone who has more than another."

"Absolutely! Absolutely right on the nailhead,
Rabbi," said the Philanthropist. "Charity is of
course both of these things, and my story will be
about both, the rewards and the obligations of
charity."

THE PHILANTHROPIST'S STORY

ONCE UPON a time, years ago, in the German town
of Wurms, there were two beggars who took up
their stations outside the Great Synagogue. Now,
one was crippled in both feet, and one was blind

in both eyes, and both stayed outside with their tin cups outstretched for alms. Whether the sun shone, or the rain fell, or the wind blew, or the snow drifted, there they were, the two beggars. And finally God took compassion on them. He sent down an angel, a messenger, who looked, however, like an ordinary man. To each of the beggars he went, and he said, the same to each: "Times have been hard for you, but now they will be better. For you will be healed, and your affairs will improve, and to start you off, here for charity's sake I give you ten gold coins."

"Well, the two beggars were skeptical, but sure enough, the crippled one regained the use of his legs and he became a prosperous horse dealer, while the blind one regained the sight in his eyes, and he became a prosperous cattle dealer. And so things continued, and times were good for the two former beggars. Each had a fine home, a wife and a family, and a thriving business that increased each year.

One day God looked down from heaven and smiled to see how the miserable were made happy. But then he began to wonder whether they were really better off inside as well as outside. So he called that same messenger to Him, and instructed him to go down to earth and make sure that these two wealthy men were proving themselves worthy of His grace.

So the angel, the messenger, went down to earth.

First he changed himself into a man with a withered arm and a limp, and he went to the horse dealer. "Please help me, sir, for the love of heaven. You see my misfortune. One breeding mare I beg from you, for my family is starving, and that would save them, and give me a start in life." But the horse dealer just frowned at him and pushed him aside. "My livelihood you ask as charity! God helps those who help themselves—leave my door and go out and work for an honest living, as I do!"

And he called his servants to chase away the beggar.

Then the angel, the messenger, transformed himself into a blind old man, led by a small ragged boy, and he went to the cattle dealer. "Please help me, sir, for the love of heaven. You see my misfortune. One breeding cow I beg from you, for my family is starving, and that would save them, and give me a start in life." The cattle dealer looked at the man, and he wept and embraced him. "Where you walk," he said, "I used to walk, and departed that way only by the grace of God. Not one cow, not two cows, but three cows shall you have."

And he took the blind beggar into his house, and sat him at the head of his table, and his wife brought him fruits and wine, and meanwhile the cattle dealer ordered his servants to bring meat and drink to the beggar's family. But the beggar lifted up his hand and stopped him.

"There is no family and I am no beggar. I am a messenger of the Lord, come to see if you are worthy of your good fortune. And indeed it is so. Because of your kind heart, you will continue in your prosperity and it will be doubled, because your fellow, the horse dealer, he that was tested and found wanting in his stony heart, all that he has will be taken from him and given to you."

And so it came to pass. The hardhearted horse

dealer once again became a crippled beggar, while the affairs of the cattle dealer flourished. Which all goes to prove that giving is the best policy, and charity is its own reward, and when it comes to entertaining angels unaware, you never know.

THE INTERFAITH CHAIRPERSON: FROM THE MOUTH OF THE DEAD

W HEN the Philanthropist had finished his story about the virtues of charity, the Fundraiser looked at him with admiration. "If I had you with me on my rounds," he said, "all I'd have to do is hold out my hand!"

There came the rustle of the Caterer's dry, precise old voice. "And then when the money rained in, what would you do with it? Nothing personal," he said quickly, with a sour smile, as the Fundraiser's normally amiable face darkened. 85

Then he continued, "I know to a penny where my income comes from and where it goes, because it's *my* money I'm getting and spending. When it's *my* money, but *you're* doing the getting and spending, then are you so scrupulous a guardian? Tax assessors, politicians, fundraisers, they're all very quick to know better than me what to do with my money. Nothing personal!"

"I'm really shocked," said the Interfaith Chairperson, indignantly shaking her fluffy blond head. "How can you talk about mere money after such an inspiring story?"

She had every intention of going on, but the redheaded Widow broke in, her green eyes blazing with indignation. "I don't know what things are like for you," she said. "But if you knew how many gross of skeins of yarn I had to sell, and how many instructions I had to give, and how many sweaters and suits I had to block, just to be sitting here on this bus today—listen, take it from me, there's nothing *mere* about money."

The Interfaith Chairperson was a little huffy at being interrupted, but she managed a smile, and she jingled her *mezuzah,* the gold good-luck one with the coral and emerald beads that she always wore on her bracelet when she presided over meetings of the Regional Interfaith Council, and she said brightly, "Well, I do think we should all make an effort to pull our minds up into realms of inspiration, like the lovely story we just heard. No offense, I'm sure." And her tinkling laugh rang out.

It was a laugh we'd all rapidly become familiar with. We'd thought it charming at first. But before very long the charm had worn thin, and I'd over-

heard someone unkind (I won't mention names)
say, "Someone told that woman early in life how
delightful her laugh was, tinkling like a little bell,
and she's been tinkling ever since, louder and
louder." And I don't like to be unkind, but it
was perfectly true, so that if any of us ever strayed
from our flock, all we had to do was listen, and
sooner or later, usually sooner, we could find our
way back by following the tinkling of our bell-
wether.

"I would now like, if I may," she said formally,
but with a sweet smile, to Harry Bailley, "to make
my own contribution to your interesting contest,
and tell you of a story, an interfaith story, of
course, that I once heard. May I?"

And Harry Bailley swept off his straw cowboy
hat with a chivalrous flourish and said, "It will
be for us our pleasure and our privilege, madam."

The Interfaith Chairperson dimpled at him,
gave a happy bounce in her seat, and began.

THE INTERFAITH CHAIRPERSON'S STORY

THIS HAPPENED hundreds of years ago in a city in
Spain, where relations between the Jews and their
Gentile fellows were, unhappily, not so good. Of
course, this was not true for all the Gentile co-
religionists. There was a small group only, six or
so, of anti-Semites, real haters, that were high up
in the government, and so they had a lot of power
to disseminate, by which I mean to spread, their
poison of hate. And where they poured their poi-

son most of all was into the ear of Don Manuel, the ruler of the city, the son of the king of Spain. But Don Manuel was a good man and a fair one, and he refused to listen to the poison. Which had the unhappy effect, I am sorry to tell you, but it is part of human nature, of making them work even harder at their devil's work. I use that word in all sincerity, because if ever there was work of the devil, this is it, to turn man against fellow man, especially in the name of the Lord, blessed be His Holy Name. Now, even though Don Manuel refused to listen, many in that city were not so wise, and these evil six gradually built up quite a group to put pressure on the ruler.

Things were at their worst in this lovely time of year we are enjoying now, on the eve of Passover, at *their* Easter. Such an intelligent group as this, I don't need to spell out, because you have already heard that infamous, I repeat infamous, accusation of long-ago Gentiles that Jews at Passover kidnap and kill little Christian children and collect their blood to make matzohs. That's more of the devil's work, to mix up an intelligence so much that it could for even one moment consider such a monstrosity of an idea. But there it is, wisdom God was stingy in dispensing, by which I mean, He didn't exactly give it out with full hands. So, these evil six were busy trying to figure out how this Passover they could work even more wickedness. And one of them had an idea.

"Listen to me," he said, "and we can destroy all the Jews, not just one here, one there, and win over Don Manuel too."

"Tell us, tell us," urged the others, excited.

And he told them a plan that makes my blood
turn to sherbet in the telling even. They would
steal away a little Gentile boy and drain his blood
and put him in the Jewish section right near the
synagogue and make the ritual blood claim
against the Jews. I know, you don't need to interrupt, this is not such a novel idea. But their idea
went one step more. It wasn't just any little Gentile boy they would kidnap and kill. It was the
nine-year-old son of Don Manuel himself, a lovely
boy, very bright, the apple of his father's eye.
They were terrible men, and it was a terrible plan,
but undeniably a wonderful plan from their point
of view to inflame the whole city, the ruler and all
the citizens, and make them destroy the Jewish
community in anger and revenge. These six were
of course among those who rush to do evil. And
so they set about the very next day, following
around the little boy, that lovely little boy, until
they knew his regular routine. And then late one
afternoon they lured him out of his path, a piece of
candy maybe, a toy, who knows? And they lured
him to a dark alley. And there, my God, I could
weep in the telling even, like he wept, the little
boy, but those six had no mercy in their hearts,
and they tied him up, a little sacrifice these good
Gentiles made to the devil, and they slit his throat,
and they caught the blood in a silver dish they'd
stolen from a Jewish house. And when it was dark
they carried that poor little body and dumped it
down right near the synagogue and spilled the
blood and threw down the bowl. And then they
hurried each to his home to be in time for evening
prayers. When the little boy didn't come home

that night, his father, Don Manuel, reacted like any father, Gentile or Jew. He was distraught, by which I mean he was almost out of his mind with fear and sorrow. Searching parties were sent out this way and that, and they searched through the city. Now, one of the search parties was made up of the six evil Gentiles. And they made sure, the six, that just before dawn they arrived at the street of the synagogue, and there they found him, the poor little white body, and his blood spilled red all around him, there where they had dumped him. Then they picked him up, and the silver dish, and they hurried back to the ruler, and they greeted him with cries and wails, but inside their false hearts were singing.

"O great ruler! We warned you of the wickedness of the godless Jews! But you were their friend and wouldn't listen, and behold! Now you are rewarded as the treacherous Jews reward their friends, see, they have stolen your only son and murdered him and drained his blood to use for their vile ceremonies. They are the worst people on earth, and surely now you see they should be destroyed."

And so they wept and wailed while their hearts were singing. The ruler's face grew black like a storm and his voice was as loud as the thunder as he called out to his servants, "Bring me the leaders of the Jews!"

Then the leaders of the Jews, the sages and the rabbis of that Spanish city, came before Don Manuel in fear and trembling.

"Traitors to my love!" he roared at them. "You have until the sun stands directly above us in the

sky to find out which among your vile Jews has
done this filthy deed. And either you will deliver
them to me for justice or I will slay all of you, and
burn your homes and your synagogue, and blot
you off the face of the earth. And now out of my
sight!"

You can surely imagine the weeping and wailing, no singing hearts in the Jewish quarter. For
what Jew would be so stupid as to believe God
demands blood for matzohs? That's craziness. . . .
So they knew no Jew had done this, and so there
was no Jew they could hand over for justice, and
so they were all going to die.

One of the great sages, Rabbi Samuel Ha-Ivri, a
big bull of a man, suggested that they arm themselves and fight. But there were only hundreds of
them, and hundreds and hundreds of thousands
of Gentiles. Then a gentle sage, Rabbi Moses Ha-
Cohen, practically a saint, said, "I will give myself
over to Don Manuel and say that I did this, I
alone, out of a sudden madness, and he will kill
me and be satisfied, and he will spare the Jewish
community."

Some of the Jews thought this was a wonderful
gesture on Rabbi Moses' part, but others said the
ruler would probably kill them all anyway so he
shouldn't slander himself, and still others said if he
confessed the Gentiles would still believe he did
it to get the blood, and that would shame the name
of the Lord, blessed be His Holy Name, which
heaven forbid. And meanwhile the sun, the hot
blazing Spanish sun, was climbing higher in the
sky.

Now the wife of Rabbi Moses Ha-Cohen was

right up front listening to the discussion, and she was getting impatient with these wise and holy men who could only think of killing or being martyred. But she wouldn't speak up in public, it not being at that time appropriate for a woman to take an active part in policy-making. So she drew her husband away by his sleeve and spoke to him in private.

"What you should be doing now is not talking about dying, but about living. You should be praying to God for His expert guidance. The Gentiles are not so bad, some of them are my friends, I know. And pity runs even in Gentile hearts, so if you pray from the depths of your heart, God will show you how to reach theirs, so that mercy will drop like the rain from heaven."

Her husband looked at her doubtfully.

"I'm sure of this!" she said firmly, and walked with him to the synagogue. Rabbi Moses Ha-Cohen was a very saintly man, and here he was in his element. He threw his prayer shawl over his head and he prayed for one solid hour nonstop. And outside in the street his wife listened to his prayers and his wails and his tears and sometimes to a silence in between. And she prayed, too, but in her heart so no one should hear.

Just at the time the sun stood directly above them in the sky, and the crowd of Jews stood silent in the street, the door of the synagogue opened. There stood the rabbi, pale, tear tracks down his cheeks, but calm and collected. He began walking toward the palace of the ruler, and the silent crowd followed him.

In the palace he went straight up to the throne

of the ruler, Don Manuel, who sat there surrounded by his counselors, and the wicked anti-
Semites were among them. Rabbi Moses bowed FROM THE
low and he said, "The Lord has told me how to MOUTH OF
discover for you the villains who have done this THE DEAD
terrible deed. But for this I need a piece of paper."

"Fetch some paper," thundered the ruler.

In the hall it was silence, and the paper was
brought. Then Rabbi Moses wrote on it the four
mystical letters of the name of the Lord, blessed
be His Holy Name, and he placed it on the forehead of the dead little boy, lying in state before
the throne of the ruler. Then everyone's blood ran
cold, mine does in the telling even, as the dead
boy sat up and bowed to his father. And Rabbi
Moses said to him, "Oh, my poor child, now in
the presence of your father and his wise counselors, tell the truth of your sad story, and who has
done this evil to you."

And the poor little boy, all ghost-white as he
was, rose to his feet and told the story, and he
pointed to each of the six who had killed him. Don
Manuel sat amazed, not knowing what to believe,
but the dead boy said to him, "If you want a sign,
then go to that alley that I told you, and dig there
and you will find a rock all spattered with blood,
and that blood is my blood."

The boy sat on his bier, by which I mean coffin,
while they waited, the ruler and the rabbi and the
counselors and the Jews. And presently there came
in a servant carrying a stone, and that stone was
spattered with blood.

"My son, oh my son!" cried out Don Manuel.
The ruler reached out to take the stone and in

the moment he touched it, the boy, his son, fell back dead and never moved or spoke again.

And the ruler was almost bursting with grief and rage. He ordered the perpetrators, by which I mean that gang of wicked Hamans, put in chains. And then he said to Rabbi Moses, "The wickedness of these false friends has driven me half mad. They would have had me kill you and all of yours, but through the power of the name of your Lord, the truth has been revealed. Now you may have them to do whatever you wish with them, and I will go to mourn my son."

Rabbi Samuel, the big one, he took those evil six and led them out and the Jews of that city punished them with torments until death, as they deserved.

But Rabbi Moses, he went and mourned with Don Manuel for a long while, and then he went to the synagogue and he fell on his knees before the Holy Ark to thank God for lending his blessed Holy Name to deliver his people. And in the women's balcony above, his wife was praying too.

And his prayers were in the Hebrew of the centuries, and were very elaborate and finely phrased and full of learning. But hers were short and in Spanish and went like this only: "Bring us speedily, O Lord, to that day when each shall sit under his vine and his fig tree, and none shall make them afraid, the Jew under his, and the Gentile under his, to each his own, amen."

After she had finished speaking, the Interfaith Chairperson gave another little bounce, I guess of satisfaction, as she looked all around the bus. And then her eyes widened as she saw the Gentile girl.

"Of course, dear," she said to her, "I mean no offense by this story, so don't feel responsible in any way, because I am well aware of the bonds that could unite us, and, besides, I have many, *many* good Christian friends." And she laughed her tinkling laugh, and she twinkled her blue eyes at the girl, who seemed about to say something, but then took a deep breath instead and turned her head away and looked out the window.

And somehow none of the rest of us were much inclined to say anything either.

THE PLASTIC SURGEON: NOT BY GOD ALONE

I T WAS quiet on the bus.

Harry Bailley had explained that late to bed and early to rise makes tourists dull and sleepy, and while we were on this mountainous stretch heading towards Safed, the little town of the mystics high in the hills of the Galilee, he would take this opportunity to give his mouth, and us, a rest. "So sleep, my little ones," he said, "while you can." And he leaned his own head back against his headrest, and adjusted his seat to recline, his shepherd's staff

resting idle beside him, and many of us followed
his example.

I didn't really relax, though. Not completely.
The bus, which was very big and unwieldy, was
running, very fast, along a little skinny mountain
road that made hairpin turns around sharp curves
without a guard rail in sight, and every time we
turned, the bus would kind of sway over on its
side, and since my window was on the outside, I
got a clear view from there to eternity, lying at the
bottom of the valleys below. So I was quiet also,
but from terror more than tired.

But then the quiet was broken by the Interfaith
Chairperson.

"Attention, attention!" she said. "This is an
emergency. Does anyone have a wash-and-dry?
I'm so grimy, I need a touch of moisture, and I'm
all run out."

There was a kind of stir of irritation, at least it
seemed to me it was irritation. But I went rum-
maging in my purse like several of the other
women. Now normally I never have anything in
my purse that's called for—you know, emergency
items like Band-Aids or rubber bands or sourballs
or a pair of scissors or Kleenex, things that *proper*
mothers always are provided with, or so my children tell me. So I was amazed this time to fish
up a wash-and-dry. It was left over from the plane
trip days ago. I'd forgotten to use it then, and it
was a little grubby around the edges, but it was a
wash-and dry, and it was still sealed, so I figured
it would do.

"Here you are," I called, and held it up proudly.
Then I got up and walked forward up the aisle

to her, or rather lurched forward, bumping from side to side as the bus went along its merry twisting way. And she was very grateful, so she said, although I thought she frowned a little as she took the wash-and-dry. Well, I know it was grubby, but it *was* still sealed.

As I made my way back to my seat, the bus made a really sharp turn, and I was thrown so hard against a seat I had to grab at the person sitting in it to stay upright, and I thought to myself, "This is it, this time we're going over the edge." And the person I'd grabbed pushed me back up, and we disentangled each other, and he was the baby-faced chorus boy, the one traveling with the balding Adult Bookstore Owner. I distinctly heard him, the Adult Bookstore Owner, I mean, muttering "Never again, never again," and even as I apologized I wondered what had made him think just now of persecutions and pogroms, that he should be quoting the Jewish Defense slogan, when I noticed the pale greenish tinge around his nostrils, and I realized he meant "Never again" a bus trip.

Now I didn't really mind anything on the trip, not even the terror, so long as the air conditioning on the bus was working. But even that was a problem, for some, at least. The Cabdriver and the Caterer had each made separate trips this very morning up to Harry Bailley, the Cabdriver to complain that the bus was too hot and the Caterer that it was too cold, and I know because they both spoke so loudly that we all heard their complaints in complete detail.

Anyway, as I walked back to my seat, I walked a little slower, not just for better balance, but looking around, making mental notes on how the rest of us were coping with the trip.

The driver, naturally, was fully occupied with his driving. His resting came when we were up and doing. And Harry Bailley, as I told you, was sitting quietly, very uncharacteristic, doing nothing. Next to the Interfaith Chairperson, who was delicately cleaning herself with the wash-and-dry a lot like a cat with its tongue and paws, her husband was reclining, fast asleep. At any rate, his eyes were shut.

Near them the Widow and the Interfaith Lieutenant were sitting together. The Lieutenant was explaining the tangle she'd got into, dropped stitches and all, trying to follow the intricate pattern of the Irish fisherman's pullover she was knitting for her oldest grandchild, and the Widow— you remember, she owned a knitting store—was explaining where she'd gone wrong. And what with the little curtains, red and orange and purple checks, primly pulled back between the windows, and the two heads bent together, one red, one gray, over the needles and the masses of yarn, it was hard to believe we weren't in a cozy kitchen back at home instead of in a tour bus hurling itself at the ramparts of the Galilean mountains.

Behind them the Art Dealer was working a puzzle in a big book of crossword puzzles, filling in the missing letters with his Mont Blanc fountain pen, and his wife was keeping a sharp lookout for dropped clues.

Across the aisle, the Rabbi and his Wife were talking quietly together, and the Cabdriver and his wife had both gone to sleep.

The Caterer was sitting on the aisle (he'd made

a fuss about that, too, because he'd wanted a window seat) while next to him the sun's rays slipped
under the tinted glass toward the top of the windows to strike full force on the Lawyer, slouched
down low in his seat, and the light glinted off his
gold-rimmed aviator sunglasses, dazzling anyone
who looked in his direction with a blinding and
impenetrable glare.

Our two young men had somehow ended up sitting together, and a picturesque pair they were,
the Scribe, slightly older, his high-buttoned black
coat and soft black hat sandwiching his pale face
in its frame of wispy blond earlocks, next to the
College Dropout, still struggling out of his teens,
his hair a blazing halo and his shirt a garden of
brilliant flowers, the one absorbed in his big thick
book, the other idly fingering his guitar, but very
softly, to himself.

In front of them sat the English Professor, the
liberal one who'd marched for Vietnam and
Biafra and civil rights. He was by the window, and
his Gentile girlfriend sat on the aisle. He was still
unhappy about having to sit one row farther back
in the bus. This is what happened. Harry Bailley
had explained that we'd rotate every morning and
afternoon from now on, each time moving toward
the back, so everyone would get a fair turn up
front. And everyone was agreeable except the English Professor. He'd protested loudly that when
people, students in a classroom, for example, had
settled themselves, then that was their proper order, and it shouldn't be disturbed. He certainly
didn't run *his* classroom that way, having them
take different seats each time they met, changing
matters and confusing issues.

So he was still annoyed, I think. At least he looked annoyed, because he was puffing angrily on his briar pipe, and the blue wreaths of smoke mounted to the overhead rack, then curled back around the heads of the Scribe and the Dropout. The Dropout didn't seem to mind, but every now and then the Scribe would frown, and without lifting his eyes from his book, he'd raise his hand and wave it slowly to dissipate the clouds and clear the air.

The Philanthropist's wife was in her seat, busily writing postcards, while her husband was on his mission. Now, you see, at every rest stop (and they came about every two hours, to accommodate the weakest kidneys) people would buy a little something to refresh themselves, orange juice, perhaps, or a bottle of grapefruit soda or a Coke, or some hard candy or a chocolate bar (Elite, made in Israel, delicious). But that wasn't the Philanthropist's way. He would return to the bus with his arms filled with whole *boxes* of chocolate bars, which he would then pass around, beaming, until they were all gone.

So that's what he was doing right now, and he'd reached the back of the bus, where the Mashgiach and the Cook were sitting side by side. The Mashgiach had been sleeping, quite loudly, but something, maybe the smell of chocolate, had woken him up. The Cook was savoring slowly, segment by segment, the extra orange he'd taken at breakfast and saved in his pocket till he'd needed it. The two men each took a chocolate bar. When the Philanthropist pressed them to take another, there's plenty more where that came from, the Mashgiach shook his head, smiling, and pointed to his paunch, but the Cook plunged his hand into the box and took as many as he could hold.

Nearer me, the Hasid was looking placidly out the window, meditatively stroking his beard, while next to him the Fundraiser was dozing, the plaid *yarmelke* over his face rising and falling with his deep, even breaths, and every once in a while a gentle snore would escape out from under it.

Across the aisle, the Executive Director, crunching Tums, had been making copious entries in his black morocco notebook, until the Merchant, next to him, began complaining in a loud voice about the outrageous dues that synagogues and temples chose to charge, and just what did he think he could do about it? (I know because I was sitting in front of them.)

Next to me was the Plastic Surgeon, and he was frowning. Now that may not sound like actually *doing* something, but he was a very big man, as I told you, six feet three and a half inches tall, and broad as well. When he got on the bus his head seemed to graze the roof, and when he sat, he had to duck to avoid the overhead racks. Just to watch him on the bus made me mildly claustrophobic. After all, even I feel tall on a bus, and I'm very short. So he was a big man, and his frown was big to match, and very *loud* too, if you can understand what I mean by that. He didn't have to *say* anything. He just sat there and glowered, like a mountain glowering, and soon we all became aware that something was displeasing him.

And then he spoke to the Interfaith Chairperson.

"Madam," he said, but the tone of his voice was not so "madam."

"Madam," he said, "I am sure you are well
aware that what you have described in the story
of the dead boy is medically impossible. Yet you
expect us to lend not only our emotions but our
rational minds to such an impossible story. This
is, forgive me if I offend, but this is a matter of
great urgency to me, this is the same tradition
of superstition and ignorance persisting in the Jewish religion which drove me out of the doors of the
synagogue when I was only thirteen, for even then
my respect and my allegiance were reserved for
science.

"Miracles!" he said scornfully, but still politely.
"Today, in the century of science, in modern Israel rank superstition still prevails. I could not
force myself to remain inside Elijah's Cave when
we stopped there yesterday. Imagine, the refuge
of the first and greatest Jewish physician, and it is
filthy, dark, unsanitary in the highest degree, and
all the invalids who belong in a hospital under
proper medical supervision flock to it to hang up
their crutches and walkers and eyeglasses and
hearing aids, as if this were the Dark Ages. It was
as bad as Lourdes! How minds can run like that, in
our enlightened age, I cannot comprehend. And
stories such as yours, madam, encourage these
tendencies toward ignorance and belief in miracles.

"It is the mind of man in which miracles are
made, madam, especially in the mind of a man
of science. Such a man was the first Jewish physician. But is he called Elijah the Physician? No,
he is called Elijah the Prophet, because the same
unenlightened and superstitious minds ruled organized institutions then as they do now. Let us

examine two case histories recorded as 'miracles'
in the Bible. The stories are similar, and they concern the senior physician, Elijah, and his younger
associate, Elisha."

Now up to this time the background to the Plastic Surgeon's lecture had been indignantly protesting soprano twitters from the Chairperson and
her Lieutenant, punctuated by alto murmurs from
the Rabbi's Wife, and from the rest of us quite a
few scowls were aimed in the doctor's direction.
But at this promise of a medical case history from,
as it were, inside out, the scowls switched to
shushing sounds aimed at the protesting trio. Because, admit it, who can resist a medical anecdote?
I certainly can't! So the doctor, excuse me, I mean
the *physician*, pressing his index fingertips together and looking grave, went on uninterrupted.

"In the first case," he said, "we have a youngster
who falls seriously ill, to the point, and I quote
from the history, 'that there was no breath left in
him.' The youngster's mother summons the physician Elijah to attend the child. Now we skip
over the nonclinical incidentals, such as prayers to
God and so forth, and look at the actions of the
physician, and again I quote, 'He stretched himself upon the child three times' and then more
about the Lord and so forth, and then we find,
'The soul of the child came back unto him, and
he revived.' Now one possible explanation might
be a sudden neurological disorder, possibly a psy-
chomotor epilepsy, or a cataleptic or narcoleptic
state, in which the youngster, certainly to the lay-
man, for all intents and purposes appears dead."

I tell you, you could have heard a pin drop on
that bus.

"If such is the case," he went on, "the state is generally self-limiting. The child would recover spontaneously, and at such a point, if one sprin- kled chicken fat all over the room, the chicken fat would be credited with the cure. But I think there is another explanation of this case. Remember that the patient had 'no breath left in him.' If we assume that 'stretching himself upon the child three times' is a dramatic, rather than a literal, version of mouth-to-mouth resuscitation (and such a possibility becomes stronger when we turn, as we shall in a moment, to our second case), then we can make another possible diagnosis, and that is Guillain-Barré Syndrome. A colleague of mine at Columbia Presbyterian has made something of a specialty of Guillain-Barré Syndrome, which is, of course, an ascending polyneuritis with paralysis caused by a massive viral infection. The youngster, once falling sick, suffers progressively until there is indeed no breath left in him. Now, if the patient can be maintained until the crisis passes, by mouth-to-mouth resuscitation in the absence of such mechanical respirators as we are fortunate enough to have in our age, then it may be possible for the patient to make a spontaneous recovery. And as for the 'three times' that the physician stretches forth, why, I regard that as a dramatic time relation and not necessarily a scientific time relation.

"Now I told you before that the possibility of having here extremely early descriptions of the medical technique of mouth-to-mouth resuscitation becomes more apparent in the second case history, a youngster treated by Elisha, Elijah's young associate. In this case, we have a youngster who goes out to be with his father, where he is reaping in the fields, and we read, he says to his father, 'My head, my head.' The father tells his servant to carry the youngster in to the mother, and the child, we read, 'sat on her knees till noon,' and he died. And we read, 'there was neither voice, nor hearing.' Let me remind you of the symptoms: we have a sudden headache, weakness (the servant has to carry the patient), and coma. Elisha, who is summoned immediately, goes in to the patient, who is apparently dead, and embarks upon a course of treatment which is thoroughly detailed, as we read, 'And he went up and lay upon the child and put his mouth upon his mouth and his eyes upon his eyes and his hands upon his hands, and he stretched himself upon him and the flesh of the child waxed warm.' "

"Excuse me, Doctor," said the Rabbi, "but in this account I clearly remember that first Elisha prayed unto the Lord."

"Yes, yes," said the Plastic Surgeon impatiently. "That's exactly what I mean about superstitious ignorance. Here is a detailed account of a medical procedure, and we find it cluttered up with these continuing appeals to the supernatural. In fact what happened, thanks to the natural 'miracle' of mouth-to-mouth resuscitation, as we read, is that 'the child sneezed seven times, and the child opened his eyes.' Now this detailed account clearly suggests a diagnosis of respiratory arrest due to some primarily neurologic disturbance, such as a viral meningitis, which would account for the sudden and severe headache. The youngster passes into a coma state in which sustained respiratory

support brings him through the crisis. These two
case histories indicate that, among Jews, the physician's art is as ancient as the Scriptures and was
handed down from generation to generation of apt
students. We all laugh when we hear 'My son, the
doctor,' but it is no joke. Jewish history is full of
Jewish sons who are physicians, in Roman days
and in the Middle Ages in Spain and Algeria and
Italy. Why, the Doge of Genoa, even the Pope himself in the sixteenth century had Jewish physicians.
And let us not forget one of the greatest Jewish
physicians of all, although his medical expertise
is often unfairly overlooked, Maimonides himself,
who practiced in Cairo in the twelfth century."

"And a cautious and wise doctor he was,"
nodded the Negligence Lawyer. "Maimonides
had a saying about the practice of medicine. He
said, 'Let me be the third physician to see the
patient.'"

The Rabbi's Wife frowned in thought, then she
said, "And what is that supposed to mean? Why
shouldn't he want to be the first doctor?" Her husband, the Rabbi, patiently leaned over to explain
to her, while the Plastic Surgeon frowned and said,
"May I remind you, Counselor, that the Book of
Ecclesiasticus contains the admonition 'Honor a
physician with the honor due unto him.'" To
which the Negligence Lawyer responded smoothly,
"As soon as we make a determination of just how
much honor is in fact due to him, Doctor, then we
can offer him exactly that amount."

"I heard a story once about a sick man," vol-
unteered the Caterer in his dry, precise voice. "He
was asked, 'What bothers you?' And he answered,

'My sins.' So his relatives asked, 'What can we get to help you?' And he answered, 'Atonement.' So they figured he was wandering in his wits, and they said, 'Let's send for the physician,' at which the sick man moaned and said, 'But he was the one who made me ill.' "

"Now, now," said the Adult Bookstore Owner, "don't you think you are being just a teensy bit unfair to the compassion and charity that are a part of all doctors' ideals?" The Caterer's owl face was still, but one eyebrow raised itself high and skeptical. The Adult Bookstore Owner ran his fingers through his thinning curls and went on in his exceedingly soft voice, "There was a doctor, I can't remember his name, but he really truly existed in history, and he never charged his patients. He simply put a box in his office instead, so people could pay what they thought they could and should pay. And this doctor's most frequent prescriptions were for bread and meat as being the best convalescent medicine, and if the patient had no money to buy them, why, then the doctor would give him the money. But I'm sure such a story is commonplace among physicians, isn't it, Doctor?"

The Plastic Surgeon went very rosy, and he opened his mouth, and at first nothing came out, so we might have been excused for diagnosing massive respiratory arrest, except that after half a minute he drew a deep spontaneous breath and said, "As I was saying, the scientific tradition is long among the Jews, and the sorrow and the pity is that it is so undervalued that a man of science, to be honored, must be styled a man of God,

and a story of personal wisdom and heroism must
be made into a miracle, something supernatural,
as we have heard in the previous story. Let me
tell you, for a change, how such a story *really* happened, heroism in its pure state, uncorrupted by
unnecessary superstition and miracle."

THE PLASTIC SURGEON'S STORY

THE TIME is again the Middle Ages, again the eve
of Easter, and the place is Italy, as I heard this
story, in a town where Jews were not shut up in
the isolation ward of the ghetto but lived side by
side with their Christian neighbors. One day, a
youngster, little more than an infant, about three
years of age, wandered through the open door of
a neighbor's house. The neighbor, an excitable,
irritable type at best, had had a falling-out with
the youngster's mother, so his response to the trespass was violent. "Get out of here, you little bas-
tard!" he shouted at the youngster. When, naturally enough, the youngster did not immediately
respond, but instead stopped in his tracks and
stared, the man shoved him toward the door. And
when the youngster did not move fast enough to
suit him, he kicked him to hurry him along. The
child was small, the man was big. The kick lifted
the youngster up in the air, and in falling, he hit
his head on the sharp corner of a heavy oak cab-
inet. The youngster hit the floor and lay there,
dead. It is true that there are recorded instances

of victims walking around for substantial periods of time, seemingly recovered, after sustaining a fatal acute intracranial hemorrhage in a concussion, a phenomenon which is useful for writers of detective stories and fabricators of miracles. But in this case, the child suffered a compression fracture of the cervical spine, that is, a broken neck, and he was dead.

Well, the man hurriedly hid the youngster's body. (The man and the child, I ought to tell you, were both Christians.) He remembered that the man next door to him, a Jewish goldsmith, was away. So when night came, he took the corpse, tucked it under his arm, crept next door, and threw it through the window of the Jew's home. The Jew's wife was home, businessmen in those times being unaccompanied on journeys by their wives. She heard a noise, got up to investigate, and by the light of her candle she found in the next room the corpse of the Christian child. Obviously she was frightened. To be in possession of a *corpus delicti* is never a comfortable position. And to be a Jew among Christians in those primitive times was not a comfortable position. She would be judged guilty before she had a chance even to begin to defend herself. And if she were lucky, the penalty would be hanging. But if she were unlucky enough to be charged, on this eve of Easter, with a ritual blood-killing, she would be burned, and perhaps other Jews along with her. And while all this flashed through her mind, she heard a noise outside, a hubbub of voices, women's and men's. One woman was screaming, "My baby, my boy! My baby, my boy! Where is he?" And

loud above the hubbub the Jewish woman heard
a man's voice boom in answer, "I saw him go ——
into the Jew's house, but I never saw him come
out alive." And then she heard, out of the con-
fusion of sound, a repeated cry, "Send to the magistrate. Send to the magistrate."

Will you all agree that this is a sufficiently des-
perate situation? Fire or the rope, and immediate
nemesis outside. What would *you* do? I have no
doubt that the orthodox prescription involves liberal weeping and wailing, tearing of clothes and
hair, and immediate prayers to invoke a deity who,
if he exists, is notoriously unwilling to get involved. Fortunately for the woman, she chose to
apply her brain to the situation instead. She took
some rags and tied the child to her abdomen. Then
she threw a loose robe around herself, and sat
down, legs wide apart, on her bed, and began to
groan and call out, as if she were a pregnant
woman in the early stages of labor. She cried loud
enough to wake her young son, and she told him,
"Run for the midwife, my time is come!"

When the midwife (who, I should tell you, was
Jewish also) arrived, the Jewish woman revealed
the corpse to her. The midwife began to attend to
her as if she were indeed giving birth. The magistrate arrived, and his men searched through
the entire house, under the beds, in the chests, in
the oven, but of course they found nothing. And
they came near the bed to search, but the midwife
had arranged a bladder, like a balloon, of water,
and the Jewish woman pierced it with a pin and
screamed, "My waters! My waters!" And the water gushed out, and the men retreated, because

there were at that time no advanced theories about men's place in delivery rooms.

The rest of the night and all the next day she groaned and cried out, and at night the news went out that the baby was stillborn. So the midwife went out with the woman before dawn and they buried the child in a newly plowed field not far away. So. The woman had saved herself by her cleverness; by what may appropriately in this case be called her mother wit, she delivered herself. And, interestingly enough, justice was done in this case, but also through no more supernatural interference than the deliverance.

The irritable Christian, a few days later, quarreled with his wife and began beating her with his fists. He knocked her down to the ground and began kicking her, and she screamed out, "Help! He will kill me like he killed the little boy!"

The windows were open, and the street was busy, and her words were heard and told to the child's mother. She went to the magistrate, who came and arrested the man. After severe interrogation, which included a regimen of blows and kicks, the man confessed to the crime and was promptly hung in the public square. Justice, assuredly—but brought about by the man's own vicious nature. Hence, *natural* justice.

Then the Jewish woman, after being reassured that she was exonerated from any blame, revealed the whole story to the magistrate. The child's body was exhumed and given a proper Christian burial. And the magistrate, in private, complimented the Jewish woman for her cleverness and quick wits. "Because otherwise," he said, "you would surely have been burned at the stake, and some of your fellow Jews as well. You saved many from death that day."

The Plastic Surgeon stopped, took out a handkerchief, and blew his nose ferociously. Then he looked slowly around at every one of us. His face was frowning and thoughtful and sad, all at the same time, and we thought he had finished speaking. But then he began again, quietly, slowly, choosing his words carefully.

"She did it, by her own efforts. Isn't that sufficient? More than sufficient? She did it, she herself, she alone. And must you take that away from us, take the easy way, give us miracles, placebos, sugar pills of fairy tales that never were or will be? People grow ill and die, everyone, we all grow ill and old and we die, and we go to rot in the earth. Look at you, at me, at all of us. Into the earth—and it would be more than anyone could bear—and they, *you*, want to take away the one thing that makes it bearable, if anything does, the heroism of the human mind. My God! It makes me sick to think of it."

THE ENGLISH PROFESSOR: A FALSE MESSIAH

THE LAWYER, when he caught the Plastic Surgeon's attention, tossed him a two-fingered salute. But the Interfaith Chairperson sulked in a huffy silence for a long time afterward, as the bus wound its way up and into the mountains of the Upper Galilee. By midmorning we were there, climbing the steep cobbled streets of Safed, following the outstretched staff of Harry Bailley.

Up and up we tramped, past the synagogues of the mystics, the masters of

Cabala who had filled this place with awe in the

sixteenth century, and past the homes of artists,

whose flowerpot gardens filled the narrow streets with brilliant color echoed in the twentieth-century canvases they offered for sale. Up and up we climbed, a few bounding like mountain goats, most of us huffing and puffing, and then Harry Bailley herded us together.

"Look!" he said, and pointed out a view to take the breath away, assuming you had any breath left after all that climbing. And mountain air, after all, is thinner to begin with. This mountain air of Safed was very thin and clear, so clear it made everything—the hills, the trees, the lakes, even us —look more vivid. It's hard to explain. It was as if we were somehow more *there*, more *real* maybe, than we had been in the lowlands. And if that sounds extravagant, well, I'm sorry. It must have been the thin air and all the exercise making me lightheaded. But all of us were quieter, more subdued than usual.

The purple mountains fell away from us to reveal, far below, a sapphire heart, and that, he told us, was the Sea of Galilee, Lake Kinneret in Hebrew, because *Kinneret* means "harp" in Hebrew, and the sound, he said, of the waves upon the shore reminded those who came here first of heavenly music.

"Judge for yourself later," he said, "when we come to Tiberias. But now, now, just look! *There* is the spot where the Jordan River joins the sea, and *there*, to the northeast, Lake Kinneret and the Lake of Hula make a heart, joined by the Jordan."

He stopped. We were already accustomed to his lively manner and his jokes. But the Harry Bailley who now spoke, spoke in a different voice.

"O God! Thou hast bound the hearts of Hula and of Kinneret with Thy rope, the Jordan," he recited. "But even Thou, O Almighty, hast not yet found in Thy possession the thread that shall unite the hearts of men together."

"Amen," I said, and so did the others say "Amen."

Quietly we filed back down through the narrow streets, our voices rising as we descended, until we were talking and laughing as always. I stopped to admire a painting of red and yellow flowers, very bright, on an easel in a garden, and when I caught up with the group they were already starting to board the bus. The Philanthropist, donor of forests and chocolate bars, was being helped up the big step by Harry Bailley's strong right arm. Behind him the Scribe, the young one with the downy blond beard, was tugging at the elbow of the Professor, the one who had been born Shimon Cohen in Brooklyn, remember? but who had been transformed long ago into Simon Priest, Professor of English Literature.

The Scribe's clear high voice rang out, "I believe with perfect faith in the Messiah's coming. And even if he be delayed, I will wait for him."

(I had no idea what had brought that on.)

The Professor looked at him as if he, the Scribe, had uttered an obscenity in the middle of one of his, the Professor's, lectures on John Milton, and without a word he stepped onto the bus.

"What was *that* all about?" I asked my neigh-

bor, the Caterer, but all I got for reply was a shrug
of the shoulders.

The Scribe, meanwhile, had stopped by Harry
Bailley's seat. "When the Messiah comes," he said,
so loud we all could hear, although usually he
spoke softly, "I think it is here he will come first."
And he went down the aisle and sat down in his
seat.

"That reminds me of a story," said the Mashgiach, and his small eyes twinkled under his
bushy eyebrows. "Did you hear the one about the
man who comes to a small town in Israel and
he can't find a job? A friend tells him to go to
the elders of the town, they're hiring someone for
some kind of a job, he doesn't know what. So
he goes, and they explain that the job is to sit at
the gates of the town from sunup till sundown and
watch for the Messiah. So he gets the job, and
every day he sits at the gates, and from sunup
till sundown he watches.

"After a couple of weeks he's pretty disgusted,
and he says to himself, 'The hours are long, all
day, every day, and the pay is very low.' So he
goes to the elders and he complains. They nod and
they're sympathetic. 'Yes, yes, we know,' they
say, 'the pay is very small and the hours are long,
but look at it this way. The job is steady.'"

The roar of the bus drowned out our laughter.
But the Scribe and the English Professor, neither
of them had laughed.

It was quiet in the bus for a while, and then
the English Professor began speaking, addressing
himself to the doctor. "Doctor," he said to the
Plastic Surgeon, "you have very forcefully and

convincingly demonstrated to us your unhappiness with the irrational and unthinking tendencies of mankind. But your mistake, Doctor, if you will allow me, is in the unexamined assumption underlying your disappointment, your assumption that most people walking the earth are rational creatures."

The Professor was clearly talking only to the Plastic Surgeon, but he seemed to be looking at all of us, and certainly his voice had the authentic ring of the lecture hall. I couldn't tell if I were eavesdropping or a regular part of his class.

He went on, "Let me point out for your consideration that one of the greatest of Western thinkers, Jonathan Swift, considered men pernicious vermin, *hominus animale rationis capax*, but only *capax*, if you follow me. Not, Man is a rational creature, but, Man is a creature *capable* of reason, and even then capable only to widely varying degrees. Why should I, Doctor, trust to reason (I speak rhetorically, as you are well aware) when I am an ignorant brute with no more sense of rhyme than of reason? I am uneducated, untrained to thought, undisciplined, and this is the condition of most men. I need hardly recall to you the Hobbesean view of the short, narrow, brutish existence of 'natural' man, or the irony implicit in Descartes' much misinterpreted dictum, *Je pense, ergo, je suis.*

"Therefore," concluded the English Professor, "it is actually 'natural' that most people hurry to take refuge in ignorance and superstition and in the unthinking conventions of a sheeplike society."

Well, I for one was very impressed. I had

counted three separate languages in less than three
minutes.

"Professor," said Harry Bailley, "you certainly
are a fine talker. May we ask for the honor of a
story from you?"

"I prefer the mask of allegory to a barefaced
story," said the Professor, "but this subject of religious credulity is so important in its implications
for our society that I prefer to take an interdis-
ciplinary approach, as it were, and invoke Clio,
the muse of history, to my aid. What I will tell you
is not fiction, but fact."

He had everyone's attention now. But instead
of beginning his story, he slowly filled his pipe,
tamped down the tobacco with deliberation, lit a
match, and drew on the pipe until clouds formed
and billowed above his head. Then, and only
then, did he begin.

THE ENGLISH PROFESSOR'S STORY

IN THE THIRD quarter of the seventeenth century,
wars, local violence, pestilence, and famine swept
over central and eastern Europe, affecting the
peasant classes adversely. In an attempt to make
some sort of sense out of these calamities, the
peasants began to talk of Armageddon, of the
end of the world, and above all, they predicted
the arrival of their longed-for Messiah to deliver
them from their troubles.

This response was most prevalent among the
Jews.

To begin with, like most peasant classes, they were poor. They were ignorant. And they were steeped in the superstition fostered by all primitive religions stressing obedience, unquestioning faith, and belief in miracles, with a deep-rooted hostility toward reason or even common sense. Add to that the clannishness and snobbishness inherent in a tribe's self-conceptualization as a chosen people, and the insularity and parochial view these of necessity inculcate, and you have a situation that is tailor-made for a charlatan. As if he had been called into being, therefore, along came Sabbatai Zevi, a false prophet with the little knowledge which, we know from the proverb, is a dangerous thing, a veneer of sophistication far above the manners and mores of rustic villagers, and a smattering of languages.

He had also the charisma of a magnetic personality and a physically attractive presence, complete to the piercing dark eyes almost obligatory for a prophet. And the final boost to his claim was provided by his birth date, which fell on the ninth day of the Hebrew month of Av, because there was an ancient legend connecting the Messiah's birth with the date of the destruction of Solomon's Temple in Jerusalem, which, you will scarcely be surprised to hear, fell on the ninth day of Av.

Sabbatai Zevi, in short, was the paradigm of a prophet, and when the young Turkish Jew (for he was born a Jew) presented himself in the city of Salonika as the Messiah, he came as an answer to prayer. A kind of Messianic hysteria, a frenzy of believing, spread like wildfire all over European

Jewry. Under the influence of this end-of-the-
world delirium, tens of thousands of poor and
credulous Jews gave away their few worldly possessions and sat down to wait for the final con-
flagration and judgment, while wealthier Jews
who fell under the spell abandoned their business
affairs and became impoverished as a result.

This fraud, this false prophet, fueled their hopes
with his ringing speeches that utilized all the mystic symbolism and irrational mythology of the *Zo-
har* and other documents of Cabalism, the magical, mystical creed that had initially plunged
these Jews into their cultural Dark Ages. Jews left
their squalid villages in droves to gaze upon this
new Messiah, and he collected an ever-larger following. He spoke, and *"Credo!"* they cried. "I believe!"

This movement, this madness, if you will, could
culminate in only one way, in disillusionment.
There is so much conflicting evidence that it is
impossible to say whether Sabbatai Zevi was a
thoroughgoing scoundrel or a self-deluded mystic. Therefore, the motivation behind his conver-
sion to Islam is also hidden from us by the veil
of history. There is one school which says that he
was threatened with his life unless he converted;
another holds that he came to believe in himself
as a prophet of Islam. Whatever the reason, the
historical fact is that he *did* become a Mohammedan, and he took the name of Mehemet Ef-
fendi.

The schism that followed tore apart the Jews of
Europe and the Near East. Many of them followed their Messiah right onto this new path and

converted to Islam. Others retreated into a belief that the convert, the Mohammedan Sabbatai Zevi, was a changeling, a double, a clone, if you will, and that the *real* Sabbatai Zevi, the Messiah, had been whisked off somewhere where he still lives in secret, awaiting the day when he is needed, an obvious parallel to the legend of King Arthur, alive and well at Avalon. But the majority of these superstitious folk, their belief shattered, returned to their homes more impoverished even than they were before, and sank into a profound cultural and spiritual apathy. And such, I say to you, are the rewards of unreasoning, mystical, wonderful, supernatural faith!

Well, some of us were angry, and some of us were apologetic, and some of us squirmed unhappily in our seats, as the professor's well-aimed shafts seemed to us to hit their targets.

But not our Hasid. He just sat quietly toward the back of the bus, rocking a little, forward and back, and humming very softly to himself. The English Professor seemed to be aiming most of his sharpest shafts at the Hasid, but the Hasid just kept twiddling his thumbs in his lap, quietly rocking and humming a little tune and looking out the window. And the more he sat and twiddled and rocked and hummed, the redder in the face the professor got, and the louder his voice and the faster his words, so the end of his story came out like the gobbling of a turkey-cock. And still the Hasid sat and twiddled and rocked and hummed. I think he might have been smiling now and then, but it's hard to tell behind a beard, isn't it?

I mean, a beard gives a person a lot of privacy. It's another natural advantage God gave to men. It *did* occur to me that a veil over a woman's face, which I have always regarded as an unmitigated evil and a product of the most virulent male chauvinism, might serve the same purpose as a man's beard, and that it could be very useful on occasion to be inscrutable. The Hasid, of course, had yet another advantage. It seems to me that if God is always walking with you and keeping you company, like He did the Hasid, this helps a lot to keep you serene.

Well, anyway, the Professor was glaring straight at the Hasid, and everyone else was very quiet, and our tour guide took a deep breath and opened his mouth, and suddenly the Hasid stopped twiddling and rocking and humming. He sat very still, and slowly he turned his head until he'd looked at all of us. Then, slowly, calmly, the Hasid began to speak. He had a curious trick of repeating single words, so that it sounded like his speech was accompanied by the tolling of a bell.

THE HASID: THE OTHER

R EMEMBER, remember, when we stood on the mountain," he began. "In the clear, thin air of Safed one sees farther than in other places. And high, so high up in the mountains, one is closer to the Lord. Which is why they came there, the true mystics, the Cabalists, the searchers for truth, whose heads were as strong as their hearts. But they left behind those in whom existed the seeds of doubt, ready to bloom at the sight of a vision too strong for them. Knowledge is a blessing, but knowledge beyond the reach of the heart's understanding can become a curse.

"And now I, I will take my turn to tell a story."

THE HASID'S STORY

YOU MUST understand, to begin with, that Elisha ben Abuyah was a great sage, one of the greatest sages in Jerusalem long ago. Even when he was a child, it was certain that he would grow up to be a scholar. He loved to learn: he loved to ask questions and he loved to debate, and he sat on the ground at the feet of the sages, his teachers, and drank in Torah the way the thirsty dust drinks in rain. So that when he was still a young man, he had already achieved a high rank for his wisdom and his learning, and the best students, among them the one who came to be Rabbi Meir, the best students came to sit in the dust at his feet. But then, something happened, and Elisha ben Abuyah turned aside from the ways in which he had walked.

This great sage and teacher would enter a house of study and stand there, silent, watching the young boys at their books until they became uneasy under that silent stare, and looked away from their books, looked toward Elisha ben Abuyah. And he would say to them, these students: "What are you doing here? You are foolish boys, to waste your hours and your days in studying the Torah. You could be out learning something useful. You could learn a trade and earn much money. You there, you could be a mason; and you could be a carpenter; you in the corner, you could be a tailor." And the boys listened, and they thought, and they closed their books and went out from the house of study, and turned away from the Torah.

Or he would sit in the center of a room of study and wait until all the young boys had gathered around him, and then he would start his questioning.

"Can the Lord do everything?"

"Yes," they would answer in chorus.

"Can the Lord make a rock he can't move?"

"Yes."

"Then the Lord can't do everything."

And the young boys would listen, and think, and they closed their books and went out from the room of study, and turned away from the Lord.

From this time, when his fellow sages and teachers discovered what their colleague (that is the word, colleague, isn't it?) was doing, they no longer called him Elisha ben Abuyah. Now, now he was called *Aher*, the Other, for he had turned aside from his fellow Jews and he walked alone. For a change in life is marked by a change in name. Remember, remember that Jacob had wrestled with the angel of the Lord, and by his strength he had survived, but he limped forever after, and his name had been changed to Israel, that is, he who strives with the Lord. But Elisha ben Abuyah had striven *against* the Lord, and so he was changed to Aher, that is, the Other. And so he would go from school to school, turning the hearts and minds of the young with false logic and

false questions and false values, planting his seeds
of doubt wherever he set his feet. And when he
walked in the street, some of the young would run
after him, and hang on him, but his fellows pulled
their garments aside lest they touch his, and they
turned away their faces. And so he grew old, old;
and lonely for his fellows and for the Lord, and
sometimes he would even try to turn again, but
something inside him made him stiff and rigid.
Then one day, Aher, who was Elisha ben Abuyah,
went walking in his garden, and he met his own
image face to face, by which he knew that his
soul had fled from him as he had fled from the
Lord, and he would shortly die, because his soul
had gone forth from him. And what he knew was
what came to pass because, first and last, he was
a man of great learning. A sad story, honored
sage to shunned apostate. Then how, how was it
that such a fearful change came to be?

Some say that one day, as he sat under a date
palm studying the Torah, Elisha ben Abuyah saw
the tongue of the martyred Rabbi Judah held in
the bloody jaws of a dog; and he was afraid and
angry, and he said to himself, "This is the tongue
that recited the Torah of the Lord? And this is
its reward? Then there is no reward, and God is
a liar." Because he had seen what he could not
understand, he spoke this way. His belief and his
worship were only in his mind, and with his
great learning, one thing he had not learned, that
the Holy One, Blessed be He, wants the heart.

But such a lesson and such an explanation are
surely too simple for men of great learning to understand. And so I will tell you what happened

to Elisha ben Abuyah according to a parable from the Talmud.

"Four rabbis entered into Paradise. One saw and died. The second saw and lost his reason. The third laid waste the young plants. Only Rabbi Akiba entered in peace and went out in peace."

A simple story this is, too simple to understand. For each simple word of the Torah is like a diamond from which shine many lights. Turn it this way, turn it that way, the colors are forever changing in their radiance. But the diamond is always the same diamond. So the story of the four rabbis holds within it the story of how Rabbi Elisha ben Abuyah became Aher.

"Four rabbis"—that is, Rabbi ben Zoma, Rabbi ben Azzai, Rabbi Elisha ben Abuyah, and Rabbi Akiba—"entered into Paradise." That is to say, they entered the Garden of Eden, our first Paradise, and Rabbi Akiba told them not to be afraid and to trust in the Lord. So they all went through the shining silver gates, only to find gates of blazing gold barring the way. "One saw and died"— that was ben Zoma, who looked upon so much splendor and so much glory, and whose heart's strength gave out with the sight. So the three passed through the golden gates into a beautiful garden, and they came to a marble enclosure. "The second saw and lost his reason"—as ben Azzai gazed upon the gleaming marble his mind gave way under the effort to comprehend his being so close to the center of Paradise. Together Elisha ben Abuyah and Akiba penetrated through the marble enclosure and stood at last at the heart of Paradise, and there in front of them, leaping

upward from the rocks, was a fountain of living
waters, and they looked upon it with awe and
trembling. "The third laid waste the young shoots"
—suddenly Elisha ben Abuyah gave a great cry,
and threw his hands over his eyes, for he was
afraid, even though Akiba had told him to trust
in the Lord. And he ran back through the marble
enclosure, and his fear had made him angry, and
he rushed around the garden like a wild boar, tearing out the young plants by their roots and fling-
ing them in the air to die. And so he raged, laying
waste the garden, tearing and destroying. "Only
Rabbi Akiba entered in peace and went out in
peace"—because he was strong of heart and mind
and faith.

Then tell me, what is this Paradise, that kills, or
maddens, or perverts the weak? There are as
many meanings as there are minds to hear this
story. But here is one. There is a Hebrew pun that
explains it. Paradise is made up of four letters,
P,R,D, and S, which form the word *Pardes*. The
first letter, P, is the *peshat*, the silver gates, the
literal meaning of the words of the Torah. The
second letter, the R, is the *remez*, the golden
gates, the meaning behind the literal meaning,
what the literal meaning stands for. The third letter, D, the marble enclosure, is the *derasha*, the
ethical meaning behind those two, what the words
teach us to do in our lives. And the S, ah! the S,
the *sod*, the living waters! That is the secret, the
mystical meaning that must be searched for
through the world, up to the gates of Paradise and
beyond to the living waters which are Torah, and
Truth, and the Holy One, Blessed be He, Himself.

The *sod* is the end of our journey, the sweet meat within the nutshell, the seed within the growing flower that grows only in Paradise. But, of course, this Paradise—we can't go there to pluck out the secret. After all, who among us is a saint like Akiba? And even he went out of the garden again. So we learn that we can only know the deepest meanings of life when we reach Paradise, after death, in the next life. Just as the S completes Paradise, so does Paradise complete the world, and death complete life. So you must go on, seeking, seeking knowledge and wisdom until the day of your death, studying and teaching, knowing that you cannot reach that which you are searching for. But you can't be frightened off your job like this, like Aher, the Other, and say, "I cannot, I am afraid, I will not." No, no, it is told to us, "You are not obliged to finish the task, yet you are not free to desist from it." And so together we have learned a little Torah, and see, out the window, this afternoon's bus trip is almost ended, and so is my story, for the Lord, the Lord is merciful in small things as He is in large ones.

And he was right, because the bus was nearing Tiberias, on the Sea of Galilee, and all around us from the brown earth sprang a spring glory of anemones, red, pink, purple, and white, the lilies of the field, to welcome us.

THE INTERFAITH LIEUTENANT: MIRACLES ARE HARD ON A MOTHER

WE STAYED the night down at Tiberias. And I do mean *down*. You can see on any map, Tiberias is below sea level, on the shore of the Sea of Galilee. Or the Lake of Kinneret. It's the same body of water. It just depends on who made the map.

Whichever it was, sea or lake, after a morning of sightseeing we were sitting right by it, admiring the diamonds sparkling on its blue surface and listening to the waves beat against the shore, trying to decide 131 if they sounded like a harp (which, if you remember, is what *Kinneret* means in Hebrew). And I really didn't think they did very much, they sounded to me more like waves beating on a shore, but I certainly wasn't going to advertise my lack of imagination. So I was relieved when the Dropout exclaimed "No way!" when I asked him his opinion, because he was, after all, our resident musical authority, with his guitar and all.

And we were also enjoying a meal of fish and chips at a sea- (or lake-) side restaurant. I must tell you that these weren't just ordinary everyday fish and chips, or I wouldn't be telling you about them. Well, the chips were ordinary. But the fish, bony and sweet-fleshed, was comb fish, which is found, Harry Bailley swore to us, in only two places in the world, here and in Lake Victoria in Uganda.

They also call it St. Peter's fish, because of a mark on its skin that looks like a thumbprint. The Chairperson of the Massachusetts, Connecticut, and Rhode Island Tri-State Area of Interfaith Councils was telling us all about it, but she was so knowledgeable that I was afraid my fish would get cold, so I ate instead of listening. I'm sorry, but if you want to know more about the legend of St. Peter's fish, you'll have to find out for yourself.

Before lunch, we had had a boat ride to the farther shore to see an ancient church, or maybe it was a synagogue, no one can say for certain. It has a mosaic of the zodiac on the floor, but that doesn't prove anything one way or the other.

It's funny, but Tiberias was like that, on-the-one-hand, on-the-other-hand. The Sea of Galilee

or Lake Kinneret, comb fish or St. Peter's fish,
synagogue or church.

Even its name. Most Christian historians say it's named after Tiberias, who was emperor of Rome when it was built. But Jewish sages claim its name derives from *tibur*, the word for "navel," because Tiberias was the cradle of the great academies of Jewish learning, the place where the *Mishnah*, the *Gemara*, and the Jerusalem Talmud were all completed and written down.

For that matter, on the one hand, in the winter months, Tiberias is jammed with mountain dwellers seeking sun and swimming. On the other hand, in summer, many dwellers there swarm up to Safed and the mountains for their cooling breezes.

As I said, Tiberias is like that. It depends on which perspective you're looking from.

Which can present problems—being able to see things from two perspectives, I mean. Like me. I'm very good at "on-the-one-hand, on-the-other-hand." I can always see both sides of a question. It's the answers I have problems with. I seem to find two. Or none.

And when you're tolerant and understanding, which I am, pretty much, it makes it sometimes very difficult to actually *do* anything. So I find I don't do very much, but I spend a lot of time looking on, and I tell myself that somebody's got to take notes, don't they? I mean, there's such a person as the Recording Angel, so even God must think it's worthwhile taking notes.

Anyway, we had had a busy morning, so when we boarded the bus again, everyone was chattering away about all the things we'd seen and heard. The Interfaith Chairperson's laugh chimed like a bell at regular two-minute intervals. The Executive Director was furiously scribbling away in his black morocco notebook, while the Lawyer was counting his exposed rolls of film and loading up for his next shooting spree. The Art Dealer was explaining in detail the history of mosaic sculpture to the Rabbi and his Wife. Across the aisle from me the Interfaith Lieutenant was bubbling away to the Widow, but not about Tiberias or any of its sights. She had out her stack of snapshots of her grandchildren, and she was going through each and every one of them, with commentary.

"That's Joshua, blond, you see how blond he is. He's brilliant, if I do say so myself. His nursery-school teacher just can't get over him. And Deborah, his sister, also a blonde . . ."

The Widow smiled politely, and oohed and ahed in the appropriate places. Of course I would never say such a thing, but the Interfaith Lieutenant made me think of all the jokes about Jewish mothers you'd ever rejected because of course they were too exaggerated, no one in real life could possibly be like that! But she was.

I won't bore you with the stories, like the one about the grandma on the boardwalk in Atlantic City who's walking with her granddaughter when a neighbor comes by.

"What a gorgeous child!" says the neighbor.

"That's nothing," says the grandma. "You should see her picture."

Or the classic of the grandmother introducing her two grandsons—"Here's my *ainichel*, my youngest grandson, he's seven, he's the brain sur-

geon, and his brother here, he's the Supreme Court
judge."

No, I won't bother telling you those stories. You
probably already know them. But I bit my tongue
and I didn't say anything, which was hard for me
because, personally, I would never *dream* of in-
flicting my children's pictures on total—well, not
quite *total* by now, to be fair—almost total strangers even though, believe me, because I saw her
pictures, my children are *much* better-looking than
her grandchildren.

As if he'd read my mind, though, Harry Bailley
leaned over and smiled. He said, very quietly,
"Who said it was only mothers who doted on their
children? Children have fathers, too. On my last
tour a man, a fine gentleman from Detroit, Mich-
igan, he told me once he got a phone call from one
of his old father's friends. I should explain the father had a fall, he broke his hip, he was in the
hospital, very sudden.

"The friend said, 'Your father comes every
morning to the *shul* for prayers, two, three, four
mornings he didn't come, and I'm worried. So I
know he has two sons, I took a chance in the phone
book, I hope you'll forgive the liberty, and how is
your father?'

"The son explained what had happened, and
he thanked his father's friend for calling.

"'It's nothing,' said the friend. 'Just give my
wishes for a speedy recovery.'

"The son started to hang up, but the man's voice
cut in again. 'Tell me,' he said, 'to which son am I
speaking, the brilliant doctor or the fantastically
successful businessman?'"

We laughed together quietly. Just then the Interfaith Lieutenant's voice rose solemnly above the other chatter.

"A child is a blessing," she said, "and a grand-child is a miracle." (Which is a consistent position for someone who'd suggested adding the Blessed Mother Mary to the Trinity.)

"Here we go with the miracles again," said the Plastic Surgeon in disgust.

"What's all the fuss about miracles?" retorted the Interfaith Lieutenant. "Surely God is entitled."

The Fundraiser, he of the three *yarmelkes* to meet all contingencies, spoke up. "I feel about miracles the way I do about ghosts. I don't say I believe in them, but it never hurts to be polite."

The Interfaith Lieutenant smiled politely and continued, "Who are we to think we know it all? After all—"

"There are more things in heaven and earth, eh, Horatio," interrupted the English Professor, puffing on his briar pipe. "You agree, naturally."

She met him with a level stare, very dignified. "I might. If I knew what you were talking about, Professor. Explain."

"It's nothing, nothing," he said, offhand. "Just some Shakespeare I assumed was universally recognizable. Obviously my mistake. Never mind, let it pass."

"No, I will not," she said firmly. "This is not good manners, to hint and pass right by. This is not how your mother taught you, I'm sure. Explain what you mean. You're a teacher? Teach."

The Art Dealer's son, he may have been a College Dropout but he was a nice young man with lovely manners, he spoke up instead, while the Pro-

fessor, struggling (I suppose) with alternative
modes of response, applied himself busily to his
pipe.

"That's from Shakespeare's play *Hamlet*," said
the young man. "See, Hamlet and his buddy Horatio have just, you know, rapped with the ghost
of Hamlet's murdered father, and Horatio's trying
to, like, explain the ghost away with some heavy
philosophy, but Hamlet says to him, like, 'There
are more things in heaven and earth, Horatio, than
are dreamt of in your philosophy.' Hamlet believed in miracles, too," he said, and smiled at
her, and struck several pleasing chords on the guitar he always carried with him, cradled in his lap.

"I am acquainted with the play *Hamlet*," said
the Interfaith Lieutenant, "and I thank you for the
reminder. That was the mother who had so much
trouble with her son after her first husband died.
The son was jealous when she remarried, and he
said terrible things to her, to his mother. That's a
terrible thing altogether for a woman, to be torn
between her husband and her child, and it is certainly worth writing a play about. You could call
it *Gertrude*, or *Molly*, or whatever her name was.
But Shakespeare is a man, he sees everything from
the man's point of view, which is understandable,
but that's how the play turns into *Hamlet*.

"You know," she said thoughtfully, absently
tapping her nose with a snapshot, "the writers of
the Bible were like that. They were all men. Wonderful men, I'm sure, I mean that sincerely, Rabbi,
very pious and very wise, but they were men. And
it seems to me that however pious and wise, they
had limits. You take the story, you all know it,

that's recited every Rosh Hashanah, every New Year, of Abraham and the sacrifice of Isaac. And what do you hear? There is God and Abraham and Isaac. My father, my son. Well, that boy had a mother. And she had feelings, and not one word do you find about his mother. A miracle happens, one that saves her son's life. But nobody bothers to let her in on the miracle. What did she think about all this? God calls Abraham, Abraham only, and Abraham says, *Hineni,* here I am. Not, Here *we* are, his mother and me, but, Here I am. And God tells him to take Isaac and go to Mount Moriah and sacrifice him. *Your* son you should sacrifice to me, He tells Abraham. And Abraham says Okay. Not, Should we ask his mother? Not, His mother will share this miracle with me. Okay, he says. And off they go. They get there and the boy, who is a bright child, says, 'Where's the sacrifice?' and his father says, 'God will provide.' And Abraham binds Isaac on the altar, and he raises the knife, and then! An angel calls, 'Abraham, Abraham, put down the knife.' And there's a ram caught by the horns in a thicket, and Abraham sacrifices the ram, and God is proud of Abraham, so pious and obedient, and of Isaac, so pious and obedient, and they all live happily ever after. A miracle. All the same, miracles are hard on a mother. Nobody told Sarah anything, but she knew something was up, Abraham was so strange in his manner, abrupt, and Isaac was excited, going on a trip with his father. She suspected something, but she didn't know what, for good or for bad. *Her* worries, *her* sorrows, nobody pays any attention to them. Only once did I find a legend, that's all it was, a legend, that ever paid attention to Isaac's mother, to Sarah. And in that legend, the only one that paid attention to Sarah was the Devil. We're each supposed to tell a story, so I will tell you a story, about Sarah.

THE INTERFAITH LIEUTENANT'S STORY

FIRST YOU MUST understand that Isaac was a menopause baby. It says in the Bible, "Sarah had stopped having the periods of women." That's how Isaac got his name; when the angels told Abraham he and Sarah would have a son, she was listening in secret, and she laughed, because her womb was barren and her husband was old. But God has his miracles, and she conceived and bore a son and they called his name Isaac, which is "laughter." And Isaac was a joy and a blessing and a source of laughter to his parents, but especially to his mother. Her old breasts grew firm and young, and she took pleasure when he suckled from her, pulling on her breasts. He was a greedy baby, and he grew and he flourished. And he was her heart's delight, the apple of her eye.

When Isaac was about nine years old, the Devil had a conversation with God. He told God that Abraham was so satisfied with his tents and camels and belongings, and so happy with his little son Isaac, that he'd forgotten God.

"He doesn't even offer up sacrifices to You any more," the Devil said, smiling.

And God said, "Abraham is my good and faithful servant. He would do anything for me. I have faith in him. He would sacrifice anything for me."

And the Devil said, kind of laughing, "Even Isaac, I suppose."

And God said, "Even Isaac."

The Devil said, "Not Isaac. I'll bet he wouldn't."

And God said, "Yes, he would."

And the Devil said, "You're on."

Well, maybe not in those words. But he provoked God to this wicked bargain, at least *I* think it was a wicked bargain. I know, it's supposed to be an opportunity for Abraham to show his perfect faith. So God called Abraham, and Abraham agreed. And Abraham got ready for a trip, and he said to Sarah, "The boy has grown, and he's learned many things, but to serve God in perfect faith, that he has not yet learned. I'm taking him away awhile that he may learn to serve the Lord our God with all his heart and with all his soul."

And the story goes on like it does in the Bible, with noble Abraham of perfect faith, and Isaac, his son, just like him. Such a son as that one in the Bible no one needs ever to worry about. But do you think this is the way of a real nine-year-old boy? Only a man, you will pardon me, only a man could create such a nine-year-old, serious, brave, biddable. This is how a man sees a good son. But the Isaac that Sarah knew, ah! That was a real child. A mischief-maker he was, with a glint in his eye. He was full of life and schemes that ended up making trouble, but they were the schemes of a good heart. And when he was afraid and he was with his father or the other boys, why, he was brave, and nothing scared him, nothing. But she knew better. She knew that the big front was just a big front, and inside was just a little boy, her little boy, the one that wept such loud and stormy tears into her arms. That little boy was sometimes so afraid of the thunder or the dark or of the thought of dying that only his proud, fierce will kept him from screaming out loud.

And that was the nine-year-old that Abraham took by the hand and set off on a trip to God knows where. Sarah kissed and hugged Isaac, and kissed and hugged him again. And she gave instructions to his father: Be sure he gets enough to eat. Be sure he gets enough water to drink at all times. Be sure he wears a hat. The sun is so hot, he needs to cover his head, and he won't want to, so you'll have to insist. And don't forget, he thinks he's such a big man, and so do you, he's only nine years old."

She followed them a while, and her heart was heavy, and at last she had to turn her head away so they wouldn't see the tears in her eyes, and when she turned around again, they were already far, far down the dusty road.

Each morning she went to see if they were coming back, but no one came. On the third morning she saw a cloud of dust far down the road, and her heart leaped. But when it came closer, she saw it was only one person, and her heart plunged, but when it came closer still she saw it was a stranger, a poor old man, ragged, like a beggar. This was the Devil, only of course Sarah didn't know that, and she hailed him.

"Did you see anyone else when you were traveling on the road?"

And he said, "No. Who are you awaiting?"

And she said, "My husband, Abraham, with my son, Isaac. He took the boy so that he should learn to serve the Lord with all his heart and with all his soul, and I wait each day until they come home again."

And the beggar said, "Your husband, Abraham, will be coming along, but Isaac, your son, Isaac, your favored one, he will never return home to you again."

And she went all white and faint and said to him, "What do you mean?"

And he said, "Isaac has learned to serve the Lord, with all his heart and with all his soul and his body also. For Abraham has offered him up on an altar as a sacrifice to his God, and Isaac is dead."

Sarah gave a great cry and fell to the earth as if she too were dead. When she came to herself, she was alone, and she remembered the beggar's words, and she tore her clothes and she sat in the dust, pouring dust over her head, and her tears fell like salt rain on the barren ground, and that was how her women servants found her when they came to look for her.

They raised her up, and she leaned on one of them and she whispered something, so low the maidservant had to bend her head to listen. She whispered, "My pretty little boy." And then she didn't speak again.

And all this while, Abraham and Isaac were coming home from Mount Moriah, hand in hand. But Sarah mourned her son, silent and dry-eyed, all night. And in the morning she arose and took two of her women servants with her, and they set out to find where Abraham and Isaac had gone, so that she could look for the last time on her son, Isaac. And they went here, and they went there, but no one had seen the father and the boy. They had come to the outskirts of Hebron when someone came toward them on the road, and Sarah looked, and it was the same old beggar who had told her of Isaac's death. She broke away from her women servants and ran towards him, begging and pleading with him to tell her where they were. And he smiled, the old beggar, the Devil, and he showed his sharp pointed teeth, only she didn't notice, and he said, "Oh, Sarah! Forgive me! I got the story wrong, it was a lie, Abraham did not sacrifice Isaac, and Isaac is not dead. It was a trick of God's, that's all, never mind."

She stood stock still and she looked at him. And when the words at last reached her understanding, she raised her hands to heaven to rejoice, and her heart leaped inside her, so that it broke from grief and sudden joy, and she died.

When Abraham and Isaac reached their home at Beersheba, the boy ran ahead to look for his mother. But she wasn't there. And the servants told Abraham of the news of Isaac's death that had come to them. And Abraham took Isaac and in a great hurry they set out to follow Sarah. And at last they found her, in Hebron. And they wept over her body, but even then the Bible says only, Abraham mourned bitterly for her. Of her son, her pretty little boy, who wailed and moaned and had to be dragged off his mother's body by the others, not a word. "My mother! My mother!" he cried. Not a word. And it was no good anyway, for Sarah was dead.

THE RABBI'S WIFE: HANNAH'S CHILDREN

WHEN the Interfaith Lieutenant had finished her story of Abraham, Isaac, and Sarah, and we had all paid it a tribute of silence, the young Scribe spoke up in a soft, tentative voice.

"Are you saying that God should have asked Sarah's permission?" he asked.

The Interfaith Lieutenant thought a little, then said, "Maybe I am. Could it have hurt if God had called Sarah too? Didn't *she* deserve to be tested?"

"But," said the Scribe,

"you've said she would not have agreed. And that's
not logical."

"So is logic everything?" retorted the Interfaith
Lieutenant. "Love is something too."

"Yes," said the Rabbi quietly. "Love is something. Sarah loved Isaac. So did Abraham. But Abraham loved God."

"What kind of God is it," the Interfaith Lieutenant burst out, "who says you have to love Him *more than?* More than parents, more than children, more than husbands or wives? I too love God! But *more than?*"

"I too am a mother," said the Rabbi's Wife, in a clear firm voice.

And I can tell you, she certainly had mothered all of us. Whenever we neared a holy place, a church, a mosque, or a synagogue, out of her handbag, like a magician's sack, would flow endless lengths of scarves to cover up the women's heads and drape about their bare shoulders, and numberless skullcaps, so that our men should not go bareheaded before the Lord. And she prefaced her comments often with "Mamma always said," so that we had already compiled a list of Mamma's wise sayings, the Mamma who had come as an immigrant to the oil fields of Texas and struck, not oil but many children, and much hard work, but Mamma always said, "Everything always happens for the best," and "What happens, happens," and in extreme cases, "Man plans, God laughs," which she translated as "God knows and you don't." So I thought we were going to hear one more of Mamma's pronouncements, but instead, she repeated what she had said.

"I too am a mother, and I too have nursed my children. And I knew that more than they wanted my breasts, I wanted to offer them my breasts. I would have given my life for them, I suppose. I still would. But one thing I know. Children are children, but God is God. And our children don't belong to us. They come as a loan from God."

"Like taking out a library book," I said, before my head could catch up with my tongue.

The Rabbi's Wife considered me for a moment. Then she said, "A foolish comparison, but it will do. The books have to be returned. So do the children. All we hope is that we're lucky enough to be dead before that day. But if we're not, then we must bear and be strong. The Sarah in that story you just heard isn't the real Sarah. That Sarah mixes up a soft heart and a soft head. Surely Sarah was strong, and could bear trials as well as Abraham. Maybe better. I remember my mamma, God rest her soul, used to tell me about Beruriah, the wife of the great Rabbi Meir, the sage. Oh, she was a Sarah, a mother in Israel! She had two sons, two beautiful boys, and they were her life. Well, the Rabbi was away teaching, and in the same day both of those beautiful sons took sick and died. Beruriah wept, you can imagine, but then she thought of her husband coming home, so she took a cloth and she covered the two bodies. And at evening she went forward to greet Rabbi Meir. She kissed him, and she gave him a bowl of soup, and when he was finished she began speaking to him.

"'A man came today with a problem to put to you. He said that a jeweler had given him two beautiful diamonds to take care of for him. And

he had taken wonderful care of those diamonds,
and he had loved having them. And then today
the jeweler came back and asked for the return
of the diamonds. The man was sad at the thought
of losing the diamonds, and angry at the jeweler
for demanding them, and he came to you to see
how he could avoid giving them back.'

"Rabbi Meir grew very angry. 'That man is a
thief!' he said. 'He wishes to keep what he knew
was only lent, instead of being grateful for having
had the enjoyment of two beautiful jewels. And
furthermore, he should be grateful that the burden
of caring for such precious jewels and protecting
them from harm lies no longer upon his shoulders.'

"With that, Beruriah rose from the table, took
his hand, and led him to the bedroom where the
bodies of the children were lying.

" 'See, my husband, we have enjoyed these precious jewels, and cared for them, and worried
about them, and today the jeweler who lent them
has come to take them back.' And Rabbi Meir
wept, but he was consoled by his own wisdom,
because of the wisdom of his wife. This is the story
my Mamma, God rest her soul, told me, and I
never forgot."

"A very beautiful story," agreed the Interfaith
Lieutenant. "But I can understand sickness. After
all, sickness happens. God doesn't do it on purpose. But to ask for a child's life, just for His own
honor— Such a jealous God! Forgive me, but *this*
I cannot understand."

"Yes, you can," said the Rabbi's Wife. "One
child, even seven children. Because He has the

right. Let me tell you of a mother who, in her
spirit and her courage, was equal to Abraham. Let
me tell you of Hannah and her seven sons." And
in her flat, even, unadorned voice, she began.

THE RABBI'S WIFE'S STORY

IT WAS IN Jerusalem long ago, when the Syrians
and their wicked king, Antiochus, had occupied
the land and were defiling the Temple. The king
commanded that the Jews come before him in the
Temple, before the Holy of Holies, and bend the
knee and bow the head before an idol that he had
set up there. And to set an example for all the Jews,
the first to be called was Hannah, a pious widow
who was known for her wisdom, her good deeds,
and her acts of charity. Because if Hannah and
her children would kneel to this idol, King Antiochus figured, then surely the rest of the Jews
would fall down beside her and their God, the
God of the Jews, would be disgraced.

So Hannah and her seven sons were brought before the king. All the things of torture were there,
iron rakes and whips and knives. He asked them
all if they would kneel down to worship the idol,
and all of them said no. So the king's men began
with the first son. They cut out his tongue, and
then they roasted him alive in an iron pan over a
flame. But he would not give in, and his mother,
Hannah, looked on, and he died.

The second son they flayed until all his skin lay
in a heap beside his body, but he would not give

in, and his mother, Hannah, looked on, and he
died.

The third son they raked his skin with iron rakes until the blood poured down, but he would not give in, and his mother, Hannah, looked on, and he died.

The fourth son they whipped with whips until the flesh hung off from the bones, but he would not give in, and his mother, Hannah, looked on, and he died.

The fifth and the sixth sons too they tortured by knife and rake and whip and fire, but they would not give in, and their mother, Hannah, looked on, and they died.

And then came the seventh son, her youngest, her baby. And even that cruel man of stone, King Antiochus, felt his heart stir within him. He said to the boy, "Look, you do not have to really kneel down. I will take this ring off my finger, and I will drop it, and you will pick it up and return it to me, and the people will think you have knelt to worship the idol, but all you have done is to return my ring."

The king turned to Hannah and he said, "You are his mother, and he is your last remaining son. Tell him in your own language to do this simple thing, and he will be spared to you."

So Hannah spoke to her seventh son, in Hebrew, which the king could not understand, and she said, "Know before whom you stand. You came to my womb, I know not how. Not your father and not myself, but the Lord your God gave you life. Now you must go back to Him who is your father and mother. But first have pity on me, because for nine months I carried you, for three years I suckled you, for thirteen years I have reared you. Look at the heaven and the earth and remember that the Lord your God made them from nothing, even as He made you. Do not be afraid, but join your brothers, so that we will one day all be together again in God from whom we came. Goodbye, my son."

And she smiled at him.

The king saw her smile, and he drew the ring off his finger and let it drop to the floor. He waited, but the boy stood straight and stiff, and said, "I will bend my knee and bow my head before no man, but only for the honor of the Lord my God, the Lord of Israel, and if I must give my life in His Name, then I will do so."

So they tortured the boy with all the tortures of his brothers, but he would not give in, and his mother, Hannah, looked on, and he died.

Then Hannah said, "Now kill me as well, for I am a dead woman already." And they did.

THE COOK:
I KNOW
A MAN

INSIDE the bus there was a kind of chill after the Rabbi's Wife's story, and nobody said anything, because what could you say? And outside all was heat and light, and there were the brown and stony wastes of the Judean desert on both sides as far as the eye could see, the hills folded like lions' paws stretching almost to the road, bare and barren like the Wild West of America, but instead of sagebrush and the tumbleweed of the West were here terebinth and saltbush. And then those folded hills were replaced by higher, sterner mountains, crags of sandstone, pitted with caves, the caves where the Dead Sea Scrolls were found and the caves where young David, not yet a king, hid, an outlaw, from the jealous wrath of Saul. We stopped and got off the bus to look at the caves, and above us arched a vast, deep-blue sky, truly the vault of heaven, and something inside me leaped toward the arid land and whispered, "I come from this desert." And then we were back on the bus, on a ribbon of road squashed between the sparkling aquamarine of the Dead Sea, its rim of shore fringed with reeds, and on our right side the mountains, rich brown, stony, crumbling, rising sheer and strong, and far on the left, shimmering in a heat haze, the mountains of Moab. And still we were quiet.

Then the Cook, who had scarcely been heard to say one word during our whole trip, but sat silent by himself, raised his voice. It came out a little harsh and rusty from lack of use, but what he said was clear enough. He said, "Orange marmalade."

Now orange marmalade, coming out of the blue like that, might have seemed a peculiar thing to say, but for the Cook, orange marmalade, or any other food, seemed appropriate. Because, without meaning to be uncharitable, we had all commented at one time or another on his extraordinary appetite. The man was a vacuum cleaner! Set the biggest heap of food before him, and he simply *inhaled* it, now you see it, now you don't. Take breakfast, for example. I don't know how many of you are familiar with Israeli breakfasts. I wasn't. But I found out. Breakfast is a buffet, at the hotels at any rate, and it consists, more or less, of (are you ready?) orange juice, grapefruit juice, ripe olives, fresh green olives, white and yellow cheeses, soft, medium, and hard, with little holes and big holes and no holes, cottage cheese, cream cheese, sour cream, creamed herring, herring salad, matjes herring, pickled herring, tomato herring, tuna fish, yoghurt plain and fruited, oatmeal, eggs boiled and scrambled, peppers green and red, cucumbers, tomatoes, melon, croissants, rolls, butter, marmalade, and honey. Is your mouth watering? Mine is. In my opinion, breakfast is the best meal served in Israel.

Well, all of us, even the hungriest, would take a taste of this and a dab of that the first time around, till we had discovered the things we liked best, and then we'd settle for a fair amount of those. But not the Cook. Two, three, four, five visits to the buffet table he would make, his plate piled high each time, and he ate his way through everything as if he were afraid he'd never get another meal. Some people thought it was funny, and some people thought it was disgusting, but all of us had noticed it. And as much as he ate, that's how little he spoke. So when he finally did say something, as I said, "Orange marmalade" seemed appropriate.

He went on, "My story will be about orange marmalade. Among other things."

THE COOK'S STORY

I KNOW A MAN, he lived in Warsaw, I'll call him Job. He was a good man, at least he always tried to be, he feared God and he avoided evil as much as a person can. And he was married, he had a nice wife and three daughters and a son. Now this Job, he wasn't what you'd call wealthy, really wealthy, but he lived okay. He had a good restaurant, and it brought in a good living. He had a house in town and even a small. cabin in the country, for vacation now and then, and he even had some servants. And he gave to the poor with an open hand, and he observed all the commandments and the festivals. Especially Yom Kippur, the Day of Atonement, he went to the *shul* in fear and trembling to pound his chest and confess and repent his sins. And he didn't repent once only, but again and again, because he was afraid that some one of his family might, in a bad temper or something, have sinned and cursed God in their heart and forgotten, so he was making sure that their sin, if it was one, would be forgiven. And this was Job's life.

Now one day, somewhere off from the world of men, God and Satan, they were having a conversation. And God bragged to Satan how his servant Job was so upright and good and God-fearing. But Satan laughed at Him. He said, "Oh, yeah? Why shouldn't Job love you? Look at him, he has all he needs, whatever he touches prospers, why shouldn't he praise You and fear You? You mark what I say, take away what he has, and see how fast he'll come to curse You to Your face." Then God got angry. He said to Satan, "Go, you have my permission, do your worst to him, only you can't kill him, and we'll see what we'll see."

Now it came to pass in Poland that the lice, the

scum, the vermin, those sons of Satan, the Nazis,
they overran the land. And one day Job in his
house got a message from a boy, all raggedy and
out of breath from running. "Your children," he
cried out. "Your children were all gathered together at your eldest son's store when a mob gathered and began stoning the windows. When your
son ran out to stop them, they stoned him as well,
and then they set fire to the store, and of them all
only your youngest daughter's husband has escaped, and he is in the hospital."

At the look on Job's face, the boy turned and
ran out of the house. But Job got up and tore his
jacket in the Jewish way, and he covered all the
mirrors, and he put on his bedroom slippers, and
he sat down on a low stool to mourn, and he beat
his chest, and he said, "Naked I came from out of
my mother, and naked I shall return. The Lord
gives, the Lord takes away, Blessed be the name
of the Lord." And he wept the night through, and
all the days after, but he didn't deny God.

So out in that somewhere God bragged again to
Satan about Job, his good servant, who was tested
and found true. But Satan said back to Him, "Sure,
those were evils, but they happened to his kin, not
to him himself. Skin for skin, all that a man has,
he'll give it all for his own life. Mark my words,
you harm his own flesh and bone, he will surely
curse You." At which God got even angrier, and
he said to Satan, "Behold, I give Job to you. Anything you want. Only spare his life."

Then came the racial edicts, those laws of injustice, that Jews couldn't serve in the government any more, or be lawyers or doctors, or teach

in the university. And Jews had to wear yellow armbands with the Star of David on them, which is Solomon's Seal, to mark them as fair game for the hooligans who roamed the streets looking for trouble. So now when Job went walking, they pulled his beard and threw mud at him and spat in his face. And the servants all left, and there was hardly any food in the house, because Job's restaurant had been taken over by a pure Aryan and food wasn't defiled any more because a Jew prepared it. Job's wife grew thin from grief and hunger. She said to Job, "And now what do you say about that God of yours? Curse Him, and let us die, I am content." But Job spoke sternly to her. He said, "What? Do we get good things only from God's hands, and never bad things?" And he still wouldn't deny God.

But one thing he did curse. He cursed the day of his birth, a cloud should blot it out. And he rocked back and forth in his ragged clothes, wailing. "Why didn't I die in my mother's womb? Why didn't I perish when they pulled me forth? Then I would be at rest, in the earth, still and quiet, in the grave, where no one wicked could torment me, and I could sleep in peace."

And he remembered what had been just such a short time ago, and he tried to be patient, but he couldn't, and he cried aloud, "Why can't I be back in the months of old, when God watched over me, His Light shone and there was no darkness, my children were with me, my house was shining and the table full. Then I walked in the streets and I wasn't afraid. Hats were tipped to me, I was a man, I did good, and I walked with the Lord. And now, the young foxes, they spit upon me in

the streets, they've stripped my house and burned
my children, all, all is past like a cloud in a summer sky, all there's left to me is affliction, dust and
ashes, and I mourn without sight of the sun."

Then a friend of his from the old days came to
see him, Samuel came, and he said to Job, "Listen,
I want to tell you something and I think you'll be
angry at me, but I can't help it, I have to talk to
you. You are a wise man, you've helped a lot of
people in their weakness, supported a lot of them
when they were falling, even me. But now evil
has come upon you, and you, you, Job, are afraid.
You try to justify yourself, you did such good
deeds always. But that doesn't mean God is unjust.
I ask you, who ever perished for being innocent?
When were the upright cut down? No, in my experience, it's the ones who plow iniquity and sow
mischief who reap them as their reward. Take you.
Your deeds were good, yes, according to your intention. But can a mortal man always be good
and just in the sight of the Lord? Can he always
be pure? Of course not. Listen, affliction doesn't
come from the dust. Trouble doesn't spring forth
from the ground, from nowhere. No, man is born
to trouble as the sparks fly upward. And anyway,
the man who God corrects, that is a happy man,
because he can recognize his sins and amend
them and be delivered by God from all his troubles. And the day will surely come when he will
rejoice again, and be borne to his grave in the
ripeness of old age like a shock of corn in its
season."

But Job refused to be comforted by Samuel, his
old friend. He said, "You teach me where I've done
wrong, then I'll hold my peace. Make me un-

derstand where I've sinned, then I'll be silent. My nights are long, and I toss and turn until dawn, and I have no answer. My clothes are in rags, my skin is diseased, my days fly by and they bring no hope. So let me speak, for my spirit cries within me. I will complain, for my soul is bitter. I only want to talk to God, to ask him why he's destroying me, he who made me from clay and is bringing me to dust again. I want to know why, because I'm innocent, and this is injustice, and how can it be that He doesn't care, that he destroys the innocent and the wicked together?"

Then the lice, the vermin, the sons of Satan, the Nazis, they came and they rounded up all the Jews of Warsaw. They herded them through the streets like sheep to the slaughterer, at machine-gun point, men, women, little children, their hands over their heads. Into the crowded streets of the old Warsaw ghetto they led them, and they ringed the walls all around with barbed wire, no one could go in or out. And this was Job's new home. There in the ghetto, in the cold with no heat, and little fuel for fires, and food deliveries few and far between, there people grew sick and children died from hunger and disease. Crying babies pulled at the withered breasts of their mothers, whose milk had run dry. Orphans fell and lay in the street, and they died. And yet even there the people settled in, they worked and they set up schools and they tried their own rationing systems, and they lived somehow, some of them, any way they could.

Time passed, and the Jews were left alone behind the ghetto walls. And then Nazi soldiers with

bullhorns began patrolling the streets offering
food and clothing to anyone who would come to
the new "work camps." But strange rumors had
even reached inside the ghetto walls, that these
"work camps" harbored something terrible, something of the devil, and so no one would go. Then
the Nazis blockaded the ghetto, and prevented
food from coming in. And the Nazi soldiers would
stand in the street with a jar of orange marmalade,
and spoon some out, and savor it, and offer it to
those who would come, to the starving people hiding in their tenements. "Orange marmalade!"
Some of those people, especially the children, they
were drawn by the shining orange sticky sweetness, and they went. "Orange marmalade!" And
they went. But others made other plans. They assembled what weapons they could find or put
together or smuggle in from outside, and they prepared to make their stand.

A young acquaintance of Job's, his name was
Mordechai, he was young and strong and fiery.
He came to Job and he said, "Now join us, stretch
out your hands toward God, lift up your face, take
heart! Here is the consolation of God. The wicked
man will hear the sound of terror in his ears. As he
sits there, in his prosperity, then the destroyers
will come down upon him, and the sword will find
him, fire shall consume him. The light of the
wicked will be put out. He will be tangled in a net
and we are the net. He will be caught by a snare,
and we are the snare. A noose dangles for him, and
we are the noose. From underneath, his roots shall
be dug up, and above, his branch shall wither,
and even his name will perish from the earth, root

and branch, because that is the portion that God gives to the wicked, and we, we are the deliverers of the portion. See, here is my rifle, and there are others among us, with rifles and shotguns and knives and clubs. We will fall upon this enemy and take our revenge. Join us."

Job looked up at him, weary. He said, "I'm sure you are the wise ones, and all wisdom will die with you. But I'm not completely ignorant, and so let me ask you a question? How do you think you're going to do all these great deeds? If you ask the animals, they'll teach you, the birds will tell you, the fish in the sea will declare, all of them, all the world was made by the hand of God, and in His hand he has the soul of every living thing, and the breath of all mankind. So I tell you, if there's a remedy to this evil, the remedy is with God alone, and it's God that my quarrel is with. I want to argue with God. But you, with your rifles and shotguns and knives, you're doctors who give soothing syrup to lepers. Beware, because your memorials will be heaped-up ashes, and your monuments, they'll be built of clay."

But Mordechai was burning within his soul, and he said, with his face alight, "To die in such a way is to live! The desire of my life is come upon me, for the Jews are rising in self-defense, and to be a fighter is my chosen fate, my bliss."

And he went off to join his friends.

After the guns had stopped, and the fires had burned out, and the dead stank in the streets, then the Nazis came into the bombed-out ghetto, and they loaded those who were left into boxcars, like cattle, Job among them, and that was how they came to Oswiecim, which is a place in Poland, but the Nazis called it, in German, Auschwitz. And the face of Oswiecim, at its gates it wore formal flower borders, and triumphal bands played music, especially Wagner, to welcome the newcomers.

But beyond the flowers and the music, Job entered into a world of beatings and forced labor and typhus and starvation, of shaved heads and severed families. They tore his wife, his wife of forty years, from his side, and sent her to the women's camp. The healthy were worked like horses, and the very old and the very young and the sick were sent to disinfecting showers, which made sense to them, because the huts they lived in were filthy, so that maggots and lice and fleas abounded in the litter, and rats and roaches rejoiced in their portion. And when they reached the bathhouses, by the miracle of Zyklon-B they were disinfected forever, free of the infection of being part of God's human race. But as the days wore into months, the gas ran short sometimes, or maybe it was that the showers couldn't operate fast enough to fill the crematoria which could handle fifteen thousand bodies a day going full blast, so the children, being small enough to manage, were thrown straight into the furnaces without being gassed first. In his hut, Job heard them screaming in the flames. And he pressed his hands over his ears to stop the sound, but still he heard the screams. And he couldn't stand it any longer, he raised his fists to heaven and he shook them, and he cried, "My God, my God, why have You forsaken me?"

Then a friend of his, Elihu, came to him, and he spoke harshly to Job. "What is all this, a wise man answers with wind, with speeches that are useless? Are you the first and only man who ever lived? Does God share his plans with you? Do you know something the rest of us don't? What is a man, born of woman, that he can be righteous? And then how dare you question God? Don't you know since the beginning of time that the triumph of the wicked is short, and the joy of the godless flashes past in a moment? And then how dare you question God? Far be it from Him to do injustice, while you, you add rebellion to the other sins you don't even know you've committed, and you dare to lift your voice against God and say, 'I am righteous before You.'

"Listen, Job. God's greatness runs far past what we know. Can we understand why the clouds form, or the reason for their crashing together? God covers his hands with lightning, charges it to strike the mark, thunders marvels with His voice. He does great things, but we can't understand them. He tells the snow to fall, and the rainshowers, and animals creep into their caves and into their dens. And then, out of the clouds comes the storm, cold out of the north, and the rain and the lightning, they do whatever He commands, perhaps for correction for His earth, or for mercy, that He makes the storm to come. Now just stop complaining and think a while. Consider the wonderful works of God. Could you spread out the sky, bring the storm, and the stars that follow it? But until the wind passes and cleanses them, men's eyes cannot see the lights shining bright in the skies. Out of the north comes splendor, like gold, and God clothes himself in terrible majesty, and

this God does not do violence to judgment and to

justice."

Then Job raised his head to look at Elihu, and he began, "Those are fine words, Elihu. Your tongue is silver. But you're neither the first or the last one, many have spoken to me, and sorry comfort have all of you brought to me. Now *you* let *me* speak, and then, when I finish, then you can make fun of my poor judgment. My complaint isn't to you, or to any man. Why shouldn't I be impatient and complain? Look at me, aren't you astonished? Can't you see? I'm frightened, and horror has taken hold of my flesh, for I have heard frightful things. Oh, if I only knew where I could find God, where I could come and charge him face to face, before His very throne! I would argue my case right before Him, and listen to His reply, and then confound Him in my turn. Night after night I call Him, call Him to account before his own bar of justice, but He doesn't listen, and I have nothing to say to you." So Elihu turned away from Job, and left him.

Late, late that night, as he lay in his rags on bare splintered boards, and the rats scurried in the litter on the floor, Job heard the voice of God.

"Who dares to challenge me? Answer me, you who question. Where were you when I laid the foundations of the earth? Answer, if you have understanding. Have you commanded the morning since your days began? Have you walked in the depths of the sea? Have the gates of death been revealed to you? Answer, if you know so much.

"Tell me this. Has the rain a father? Who begat the dewdrops? From whose womb came the ice?

Can you bind the Pleiades with chains, or loose the bonds of Orion? Can you send forth lightning, and make the wind blow? Have you sent the raven his prey, to feed his little ones when they cry out to God from hunger? Did you give the horse his strength and clothe him with fierceness? Is it by your wisdom that the hawk soars? At your command that the vulture mounts the skies? Who has given me anything that I need to repay him? Who are you, that I should be mindful of you? Everything under the whole heaven is mine. He that argues with God, now let him answer Me."

And Job raised his head from the boards, and he looked through the roof of his hut into that somewhere far from the world of men, and he spoke.

"I know what is the proper thing for me to say to You. But the time for those words has come and gone, long ago. What am I, that You should be mindful of me? Nothing. I am a man. But You have made me, made me a man, I am your creature. And is this how You care for me? A boy cares better for his cat, and You, You are God!

"You've said that you can do everything, nothing is hidden from you. So it's out of Your own mouth that I charge you. What is all this of the Pleiades, and the seas and the heavens? I tell You this, the stars themselves look down and weep at what they see, while You turn away dry eyes. There's food for the young ravens, yes, but none for us who starve, no longer men of flesh and blood, only shadows and skeletons. And your whirlwinds, those fiery whirlwinds in which You chose not to speak to Moses? For Your own sake I hope that isn't Your voice I hear in the whirlwinds that rage

every day from the chimneys of Auschwitz. For
man is born to trouble, they quote You, as the
sparks fly upward. So is this what man is born to?
To the ovens? Is this some kind of a cosmic joke
beyond human understanding? If so, I spit upon
such an understanding, to understand such a
joke. I, I may have sinned. I've tried not to, but
I am a man. But tell me. What is the sin of the
children? What is the glory of their martyrdom?
With what weapons do they fight Your battle for
You?

"Oh, if my words were only written down! Oh,
that somebody would print them in a book! Hear
me, God. A Jew I am, and a Jew I'll stay, despite
You, God, to spite You, God, and to bear witness
against You. And if I should happen to live beyond these daily deaths, then I'll go on observing
all the rituals and all the religious obligations. But
don't fool Yourself. It won't be to honor You, the
God who turned a deaf ear and a dry eye. It'll be
so that Satan, that Hitler, shouldn't have won. But
as for You—I don't believe in You, not any more.
I won't worship You, no more. You are the living
God, and I *will not* worship You. I curse You, do
You hear me? And now, let me die!"

But Job did not die, because God was ashamed.

"This is what that man said to me," said the
Cook.

The Art Dealer spoke mildly. "You curse God,
but you are still fighting His battles."

"Who? Me?" said the Cook, wrinkling his forehead and smiling. "It wasn't me. I wouldn't talk
such a way to God. And what do I know anyway?
I'm only a cook. I got no education. All I ever

studied was the Bible. No, this was only a man I
know. But I understand that man. The Bible story
of Abraham and Isaac is nice, very nice. God
saved Isaac, He sent a ram for the sacrifice. But
God didn't save Hannah or her seven sons. No rams
for them. He accepted the sacrifice. And when six
million were sacrificed, God accepted them, too.
We called and called. But He never answered.
Maybe He was too busy with the Pleiades. Or
maybe He'd heard it too many times before. Who
presumes to know? After all, He is God. But just
tell me this. God called Abraham, and Abraham
answered, *Hineni,* here I am. Hannah too, she
answered *Hineni.* Now, if Abraham answered, and
Hannah answered, does God also have an obligation to answer? Tell me!"

The Cook turned his eyes like blazing coals
toward the Rabbi in his corner, but the Rabbi simply sat there, head bowed, eyes closed. He might
have been sleeping, or praying, or mourning, and
all of us were silent.

And then the mountains on our right thinned
and receded, till they stood out like loaves of
whole-wheat bread on end, and scattered on the
pale sandy plains between were curious low, flat
hills, for all the world like little sand cupcakes
turned out of tins on the desert floor by giant
children. In the distance Harry Bailley pointed to
one high steep hill with a flat top, a loaf whose
end slice was missing, rising almost to heaven,
and that was Masada.

THE SCRIBE: KING SOLOMON AND THE ANT

WE HAD passed the night in a guesthouse in nearby Arad, so that we could set out for Masada at dawn, when it is still cool there in the desert. Now there is a path that twists and coils its narrow way up to the top of Masada, clinging for dear life to the sheer stone walls. They call that path "the snake," the way of the serpent, and it is the way up for anyone who is young, strong, and very, very brave.

The rest of us take a cable car.

167

That is the easy and uneventful way unless, like me, you suffer from acrophobia, what one wit of our time has dubbed "high anxiety," although to me there is nothing funny about it. If I had known just how high the fortress of Masada is, I might have hidden on the bus. But face to face with the very emblem of courage and endurance, how could I shirk?

So I stood in the exact center of the car, people pressing all around me mercifully blocking out the windows for me. I squeezed my eyes tight shut and clenched my fists. My palms were already sweating. The Rabbi's Wife patted me on the shoulder, and the car rose. Only once I opened my eyes, but one dizzying glimpse of the desert floor dropping away beneath us was enough, and I closed my eyes again, and I prayed. When we reached the top I stepped gratefully out, only to discover to my horror that we were *not* at the top. To reach the top it was necessary to climb still higher, and the staircase was the worst kind, the kind with open wooden risers and the void beneath plainly visible between them. All there was between me and the desert floor was a flimsy handrail that wobbled, like my knees. Somehow, by some miracle, after ten thousand thousand steps (there probably were fifty) I was there.

The fortress itself was an enormous plateau, vast, like a football playing field, but magnified. Above us was the limitless blue sky, and far toward the horizon a pale aquamarine rimmed with white that was the Dead Sea with its salty beaches, and everything else in that vast world was one color, sand color, the desert floor, the walls

of living stone, the dead and ruined stones of
the buildings, the homes, the synagogue, the store-
houses that had served the zealots of the second
century as they lived and died in their city in the
sky.

It was almost impossible in that sandy world to
imagine the river of scarlet that had run here centuries ago, thick and scalding under the desert sun.

And everything was silent, except the rushing
of the wind if you approached the edges. After
one timid try, I didn't.

Fortunately, Harry Bailley chose a comforting
spot in the very middle of the plateau to tell us
the story of Masada, last stronghold of the Jewish
rebels against Rome. For three years, nearly one
thousand Jews ate, slept, and raised their families
in this mountain fortress, while far below the
Romans tried in vain to capture it.

In the year 73 of the Common Era, after giving
up on direct assaults and food blockades, a Roman
commander began building earthen ramparts up
from the ground. Despite attacks from the defend-
ers, the walls rose higher and higher. It became
evident that the Romans would inevitably reach
the fortress. And then the people, with their commander, Eleazer ben Yair, took a solemn oath to
kill themselves, men, women, and children, rather
than be captured by the Romans and their faith
humiliated. So ten men were chosen by lot to kill
all the rest. Families lay down together, wives with
their husbands, grandmothers and grandsons, all
lay down together, and all were slain by the
swords of the ten. Then those ten men drew lots,
and one killed nine and then himself.

At that moment in time, Masada stopped. The blood dried. Stones eroded from the wind and heat and blowing sand. Pieces of wall fell down to the desert below, and the stone crumbled back into sand.

And here we were, riding up by cable car with our cameras and our guides and our tourist books.

There is also on Masada a pleasure palace, built by Herod, with a swimming pool and Roman baths. But since that lies on the second level, and is reached only by another narrow stairway at the edge of a precipice, I can't tell you about it. I wasn't going down there, not if Herod himself were to greet me.

I stayed alone, near the water barrel, under a small, dubious sun shelter of thin wooden slats. I looked out over the ruined walls to the barren land beyond and to the Dead Sea. Dead. Everything was dead. All I could hear was my breathing, and the wind. But then I heard another sound, at the same time peculiar and familiar.

It was the sound a small boy makes when he imagines he is a machine gunner, and it came from my left. I looked over.

The College Dropout was standing by a rampart, or what was left of one, holding his guitar in a very strange fashion, cradling the big end, with the neck pointing out across space, and making those strange sounds that I had heard.

Then I realized that I had seen someone else acting that way—my small son, when he played at soldier, or cowboys and Indians, or cops and robbers.

Surely the Dropout was playing zealot, strafing

imaginary Romans with his imaginary machine
gun. I would have laughed (to myself only, of
course) but his face was bright with exaltation,
and in a flash I saw Masada through his eyes, alive,
flaming torches at sunset, the way it must be for
young Israeli soldiers when they take their oath
of allegiance there: Masada will not fall again.

Never again.

Then I was seeing through my own eyes again,
Masada, ruined and desolate.

As for me, just to make the return descent on
the cable car took all my courage.

It was a somber group of pilgrims that stepped
off the cable car onto the shaded platform below,
waiting to be rounded up and marched off to our
bus. The Rabbi's Wife was dabbing at her eyes
with a bit of crumpled Kleenex. The Philanthropist
had his arm protectively around his wife, and he
was patting her, the way you do to steady a
frightened horse, while the Plastic Surgeon fiercely
and repeatedly blew his nose, like trumpet blasts.

And then the Mashgiach, the certifier of ritual
cleanliness and fleshly pleasures, his red face posi-
tively flaming from the morning sun, threw back
his head and laughed, a full-throated roar of
laughter that made us all smile despite ourselves.

"Weeping lasts the night," he announced, "but
joy comes in the morning!" He looked up at the
sun which stood noon-high in the sky, then held
out his watch and said, laughing, "By midday, at
the latest!" Some of us looked a little shocked, I
suppose, and the Interfaith Chairperson began jin-
gling her *mezuzah* ominously, when he quickly
said, "I mean it. Listen! They're dead, it's true, it's

terrible, but we, we are alive and well, here in God's sunshine, and the world is full of good things, air and water, wine and women. It's an insult, then, to God, to turn aside from his good things, and weep and wail when we have no cause. So let us give thanks for wonderful things, air and water, wine and women. Especially women!" And he raised his hand in a gallant toast to the ladies of our company, then lowered it and laughed as he realized he had nothing to toast with. "One should always drink to the ladies whenever possible," he said, "for a woman's charms are upon her."

"Weapons," said the Merchant bitterly. (He was the retired one, from Harrisburg, Pennsylvania, and Miami, and now New York, who only seemed to come alive when matters of finance were talked about.) "The saying goes, a woman's *weapons* are upon her."

"Charms, weapons, what's the difference," responded the Mashgiach cheerfully. "They use both the same to fight the good fight, and we are good soldiers, aren't we?" And he clapped the Merchant on the shoulder and, ignoring his protests, led him and the rest of us to the bus, marching and waving his free arm.

Well, we were all back on the bus and the Mashgiach was settled quietly, where he customarily sat, in the back of the bus, bathed in a haze of good nature and what might possibly have been the fumes of a quick nip of schnapps when the young Scribe, a delicate flush rising to his forehead, twisted around in his seat and addressed him.

"Excuse me," he said, "but such talk is highly improper."

Now I have to tell you that this pale young man,
with his ear curls and his tender beard and his pink
skin, spoke in a very curious way, a singsong, as if
he were reciting *pilpul*, the question-and-answer,
the "on-the-one-hand, on-the-other-hand," the
"supposes" involved in the study of Talmud. It's
unmistakable if you've ever heard it before, but
difficult to describe, to convey the characteristic
quality, the dip and rise in the voice matching the
dip and rise of the thumb as if it were searching
out plums in Jack Horner's pie, and this is hard to
convey just with words. I warned you when we
began, I'm no writer. I'm sorry, but there it is.

"I mean no disrespect, especially to my elders,"
said the Scribe, "but right is right, wrong is wrong,
and such talk is improper and misplaced."

Well, I had to smile at that. At this choice of the
word "misplaced," that is, because if ever anyone
was constantly misplaced, it was the Scribe. He
was our lost sheep. I guess there's one in every
group, and he was ours. It must be that he had
been searching for the truth for such a long time,
first at Princeton, then in the Vermont woods,
finally in his wonder rabbi, that even after he'd
found (at least for the time being) his True North
in Far Rockaway, he couldn't get out of the habit
of seeking. So wherever we went, at least half the
time when we were ready to move on, the Scribe
wasn't with us, and Harry Bailley had to set off
with his shepherd's staff to find him, while the rest
of us obediently huddled together, waiting, until
he reappeared with the wandering one, who, more
often than not, had been found with his nose
pressed against an ancient stone trying to decipher
the lost letters of an almost obliterated inscription.

The Widow turned to the Scribe. "But," she said, "is it not written, the Lord our God commanded Adam and Eve, saying, Be fruitful and multiply?"

"Yes," said the Scribe, but keeping his eyes modestly lowered so he would not look directly at a woman not his wife. "It is so written. But such things are for the darkness, they are behind closed doors, and furthermore, they are not for pleasure but only for God's glory and to honor His commandment.

"It is true that I am young. I am not even a scholar. I am only a teacher of the *Alef Bet*, of the alphabet. But look what we can learn from those first two letters only, from *Alef* and from *Bet*.

"The *Alef* is the first letter of all, of God, who is *Elohim*, and of *Adam*, who is the first man, and of *Abraham*, who is the first Jew. And we dig deeper still, for *Alef* is also the first letter of the first word of the first commandment, *Anochi*, I, I am the Lord your God, who brought you forth from the land of Egypt, out of the house of slavery, to be your God.

"And *Bet*, *Bet* is a little house with its back to the past and its door open to the future, which teaches us not to waste time on the mysteries of our origin, but to look toward our future deeds. *Bet* is also God's house, the holy house, *Bet-El*, a house of study, *Bet Midrash*, a house of prayer, *Bet Tefilah*, and a house for teaching children, *Bet Sefer*, all houses within the great house of God which is the world, and which was created with a *Bet*, the first word of the Torah, *Bereshit*, God created.

"And this is only the *Alef* and the *Bet!* There
are twenty more letters in the alphabet, and in
twenty times twenty years I could only begin to
study and to learn. And therefore it may be bold
in me to speak up to my elders in this way. But
even an ant was not afraid to rebuke the mighty
King Solomon when there was need. I love to tell
the children stories, but they do not always love
to listen, and they fidget and they make noise and
sometimes my story gets lost. I will tell you all
the story of King Solomon and the ant, you may
not love to listen and you may fidget, but I know
you won't make noise, and this one time, at least,
my story will not get lost."

THE SCRIBE'S STORY

KING SOLOMON, the son of David, was the mighti-
est of the mighty. He sat on his golden throne in
his crystal palace, and the temple which he built
was of olive wood and cypress and cedars of
Lebanon. He could speak the language of all the
animals, the beasts in the fields and the forests,
the fish in the sea, and the birds in the air. He
ruled over the sons of men, and the angels and
the demons and the spirits of the four elements,
and he could fly through the air on a magic carpet
of green silk with golden threads woven through
it, a carpet sixty miles long and sixty miles wide,
but the mighty eagle was his messenger and his
favorite chariot.

One day Solomon was flying over his kingdom

on his eagle when far below him, on the bank of a river, he heard one black ant speak to its neighbors.

"Hurry home," said the ant, "or you will be destroyed by the hosts of King Solomon."

Solomon was angry, and he had the eagle plunge down to the earth. He dismounted and demanded, "Who said this thing, to hurry home lest you be destroyed by the hosts of King Solomon?"

One small black ant said, "It was I."

Solomon knit his brows and frowned at her. He said, "Why did you say this thing?"

The ant replied, "Because I feared that the ants would stop to watch the procession of the hosts of Solomon, and be distracted, and thereby leave off praising God, our Father, our King, who then would be angry at us and destroy us."

Solomon said to the ant, "Who are you, who are the only ant to say this thing to the others?"

The ant said, "I am their queen, and my name is Machshemeh."

Solomon was still very angry, and he said, "I wish to question you."

The ant said, "It is not appropriate that the one who asks should be above and the one who is asked should be on the ground."

So Solomon picked up the ant and set her nearer him, but she said, "It is not appropriate that the one who asks should be higher and the one who is asked should be lower. Take me up into your hand, and I will answer you."

So Solomon took the ant onto the palm of his hand, and he said to her, "Is there anyone in the world greater than I am?"

And she said, "Yes."

And he said, "Who is it?"

And she said, "It is I."

Solomon said, "How is this possible, that you should be greater than I am?"

And the ant said, "If I were not greater than you, then God, our Father, our King, would not have sent you to me to raise me up on your hand."

Solomon was furious, and he threw the ant down on the ground.

"Ant," he said, "you cannot know who I am. I am Solomon the mighty, King in Israel, son of David the King."

And the ant said to him, "I know before whom I stand. You are Solomon, and your name begins with *Shin*, a crowned letter, and it is the same as the first letter of God's most mysterious name, *Shaddai*, and His divine presence, *Shechina*. And it begins the day of rest, *Shabbat*, and peace, which is *Shalom*, and wholeness, which is *Shalem*, and peace and wholeness together are perfection, and in your majesty and your glory you may think of yourself as perfect. But that is vanity, power and glory are vanity, all is vanity. I am here to bid you remember that *Shin* also begins a lie, *Shav*, and a falsehood, *Sheker*, and you must beware lest you fall into the pit of lies and falsehood that vanity shall dig for you. Remember then thy Creator in the days of thy glory, before the evil days come. I am a lowly ant, but I know before whom I stand. And you, O mighty King, know then before whom *you* stand, before the most Holy One, Blessed be He, and cast out vanity, and know too from whence you came, from a handful of dust, and a single drop of evil-smelling fluid."

Then Solomon, the mighty King, was ashamed, and he threw himself face down upon the ground beside the ant, to worship his Maker in humility and in prayer.

THE MASHGIACH: RABBI AMRAN'S LADDER

I THOUGHT to myself that for a young man with a pretty wife and three small children, all under five, at home, the Scribe had a peculiar sort of attitude toward our common origins, and the Dropout may have agreed with me, because I'm sure I overheard him exclaim "No way!" to himself, just loud enough that I could catch it. (I have very sharp ears. In fact, part of the fun of eating out in a restaurant for me is listening to the conversations at the tables on either side of me as well as at my own. There's a kind of collage effect that's fascinating— But that belongs to another conversation, some other time. I was telling you about the aftermath of the Scribe's story.) The much-traveled, much-married Widow beamed upon the Scribe and said to him fondly, "You're a fine young man, still a little green behind the ears, but that's all right, you'll outgrow it."

"What can a little ant know?" said the Interfaith Chairperson impatiently, and she jingled the *mezuzah* on her bracelet loudly. "Quoting from ants!"

The English Professor spoke up. "Citing truth in the form of an animal fable is actually a commonly employed literary device with vast philosophical implications. For instance, consider Aesop's *Fables*—but I am digressing. What is pertinent is that the animal fable is akin to the parable, which . . ."

"Parable, shmarable," said, of all people, the Rabbi's Wife. "People are not ants, and ants are not people."

"If they were, would that be ant-thropomorphism?" I asked, with a little laugh. (No one else laughed.)

But the Mashgiach looked across at the Scribe with a kindly leer, and he said, "Do you know what is a pious fool, my young friend? A man who sees a woman drowning in the river and says, "It is improper for me to look upon her, so I cannot go in and save her." You know, we Jews have not survived for four thousand years on pious talk alone, my young friend. But we are a funny people, funny-peculiar, not funny ha-ha, and we insist on pretending that there is something unnatural and dirty about what is really the most natural thing in the world."

"Which is what?" said the Cabdriver boldly.

Our tour guide, Harry Bailley, was squirming in his seat. "Please," he said in a stern voice, "remember that there are ladies here present among us."

The Mashgiach grinned and said, "S–E–X. Okay? Delicate enough? Listen, the way I see it is this, if God created it, it must be good, and if it weren't good, He wouldn't have created it."

"Q.E.D.," said the Lawyer, and "More dirty spelling!" hissed the Interfaith Chairperson to her husband, silent beside her.

"For all that you're so young, my friend," said the Mashgiach to the Scribe, "you remind me of the old painter in the story. Mrs. Goldstein has her apartment painted, see, the painter's all done except for some finishing touches, he leaves, and Mr. Goldstein comes home. Before you can say 'Wet paint,' he leans with his hand on the wall and he groans, 'Oy, am I tired!' She screams, he takes his hand off the wall and sure enough, there's a big palm print in the middle of the freshly painted wall. '*Gevalt!*' she cries, 'what am I going to do? The painter's finished, he'll charge me for a new wall!' Her husband says, 'Calm down, Becky, you'll be nice to him, you'll smile at him, be pleasant, he'll fix it for free.'

"So the painter comes back to finish up the next day, and there's Mrs. Goldstein smiling with all her teeth. She smiles at him, and she praises his painting ability, and she coos with her voice, and she kind of wiggles a little, and finally he says, 'Look, Mrs. Goldstein, is there anything else I can do for you?' And she says, 'Yes, Mr. Painter. I'd like to show you where Mr. Goldstein put his hand last night.' And the painter, he looks at her and he says, 'Look, Mrs. Goldstein, I'm an old man, better you should give me a nice glass of tea.' "

There were some scattered laughs and plenty of smiles and some little pockets of silence on the bus, and the Mashgiach beamed.

"That's a typical Jewish sex joke," he said. "Like a ten-minute Jewish porno movie, you know what that is?"

No one seemed to know.

"It's one minute of sex, and nine minutes of guilt!"

This time there were fewer smiles and more silence.

"Being suspicious of sex, that seems to be a Jewish trait," he said. "There's another story I remember, about a rabbi and the Sabbath candles. How does it go? A pretty young woman comes to this rabbi for a blessing. So he stretches out his hands over her head and he says the blessing. 'But, Rabbi,' she says, 'you held your hands so high above my head! Isn't the blessing more powerful if you touch the head?'

"The rabbi looks at her and he says, 'My child, when you light the Sabbath candles and you bless them, do you hold your hands above them, or do you touch the flames?'

" 'Of course above them! If I touched the flame, I'd burn my hands.'

" 'Aha!' says the rabbi. 'And do you think it's any different for me?' he says. 'If I touched your head with my hands, I too might burn them!'

"So it seems that the Jewish sex hero is someone
who *avoids* it, as a fate worse than death. I told
you we were a funny people! I do know one story,
though, about a rabbi and temptation, when
temptation won—"

THE MASHGIACH'S STORY

RABBI AMRAN, the pious, lived in a small town in
Samaria. He averted his eyes when he passed
women walking in the streets, and he would not
even receive a dish at the table from a woman's
hands, that's how pure he was. So when a band of
kidnapped Jewish girls were ransomed by their
kinsmen of Samaria, whose house was selected to
shelter them? Naturally! Rabbi Amran's.

The rabbi had an attic which was reached only
by a ladder so heavy it took ten men to lift it.
The men moved the ladder into position and the
girls, in their torn and scanty attire, climbed up
the ladder and into the attic. The ladder was then
removed. Rabbi Amran, as was his custom, had
glanced aside as the girls went by, but just for a
moment his glance went left instead of right, and
what he saw went like a flaming arrow to his
heart and set it on fire.

Beautiful young girls, ripe like peaches and the
tender bloom still on them. Silky clouds of hair,
black shining eyes, lips of pomegranate, olive
skins, breasts like melons, swelling to bursting
point with juice. It was a feast that was passing
before him! And he had been starving all his life.

And all this at a single glance. What if he had *really* looked?

That night Rabbi Amran lay on his pallet and he thought of the banquet that awaited in the attic. His mouth began to water. But sternly he pushed the vision deep down under the surface of his thoughts, and he fell asleep. But he dreamed a dream. In his dream there was a great ladder that stretched from heaven to earth, and on it, going up and down, were beautiful girls, like angels, in diaphanous nightgowns, up and down, up and down. And Rabbi Amran's heart burned within him, until his heartburn wakened him. And then began a struggle in Rabbi Amran! Should he go up the ladder? Should he not go up the ladder? Down here was piety and holiness, but up there were beautiful girls like angels. Rabbi Amran wrestled and wrestled, and then—he lost!

Like a madman whose strength is as the strength of ten, he ran to that heavy ladder and like a feather he lifted it and moved it to the opening of the attic. And then he began to mount the ladder, rung by rung, higher and higher.

Higher and higher he mounted, faster and faster he came. He was almost at the top, when by some superhuman effort he erupted and began to yell at the top of his lungs, "Fire! Fire!"

Well, he woke all the neighbors, who came running, and the fire brigade, who came with their buckets of water, and they all gathered at the foot of the ladder and stood gaping at Rabbi Amran.

"Where is the fire?" called the head of the fire brigade.

"It was in my heart," said Rabbi Amran, "but
I have just quenched it."

"Shame, shame!" cried out the neighbors,
and they pointed a finger. "We are ashamed of
you, Rabbi Amran."

But the rabbi said as he came slowly down the
ladder, with dragging feet, "It is better that I
should be ashamed before you in this world than
that I should be ashamed before God in the next
world."

"And now," said the Mashgiach, "I will be
ashamed before you in this world in my bathing
suit, for here we are at Ein Gedi, to enjoy."

That was an afternoon to remember, the afternoon at the oasis of Ein Gedi, on the shores of
the Dead Sea. First we had lunch at the restaurant
run by the kibbutzniks, the settlers of Ein Gedi,
and then we drifted over to the beach and the
bathhouse.

Not all of us, of course. As you might expect,
the young Scribe refused to have anything to do
with mixed public bathing, so while the rest of us
sunned and swam in the Dead Sea, the Scribe
and the Hasid sat, fully clothed in sober black coats
and hats, in the air-conditioned restaurant and,
oblivious of the hundred-degree weather outside,
drank innumerable glasses of tea and talked, like
father and son. (And how much more appropriate,
it seemed to me, the Hasid would have been as the
young Scribe's father rather than the aggressive,
agnostic, womanizing Oklahoma oil millionaire God
had absentmindedly provided for him.)

But the rest of us were there. The sky was blue,

but not just blue. It was a blue of such intensity
that it dazzled your eyes and hurt them, and it
turned the sandy shore into a snowbank, and
whole stretches of the Dead Sea into fields of diamonds, which also dazzled your eyes until you
had to shut them against the color and the light.
The sand and the stones were so hot under your
feet that you had to wear your shoes or sandals
or sneakers right down to the very edge of the
water, and take them off just as you stepped in.

The water, too, was warm, the temperature of
a bath, and faintly oily, so that it filmed your
skin, and transparent, so that you could look down
and clearly see the round, smooth rocks on the
bottom. But if you stood still and stared at the
surface, it shimmered with an iridescent oily film
that swirled lazily, like moiré ribbons moving
gently in the gentlest of drafts.

And all you had to do was lean back on the
water and it bore you up like an armchair! It was
the strangest sensation, to lean against what was
clearly a liquid (you could pick it up in your
hands and it would run right through your fingers,
it was definitely water) and then have it behave
like a solid, to uphold you so that you could sit on
it, your head up straight, your feet stretched out,
and your toes above water pointing straight at
heaven, and there you'd float, uplifted by this
solid-seeming water, and the slightest gesture of
your hand would propel you along as if you were
the rowboat and your hand the oar.

If you're a swimmer like I am, that is, a very
timid and bad one, you'll understand better
(maybe) if I compare it to floating on a rubber

raft, without the raft. And it was wonderful!
Everybody who went into the water was oohing
and ahing in surprise and glee, and those who
hadn't ventured in were sitting smiling at the
antics of those who had.

The Rabbi wasn't swimming, but he sat benevo-
lently on the beach and watched our group at
play like children at recess.

The Mashgiach was clowning. He had put on
eyeglasses and a hat, and was floating reading a
newspaper while the Lawyer and the Interfaith
Chairperson busily snapped his picture from all
angles and argued over f-stops and shutter speeds.

The Cabdriver and his wife were in the water,
encouraging the Fundraiser's efforts to teach the
Widow how to swim. He would pat her reassur-
ingly as she leaned back on his arm and every
time her feet began to leave the bottom she would
give a little scream, and the Cabdriver would bellow with laughter.

The Caterer was sitting well back from the
shore, under a palm tree, and eating a handful of
dry dates, his owl eyes unblinking. He only
laughed once, when the Fundraiser, trying to demonstrate to the Widow how she couldn't possibly
drown, accidentally swallowed a mouthful of the
bitter waters and came up spluttering and spitting.

The English Professor and his Gentile girlfriend
were off by themselves in the sea halfway to the
other shore, to the mountains of Moab.

The Chairperson's Husband was also floating off
quietly, all by himself, his eyes closed and a smile
on his upturned face.

The Executive Director and the Merchant were

floating side by side discussing the stock market, while the Plastic Surgeon stood thigh-deep in the water discoursing learnedly to the Interfaith Lieutenant and the Rabbi's Wife on the saline content of the water and its chemical components, and on the barbaric Biblical ordeal of swallowing a bitter draught as a kind of truth serum, whereby the innocent (theoretically) would live and the guilty would be poisoned and die, vastly different, he pointed out, from such scientific methods of detection as truth serums and lie detectors.

"And what's the difference between them?" asked the Rabbi's Wife, but I didn't hear his answer, which went on at length, while she kept shaking her head dubiously.

The Philanthropist and his wife were frolicking in the water like children, taking turns plopping straight down with their toes sticking straight up, and laughing immoderately.

The Art Dealer and his wife were relaxing comfortably in beach chairs which they'd mysteriously procured from somewhere, in the shade of some palm trees. Their son, the Dropout, wasn't with them. It turned out he had gone across the road to the kibbutz and insisted on helping out in the fields driving the tractor, even though everyone else was lying down inside for afternoon siesta, and he came back later all sunburned scarlet like a boiled lobster, and his hands were blistered and bandaged.

The Adult Bookstore Owner and his young companion were also missing. I think they'd gone into the locker room, but no one had seen them come out again.

The Cook was stretched out on a towel on the
beach, broiling under the sun.

I had gone out of the water and showered myself off under the hose rigged up on the beach, and
I was sitting and thinking about the Dead Sea before me.

Here we were, more than a thousand feet below sea level, beside a body of water whose salt
and mineral content was four to five times greater
than that of ocean water—a body of water in which
fish don't live and plants don't grow, a despised
and rejected thing.

But not to the settlers of Israel.

For them the Dead Sea is the wealth of the
nation, its greatest single natural resource, mined
for its potash and its other minerals, which collect as a result of the constant inpouring of waters
which then have no outlet and evaporate under
the sun, while the salts and other minerals accumulate and accumulate.

And then I thought how the Dead Sea might be
a metaphor for the Jewish people, despised and
rejected, all outlets blocked, accumulating a store
of experience and ethics and wisdom that has been
a treasure to mine for those who have had eyes to
see. Even the bitter wit that is so characteristically
Jewish seemed to me to be like the waters of the
Dead Sea, bitter but cooling.

And then I thought how like America this land
of Israel was, also a nation peopled by the castoffs,
the rejected, the poor, the hungry, the religiously
persecuted, who had come, as Americans had
come, from all over the world, *away from* something as much as *to* something, and then settled

a land and made it bloom, from sea to shining sea.

Look. Here at Ein Gedi there were groves of date palms flourishing in tidy rows, a garden in the desert, blooming not of its own accord, but in testimony to the technology of irrigation and emblem of man's eternal mission to be fruitful and to multiply.

I thought of how all over Israel I had seen the dry bones beginning to be fleshed again, mile after mile, or rather kilometer after kilometer, neat orchards of citrus trees, for instance, outside of Tel Aviv, glossy leaves lit by the pale fire of lemons and grapefruit, and the deeper globes of oranges, a fruited plain under spacious skies, O beautiful. And fields of ruby-studded green where tomatoes were being harvested, and fields of grape vines, so low they looked like bushes, bending under the weight of heavy clusters, and everywhere the children, black-haired, blond, brunette, redheaded, skins of brown and olive and palest peach, new fruit ripening on an ancient rootstock.

And I thought of those who discoursed learnedly on mandates and truce lines and natural boundaries and fact-finding missions, wise, astute men, whose conclusion was that all this had no right to exist, if only one understood politics correctly. But I, I am only a housewife who understands little about politics, so to my ignorant eyes all this, which should not exist, is a marvel, a wonder, maybe even a miracle (if you don't object too much to the word, like my friend the Plastic Surgeon).

And then I thought, What is all this? I'd better

stop thinking, I'm no philosopher, I'm not even a
poet. So I went from the beach over to the restaurant and bought some grapes and ate them instead in the shade of a palm tree, which is where
Harry Bailley found me, when he came to gather
his flock for the drive to Beersheba.

THE
CATERER:
THE
SCHNORRER'S
WIFE

THE BUS had entered the sandy wastes that would take us to Beersheba, capital of the Negev, and we were all slumping in our seats, tired out from sun and water, and no one was very lively or talkative, but relaxed and lazy, most of us unbuttoned both figuratively and literally. But not the Caterer. He was huddled into his jacket. It was funny. No matter how hot it was, the sun never seemed to penetrate through to his old dry bones, and he always wore a jacket even when the Cabdriver's red bandanna handkerchief

was soaked clear through from mopping his steaming brow. I think he must have suffered from some
ailment or other. All during lunch at Ein Gedi,
while we were enjoying chickpea spread, *hum-
mous*, with its sesame-seed dressing, *tahine*, and
various salads of eggplant and cucumber and tomato, and warm *pita* bread and melon and fresh
figs, the Caterer sat crumbling a dry roll and saying
very loudly, "You can have all this *hazzerai*, just
give me a good American hot dog on a real hot-
dog roll," which didn't exactly enhance our meal,
and then he'd complain how expensive all the
food was and how it only gave him heartburn.
Really, I tried to be patient, and I was just about
able to hold my tongue, but he really was the
sourest man, and you couldn't blame it on a nagging wife or rotten kids because his wife was long
since dead and they'd never had any children.
Frankly, I could believe him about the heartburn, because he was a very poor color, and I
think he must have suffered from chronic consti-
pation.

Anyway, he clearly bore some grudge against
our Fundraiser, he'd been sniping at him from the
beginning of the trip. Now whether it was our
particular fundraiser or just the class in general I
don't know because basically the Caterer was
very close-mouthed, and the Fundraiser had chosen the technique of ignoring him rather than confronting him. But whatever it was, it made for an
uncomfortable atmosphere for the rest of us whenever the old man chose to loose his barbs. And it
was now, at the very ebb tide of our energy, when

we were all at peace and calm, that he chose to tell his story.

"Times change," he said, "and fashions change, and even words change. But the things those words describe, they stay the same. For instance a man who goes around asking for other people's money is now called by a fancy title. He is a *fundraiser*. But once, and not so long ago, he had a plainer name. He was a *schnorrer*, a beggar. And so he is still, a beggar of other people's money. You have to have a taste for it, I think, to be able to do such a thing. And most people don't have the heart. Or the stomach. But some do, and give the devil his due, some even have a real talent for it. They're good at their job. But then they can become a danger, they can become contagious, like a typhus germ. Let me tell you a story of what I mean."

THE CATERER'S STORY

ONCE UPON a time there was a widow who lived in a small town, not rich, but comfortable. She was courted by the respectable widowers among the town's businessmen, taken out, sent flowers and presents, but no, she wasn't having any of them.

"I will never marry again," she said, even as she was eating a dinner of brisket and noodle pudding, out with one of her suitors.

And things went on this way until one fine day a *schnorrer* came to town. But he was not very raggedy, and was, to give the devil his due, tall and

well set up and not bad-looking, and he had the
schnorrer's gift, a pleasing tongue, so that he
could say just what his companion wanted to hear.
So he did very well. And the ear that was most
pleased by this *schnorrer* was, what else? the widow's. To make a long story short, she fell madly in
love with him. So crazy over him she was that *she*
proposed to *him*. Now she was a handsome
woman and she was comfortably off, but this
schnorrer liked his freedom, too, and he was a
proud man, even *schnorrers* can have some pride,
so he didn't exactly jump at her offer. Instead, he
made her a counteroffer.

"I will marry you," he said, "on one condition—
that for a year you will travel around with me,
living a *schnorrer's* life, and you will learn my occupation and beg side by side with me."

And people in town could hardly believe it, but
the widow was so crazy for him that she said yes!

So they were married, and she left her comfortable house and her nice clothes and her respectable neighbors, and for a year they traveled on the
road, begging from town to town. And the widow
did all right, the *schnorrer* was surprised to see.
She had a sympathetic eye and a pleasing tongue
in her own right. So they did very well, this pair,
but at last the year was almost over, and he was
getting tired of the roaming around. He was looking forward to settling down in the widow's house
and *schnorring* from only one client for the rest of
his life. So it was with relief, as twilight began to
fall one day when they were walking down a middle-class street in a small town not far from her
home, that he turned to her and said, "I see a star

in the sky. At this moment the year is up in which you promised to beg with me, and we can now return together to your home."

And she looked at him, this respectable, well-off widow, and she said to him wistfully, "First please let's finish the houses on this street."

THE FUNDRAISER: THE JUDGMENT OF THE TRAVELERS

WHEN the Caterer had finished his story, he snapped his mouth shut like a purse, then grudgingly opened it to count out a few more words.

"You understand," he said, "it's just a story. Nothing personal." He smiled, or at least he showed his teeth, and the creases, like parentheses at the corners of his mouth, deepened.

"Of course," agreed the Fundraiser, from where he sat beside the Widow. And he also smiled, a real smile, wide and glittering. "Noth- 197 ing personal. It never is. And there is nothing personal in the story I now choose to tell." He cleared his throat a couple of times, leaned back in his seat (I noticed he was wearing his plainest black rayon skullcap), and he began.

THE FUNDRAISER'S STORY

ONCE UPON a time two men were traveling together for protection against highwaymen, and upon the eve of Sabbath they found themselves on the outskirts of a forest. Now one man was a fine strapping figure in his prime, who traveled far and wide raising money for an orphanage, and the other man was an innkeeper, a dried-up old stick of a man, but very well off. Now both these men were carrying gold pieces with them for their traveling expenses. And both these men were Jews, which meant they were not allowed to carry money on the Sabbath. What could they do?

The old innkeeper suggested to his companion that they dig a hole near the roots of a big oak tree, quickly, before darkness fell. Then they'd bury the gold, and when the three stars marking the departure of the Sabbath queen appeared in the sky the very next evening, they could dig it up again. The fundraiser, who was a frank and trusting fellow, agreed, and so they did. Then both the men went to sleep, and the following day they went about their prescribed worship, each in his own manner and place.

Now when the third star appeared in the evening sky, they met by the oak tree as agreed to dig up the gold, which they did. But after they had dug a hole twice as big as the one the day before, and still found nothing, the two travelers were forced to conclude that their gold was gone. Now the fundraiser was trying to make sense of this: "On the one hand, perhaps a robber watched us bury the gold and then stole it. But on the other hand, since neither of us saw or heard anyone, perhaps it was one of us two—"

But he had got no further than this when the old innkeeper leaped upon him, hammering him with his fists, and screaming, "Thief! Robber! Thief!" Now to tell the truth, the old man's attacking him meant no more than a mosquito, but the fundraiser had his good name to lose, not to mention his gold.

So he held off the innkeeper with one hand, and he said to him, "There is a town little more than half a day's journey away, and they will have a magistrate there. You and I will go and put this case before him." Which they did, but the innkeeper muttered "Thief" with every other step, and "Robber" on the steps between.

At last they came to the town and they found the magistrate, who was known far and wide for his wisdom and his justice, which were so great that he was known as Solomon.

"What happened?" he asked the two travelers. They told the story, each in his own way. Now the fundraiser concluded, "So you see, Mr. Justice Solomon, perhaps on the one hand a robber watched us and later stole the gold, but neither of us saw or heard anyone, so perhaps it was one of us two. But as for me, I never touched the gold after we buried it." While the innkeeper concluded, "I am an old man and sleep sound, and while I slept this young scoundrel dug up his gold and mine too, the thief, the robber!"

Now this judge, this Solomon, reasoned to himself, "A robber might slip past one sleeping man, but it is very doubtful that he could slip past two. So it would seem that one of these two men is the thief. But which one?"

And the more he thought the sadder he became, because, he said to himself, "On the one hand, if I refuse to judge this case, my reputation for wisdom will fly from me. But on the other hand, if I make a decision without any more facts than I have now, then I have a fifty-fifty chance of wronging God by an injustice. What can I do?"

And as he looked at the two travelers standing before him, inspiration came to guide this Solomon.

"Come closer to me," he said, "because I have a problem in which I need your help. The overseer of this district put this problem to me: Once there was a little boy and a little girl who pledged themselves to each other and vowed never to marry anyone else. You know how little boys and little girls sometimes do. Then they grew up, and the girl's father had arranged a proper marriage for her to a fine young man, a distant cousin. But on the night of the wedding, when the eager groom came in to the bride she said to him, 'You must not touch me, for I have pledged myself long ago to another, and first you must give him money so that he will release me from my vow.' The girl was very beautiful, and her new husband was all on fire, but he contained himself and said, 'So be

it.' And they traveled the next day to a faraway
village where that grown-up boy now lived. The
young groom came with his bride to the man, and
he offered him purses of gold and silver to release
the bride from her long-ago vows. The man
looked at the money and said, 'Put that away and
take your bride. Since you were honorable and
heeded her vow, your honor has redeemed the
pledge and I need no further payment.'

"So the young bride and groom happily were
returning along the lonely road to their own village when suddenly a highwayman appeared, old
and cruel, with two pistols, and he took all the
money, but as he was about to lay hands on the
bride, she fell down on her knees before him. 'Take
the silver, take the gold, but do not dishonor me
and my husband,' she cried. Then she told him
their history, and she said to him, 'If my husband,
who is young, could conquer his desires and leave
me untouched, surely you who are a mature man
can do no less.'

"Something within the highwayman was
touched by her words, and not only did he leave
the bride untouched, but he returned the purses
of gold and silver, and the couple returned un-
harmed to their village.

"Now this is the problem put to me by the overseer of the district, which I now put to you. Of
these three people, the girl, the groom, the highwayman, which displays the most virtue?"

The two travelers thought a while, and then the
fundraiser spoke up. "On the one hand, the girl is
virtuous indeed for honoring a far-off childish
vow, but on the other hand, the young bridegroom

displayed great virtue in a situation of severe temptation."

But the innkeeper brushed him aside with an explosion of words, like a breaking of wind: "The highwayman! The highwayman is virtuous beyond belief. What is it so wonderful with the girl, to keep a vow is expected, and women feel little enough desire anyway. And her young husband, what is it so wonderful? So he could wait—after all, if it wasn't tonight, it would be tomorrow night. But the highwayman! It's something that he passed up a tasty tidbit that was free for the taking. But there's more where that came from, even though when you get older, sometimes more is less. But to have gold and silver within his grasp, purses of it, and then to return it, this is virtue almost passing belief!"

"From your own mouth let it be," said the magistrate coldly. "The avarice that pants thus after gold and silver which you have never even seen, which exists only in a story, how then does it pant after money you have actually taken into your hands! You are the thief!"

And the old innkeeper fell down before the judge and confessed his crime, and was to be hanged. But the fundraiser took part of the blame upon himself, saying that he should have known better than to set golden temptation in the path of the avarice of an old man, and so the innkeeper escaped with no more than the beating he so richly deserved.

THE WIDOW: A LOVE STORY

THE Caterer and the Fundraiser were glaring fiercely at each other, and we were finally expecting an outbreak of open warfare, when the Widow squirmed around in her seat a little, settled herself comfortably, patted her red hair, and commented, "Yes, I do like to hear a story about a happy marriage." That sort of startled everyone, especially the Fundraiser, but she went on, "And speaking of marriage, how holy is this place we're coming to!"

We all stirred and looked

uneasily at Harry Bailley. If Beersheba were such a holy place, how come he hadn't told us? But he was looking puzzled too, and he said to the Widow gently, "Tell me, dear lady, what is this holiness?"

She opened her green eyes very wide and gazed at him reproachfully. "There's David's birthplace, and Jesus's birthplace, and the field, the field where Boaz and Ruth first laid eyes on each other, and you ask what is this holiness?"

Harry Bailley's voice was grave, although in the depths of his eyes a little light twinkled.

"But dear lady," he said, "David was not born in Beersheba, nor was Jesus born there, nor did Boaz meet Ruth there."

"So who's talking about Beersheba?" said the Widow. "I'm talking about Bethlehem."

"Ah!" said Harry Bailley. "But, dear lady, the bus is taking us now to Beersheba, not to Bethlehem."

"Oh," said the Widow. I was preparing to feel a little sorry for her, she clearly hadn't been paying any attention to our itinerary, or maybe it was her little touch of deafness, although it hadn't seemed to bother her up till now, when she asked, unperturbed, "Surely we *are* going to Bethlehem?"

"Yes, indeed," said Harry Bailley. "The day after tomorrow."

"So we *are* going to Bethlehem, if not sooner, then later, right?"

"Right," said Harry Bailley.

"And Bethlehem *is* a holy place."

"Right," said Harry Bailley.

"So that's what I said in the first place," she con-

cluded triumphantly. "How holy is this place we're
coming to!"

And she added in a firm voice, "This Bethlehem."

And I could have sworn I heard the Dropout
whisper, almost under his breath, a long-drawn-
out "All right!"

Then the Interfaith Lieutenant (a lovely
woman, a grandmother three times) said in a
positive voice, "Bethlehem, the holy shrine, the
tomb of Rachel, our grandmother. I look forward
to it."

"So do I," agreed the Widow. "But Rachel's tomb
isn't why."

"The birthplace of King David is naturally a
holy of holies," commented the Art Dealer.

"True," agreed the Widow. "But I didn't mean
David's birthplace either." And she smiled at him.

"It can't be that you mean the Church of the
What's-it, the Nativity," said the Cabdriver.
"That's for the *goyim*."

The Interfaith Chairperson fired up and said to
the Cabdriver, "Where is your sensitivity? Don't
you realize that *she* has feelings?" She turned to
the Gentile girl. "Don't you, dear?"

Well, the Gentile girl just looked at her. It's
hard to describe that look. It wasn't nasty or glaring or even really angry. It was just a look. Even
so, I can tell you, I wouldn't like anyone to look
at me like that. But the Interfaith Chairperson had
turned away the minute she'd stopped speaking,
so she never even noticed.

The Widow looked straight at the Cabdriver, her
green eyes open wide. "Those are *all* holy places,

the church, too, you should know better, Mr. Cabdriver." And she smiled at him.

"Call me Sam," he said boldly, before his wife's
elbow caught him in the ribs.

"Okay, Sam," repeated the Widow. "What I
mean is the field, the holy field. The field where
Ruth met Boaz."

There was a small silence while most of us tried
to remember just who were Ruth and Boaz.

"I don't think holy is exactly the . . ." began
the Scribe, in his soft young voice, but the Widow,
in full flood, sailed right over his low tidings.

"Not holy? What's more holy than marriage?
The field is a holy place because a marriage was
arranged there, and marriage is a holy thing. And
don't laugh, you in the corner, my friend the Merchant, because I'll prove it to you from the Bible,
from the Holy Scriptures. First off, didn't the Lord
himself say, 'It isn't good a man should be alone,
I'll make him a wife'? That was in the very beginning. And then later, when Rebekah was going off
who knows where to get engaged to Isaac, her
father wasn't too thrilled about her going so far
away, but he wouldn't make a fuss because he
said, 'It's fated from the Lord. This thing is from
the Lord.' He knew. And when Samson's mother
and father were carrying on, he was marrying that
shiksa Delilah, a Philistine girl, they didn't know
what *we* know, that the Lord was the one who
had Samson fall for her because He, not Samson,
He the Lord was looking to pick a fight with the
Philistines. And furthermore, doesn't it say straight
out in Proverbs that your fancy house and your
pots of money you can inherit from your parents,

but a good wife comes direct from the Lord? And
if the Lord is taking a direct hand in all these
marriages, then marriage is holy, good marriages,
bad marriages, all kinds of marriages, all holy.

"And I know, believe you me, because I've been
married three times myself. My first husband, we
were very happy, he was killed in a car crash. To
tell you the truth, I was a child and he was a child,
and it's all a long time ago. So I had the insurance,
and I went off to Grossinger's and I met a nice
substantial man, no kid, but a nice, kind man, he
was good to me, and we got along very nice, the
two of us, but he had two children, they made my
life such a misery that when he had a heart attack
and died I didn't know whether I was crying for
him or laughing to be rid of them. And they con-
tested his will, and I didn't get much, but I opened
my shop and with the Lord's blessing I made a
nice living, I didn't need to get married again. But
I fell in love. He was handsome, so handsome, and
younger than me, but I don't really look my age,
now tell the truth, do I look my age? and he tried
this job and that job because he wasn't quite 'settled' yet, and I was steady, and I could guide him.
And, of course, my shop brought in a nice living.
I know. But, oh, he was handsome! Sometimes he
would drink a little too much and get mean, and
he didn't care about going to synagogue, and he'd
tease me, not cute, *nasty* teasing, and tell me stories from the Bible, stories about Lilith and Delilah and Jezebel, that's what wives are, he would
say. So one day I threw a prayer book at him, I
was so mad, and he smacked me across the ear, I'm
a little deaf to this very day, and of course I had

to throw him out, didn't I? and he went to live with a seventeen-year-old *shiksa* who made him feel young again, that's what he told me, 'She makes me feel young again.' But we had our good times before it ended. I don't regret it, I don't regret anything, and to this day it tickles my heart to know that I have had my world as in my time. So I can tell you, marriage is marriage, good, bad, and indifferent, they're all good, as it is said, 'Whoso finds a wife finds a good thing.' Like Boaz —but you all remember the story of Naomi and Ruth? No? So. We're supposed to be telling stories, we shouldn't be bored on the bus, all right. Now it'll be my turn. Let me refresh you with the memory."

And she didn't more than pause to draw a deep breath, and she began.

THE WIDOW'S STORY

IT ALL BEGAN once upon a time, long ago, right there in Bethlehem, as it is written, there was a woman named Naomi, which is, in Hebrew, "pleasant." Now she was happily married to a man named Elimelech, and they had two nice sons, fine young Jewish men, and what could be wrong? But a famine came to the land, and the Elimelechs, they packed up and went to sojourn in the country of Moab, which is how you know they planned to come home again when times got better, because they were only sojourners and not one hundred percent immigrants. But life was

pleasant in Moab, and the two boys, they got
older, and they met two nice girls from Moab, and
they got married, what could be wrong? All right,
maybe Naomi would have rather had daughters-
in-law from Bethlehem, but these were nice girls,
and she was happy, they were all happy. Then
bang! First Elimelech died, and then her two sons
one after the other, one, two, three, and they were
all dead. Well, you can imagine! The wailing and
the lamentation, the three women, and no man
left for any of them. So Naomi decided she might
as well go back to her hometown, to Bethlehem,
she still had a little family there. So she set out for
Bethlehem, but she said to her daughter-in-law,
one was named Orpah and the other was named
Ruth, she said to them, "You're two fine girls, and
I love you both, and if it weren't for the terrible
thing that's happened to us, I wouldn't be saying
goodbye to you until it was time to close my eyes
forever. But as it is, you, Orpah, and you, Ruth,
you each go back to your mother's house, and I'm
going back where I came from." And she said to
them, as it is written, "May the Lord deal kindly
with you like you did with the dead and with me.
And may He grant that each of you find a home,
each in the house of a new husband, where you
belong." And she kissed them, and they kissed her,
and they were all crying together, the tears were
all mixed up together, and Orpah said, "No, I'll
go with you back to Bethlehem," and Ruth said,
"No, I'll go with you back to Bethlehem." And the
tears flowed like a summer storm, and it was "Yes,
yes, yes," and "No, no, no," until finally Naomi said
to them, "Why should you come with me, my

daughters? Am I young enough to have more sons to marry you again? Go back, go back. Even if I were to marry again, and even if I could have sons, would you wait to marry until they were grown up? Don't be silly, don't worry about me, I'll manage, and you go home and find a husband. If it were only me, so it would be, but for your sakes I find it bitter that the hand of the Lord is stretched out against me."

You don't need to raise your eyebrows; she really meant it. She was a very sincere person, Naomi was. Well, you can imagine the tears and the crying, but finally Orpah kissed her mother-in-law and kissed Ruth, and went back to the house of her parents. And Naomi said to Ruth, "Look, my daughter, Orpah's gone back to her parents' house, and to her people, and now you do the same. But Ruth hung onto her, and she said to Naomi, as it is written, very famous, "Don't tell me to leave you and go back home, because wherever you go, there I'm going, and wherever you live, there I'm living, and your family will be my family and even your God, He'll be my God. And wherever you die, there I'll die, so even death won't us part." And Naomi saw she was bound and determined to come along, and she was really very happy about it even though she didn't let on much, and the two widows, the mother-in-law and the daughter-in-law, they started out for Bethlehem together.

Well, when they got there, naturally the people turned out to see who these strangers were, you know what a small town is like, and some of the women said, "Can it be? Is this our Naomi?"

And Naomi said to them, "Listen, don't call me
that anymore, because Naomi means pleasant,
and my life's been anything but pleasant, and if
you call me Marah, bitter, it would suit me because the Lord has dealt bitterly with me. You
remember when I left, I went out full, with a husband and two sons, and now I come creeping
back empty and alone and afflicted of the Lord."
But of course she wasn't alone because there was
this beautiful young stranger from Moab, this
Ruth was with her, but you know how it is when
you're upset, you say things, you don't know what
you're saying. That's how it was with Naomi. Anyway, it was the beginning of the barley harvest,
and nobody had much time for small talk, so Naomi and Ruth went off to live in a small tum-
bledown shack which was all they could afford,
but they weren't complaining.

Now it was the custom in that time that rich
people who owned the barley fields didn't mow
them altogether, like now the big efficient farmers
do, but they left the edges standing and they
didn't gather up all the cut grain, but they left
some, because the poor people, it's written in the
Torah, I could show you, the poor people had the
right to go out after the reapers and glean what
was left over and in the corners, and it wasn't charity from the rich people, you understand, it was
the right the Lord gave to the poor people. Which
makes the difference, right? Now Naomi was still
a good-looking woman, but of course she wasn't a
chicken any more, so Ruth said to her, "You stay
home, and I'll go out and find a likely-looking
field, and I'll glean enough for supper for a few

days." Now I ought to tell you also that Naomi herself might have been poor, but she had a very wealthy cousin there in Bethlehem, a bachelor. His name was Boaz, and he owned a lot of real estate, including the best barley field around, and he was supposed to be very charitable, but she didn't want to be pushy. Anyway, when Ruth announced she was going out to glean, Naomi said, "Fine. Go, my daughter. But first change your old shawl and put on the green one that goes with your eyes, and the Lord be with you." That's maybe not exactly word for word the text, but you have to read between the lines sometimes. And you know how it is, you start out in the morning, where you'll go and who you'll see before you get back home again, you never know. And a pretty green shawl to match the eyes, it couldn't hurt. So Ruth changed, and she went out to pick a likely-looking field to follow after the reapers. And lo and behold! it just so happened the field she picked belonged to Boaz, you remember, Naomi's rich bachelor cousin. And it just so happened that very morning that Boaz woke up and said to himself, "Today I'll go out and check up on the reapers in my barley field, they're leaving enough for the poor." So he did, and when he got there, a green shawl glided past and he said to his head reaper, behind his hand, "Who is that?" And the head reaper said, "That's the new girl in town, the one who came back from Moab with your cousin Naomi." When Ruth saw them staring at her, she glided over and she kneeled down, which is not very liberated, but men did it too, they kneeled down before a lord, she kneeled down, and she

said in a very pretty small voice, "May it please
my lord to let me glean and gather among the
sheaves, even though I'm a stranger?" And Boaz,
naturally, said, Of course, and all morning he
watched the green shawl gliding here and there
gathering barley and never resting for even one
minute, because Ruth was a strong worker, which
was something men kept an eye out for in a wife
in those days. And finally it was lunchtime, and he
went over to her and he said, "My daughter." I
should tell you that he was an older man, older
than Ruth, a substantial man, but not *too* old, he
was younger than Naomi, and very distinguished-
looking. And he said, "My daughter, don't go looking for other fields to glean in. You stay right here
with my maidservants, and I've warned off the
menservants they won't dare get fresh with you,
and whenever you're thirsty you'll share the water
they brought to the field." And she said to him,
with a shy kind of a smile, "Why are you being so
nice to me, and I'm a stranger, a foreigner?" And
he said to her, "I've heard all about you, how you
left your home and family to come here with
Naomi and you've been so good and devoted."
And she said to him, "That's very kind of you to
say." And he said to her, "Come sit here, and share
my bread and dip a morsel in the vinegar." Which
is of course not possible, bread and vinegar. Who-
ever had such a lunch? It was surely something
else, and a scribe mixed up a letter or two, but
whatever it was, they shared it. And then she went
back to her gleaning, only Boaz had ordered the
reapers they should spill a lot, careless-like, in her
direction, so by the time she got back to Naomi,

she had with her a whole ephah of barley, I don't
know how much it is, but it was surely a lot. And
Naomi said, "Where on earth have you been to
bring home such a heap of grain?" And Ruth said,
"You can't imagine such a coincidence! I happened to glean in the field that belongs to Boaz,
and he was very nice to me, and he even said to
come back every day until the end of the harvest."
Well, you and I may not recognize the hand of
the Lord when we see it, but Naomi certainly did,
especially when the Lord's hand was doing something pleasant for a change. But all she said to
Ruth was, "That certainly was a coincidence, and
it's a good idea that you glean only in his field.
After all, family is family."

So for the next week or so Ruth went gleaning
every day, and she shared his bread and vinegar,
or whatever, with Boaz, and they would talk for a
while of this and that and the other thing. But
finally the time came when the barley harvest was
finished. And Naomi got up very early that morning, and she thought and she thought, and then
she went in and she shook Ruth to wake up, it was
time they had a talk.

"Listen, my daughter," she began. "You know
how it is written, It is better to live in companionship than in widowhood. And it's also true that
marriages are made in heaven, but that doesn't
mean even angels don't need a little push, a
nudge. The Lord helps those who help themselves, and it's time now for you to help yourself.
You sit back to wait like a princess, you'll never
meet Mr. Prince Charming. And speaking of
Prince Charmings, you should also know, it's just

as easy to marry a rich man as a poor man. Now
I'm speaking to you like a mother, you're my
daughter now, I can't rest easy until you're settled in a nice place of your own. Now you pay attention, you listen to me, you do what I tell you,
it's the happy ending, I guarantee. This time I
can see it, the Lord is holding out his hand for
good and not for bad. Now, down to business. Tonight Boaz and his servants are going to winnow
the barley on the threshing-floor in the barn. You
go have a bath, you put on some perfume and
that new dress I made you, and you get over to
the barn. But stay in the shadows and don't even
let anyone see you until the men finish eating and
drinking. You have anything important to say to
a man, you wait till after he's had a good dinner.
Then they'll all be a little, what shall I say? tipsy,
and they'll lie down for the night. You keep your
eyes open and spot the place where Boaz is. Then
you tiptoe over to him, and you curl up at his feet,
and you lie there, quiet like a little mouse, and
he'll take it from there."

And Ruth was no fool, she listened sharp, and
she did everything her mother-in-law had told her
without one bit of back talk, not like kids today.
And when Boaz had eaten and drunk, his heart
was merry, that's the way they put it in the Bible,
his heart was merry. He was drunk as a lord, he
was, but it's all right, he was probably plenty
merry, the whole bunch of them. So they all lay
down, and Ruth tiptoed over, quiet like a mouse,
and she curled up at his feet and she waited. And
it came to pass at midnight, Boaz got up to, what
shall I say? relieve himself, all that drinking, and

imagine how surprised he was, he trips over a woman, and he says, "Who is it?" Because it was dark in the barn, and she said, "I am Ruth, your maidservant, and I want just the edge of your robe for warmth and to protect me, because you are my relative through Naomi." And she sat there and he stared at her and he held her hand and he said, "Blessed are you in my sight, because you have come to me instead of following after the young men, even the rich young men. And don't worry, my daughter (he still thought he was too old for her), I'll take care of you, and settle you here in Bethlehem, like an uncle or a father, I'll take care of you. Stay here tonight, and tomorrow I'll introduce you to another relative, a young strong handsome one, and I'll see you settled with him if he will, and if he won't, well, then, I'll think of something."

Now this is an amazing thing. You women, you know, and you men who know women, you also know perfectly well, Ruth didn't just sit there like a dummy this whole time. But the Bible doesn't record one word, not one word, not one single solitary word that she said. Isn't that amazing? And I figured out, maybe it was the kind of thing, you had to be there, it was blushes and sighs and looks and little words, you know what I mean, it loses in the translation. But maybe also it was some young scribe copying it out, he knows the words but not the music, and all that openness and frankness and love and tenderness, it embarrassed him, so he left it all out, all Ruth's words got left out. So we don't know what Ruth said to Boaz, but we do know one thing, whatever she said, it was the right thing.

So she stayed there curled up at his feet all
night, but don't worry, it was perfectly kosher,
there were all these other people around and
anyway you can't get top price for damaged merchandise, so it was all right. And the two of them
knew it was all right, but Boaz wanted to make
sure nobody got any funny ideas even so, so he
woke her up while it was still too dark to tell one
hand from the other, and he gave her some barley,
six measures, it weighed down her new shawl out
of shape, and he sent her home to Naomi, she
shouldn't go empty-handed. And when Ruth got
home, Naomi looked at the barley and she looked
at Ruth and she listened to the whole story, and
then she said, "Sit tight, my daughter, because the
rest is up to him."

Now back in Bethlehem, Boaz went home and
changed, there was barley straw all over him, and
he went out to the gate where, what with all the
comings and goings, it's a small town, you could
count before long on seeing everybody. And sure
enough, behold! along came this relative, the
young rich one Boaz was talking about. And, according to that scribe, Boaz said to him, "Hey,
you!" And I'm sure he didn't, Boaz was a gentleman, but at any rate we don't know this young
fellow's name. But Boaz buttonholed him, and
there were ten friends along for witnesses, and
they all sat down together and Boaz began like
this.

"Naomi, our relative who came back from Moab,
is selling a piece of land that's all her husband
left to her, and I said I would tell you, you're
closer family than I am, you would have first
chance to buy it, and these are witnesses. But if

you don't want to buy, there's nobody else except me, I'll have to buy it." And the young fellow said, "Sure, I'll buy it." And Boaz said, "Okay, it's a deal. There's only one thing, though. Along with the land comes her daughter-in-law Ruth, you know, that skinny foreigner with the carrot hair, and Naomi says the buyer has to marry Ruth so the family name won't be lost." And the young relative said, "Thanks, but no thanks, my fiancée would have my head. You buy the land if you're willing to take the girl." And Boaz sighed a few times and he shook his head a few times, and then he took off one of his shoes and he handed it to one of the men, which was what they did in those days to seal a bargain. I don't know why, a handshake is much more sensible, but they used a shoe. And he said in front of everybody, "You're all witnesses, today I buy Naomi's land, and I take Ruth from Moab to be my wife so that Naomi's house may be rai ed up from the dead."

And everyone congratulated him, wished him *mazel tov* and long life, and you know the usual. And you will wonder why Boaz didn't just scoop up the girl, but went around and around that way. And I'll tell you. No matter how rich and handsome and successful a man is, he's still got a lot of pride that gets hurt easy. We women know that the stronger they are, sometimes the easier you can hurt them with a thought or a word or even a look. We're the tough ones. The men need protection. So it was obvious what Boaz was afraid of, that the town would laugh at him for a middle-aged lecher, running after a young girl with his tongue panting out, and furthermore, he's rich, she's poor, how does it look? Like he's buying his way into bed! And people should whisper such things, it would kill a man like that. But a dignified man to take on his family responsibilities, now that's a *mitzvah*, a good deed, and worthy before the Lord, not to mention the people of Bethlehem. So they got married, it was the social event of the year, and just like it should happen, the Lord blessed them and Ruth had a baby boy. And then the congratulations to the grandmother! And the good wishes, and the kisses, it was a wonder, and Ruth and Boaz had a built-in babysitter from the very beginning. In fact, the women, her neighbors, when they came for the naming, they said, "There is a son born to Naomi," not to Ruth, to Naomi, and they called the baby Obed. And this is the most beautiful thing of all, Obed grew up to be the father of Jesse. And Jesse grew up and he had a son, and you know who he was? Of course. King David! Whose city is Bethlehem we're coming to, if not today, then tomorrow, and all because marriages are made in heaven, and then finished off by us here in a little field, on earth.

THE CHAIRPERSON'S HUSBAND: THE FARMER AND HIS GOOD WIFE

ALL THIS way to Beer-sheba we had been driving through miles and miles of nothing, sandy nothing, punctuated here and there by black dots that were goat-hair Bedouin tents. Camels in camouflage blended into their sandy surroundings. Purple mountains brooded on the far horizon. Only the air conditioning of the bus marked our modern condition. Otherwise, everything looked like it must have done to the eyes of Abraham, thousands of years ago.

At one stretch of sand, which looked to me identical to all the other stretches of sand, Harry Bailley pointed out the window.

"Out there," he said, "is the village of El-Huzeil,
ruled by the legendary Sheik Suleiman, who has
thirty wives and two hundred camels, all in great
condition. Some people know how to take good
care of their possessions." He paused. "You can
laugh. I'm only kidding. Besides, there are women,
and there are women. It all depends on the woman
in the case."

"You can say that again," spoke up the Widow.
"In every partnership, how it is depends on the
woman. There was once a good man married to a
good woman but it was a pity on them, they had
no children. So, because they were good Jews and
observed the religious laws, they divorced, because
they were no profit to God. The man married
again, a bad woman this time, and she made him
bad. The woman married a bad man, and she made
him good. So you see, it all depends on the woman."

"Certainly it all depends on the woman."

The voice that echoed the sentiment was un-
familiar. We all looked around and craned our
necks to see who it came from, and the Cabdriver
was the first to spot the source.

"Well, well, another county heard from," he
said. "Come on, spit it out. You can talk."

It was the Husband of the Chairperson of the
Massachusetts, Connecticut, and Rhode Island Tri-
State Area of Interfaith Councils. I don't think
any of us had ever heard him speak before, and
I'm afraid we were all maybe a little bit rude,
staring at him. Even his wife looked at him.

"It all depends on the woman," he repeated. "A man's life, even, can depend on his woman. I am reminded of a story my father told me, the night before I was married. From that night to this day, the memory of it has never crossed my lips, but now I remember, and I will tell you. It happened long ago and far away, in the town where my father's father came from, in Zwierzyniec, in Poland, or in Austria, or in Hungary, it depends what year you look at the map. And you must understand, it's sort of a fairytale, not to be believed, divorced, if you'll excuse the expression, from real life, and without any moral at its tail whatever.

"But what's the sense of a long prologue and a short story?" he said, with a smile. "Without further to-do, let me begin."

THE CHAIRPERSON'S HUSBAND'S STORY

THE ZWIERZYNIEC *Rebbe* was known far and near as a miracle worker, a wonder rabbi, and his blessings were eagerly chased after, the blessing for long life, the blessing for good health, the blessing for nice steady husbands, the blessing for good laying hens. One time a Jewish farmer came to the Zwierzyniec *Rebbe*, bringing him many rich gifts. The *Rebbe* thanked him and said, "You had no need, my son. Your reputation precedes you as a good and virtuous man, a patient husband, a gentle master. What is the blessing that you seek?"

The farmer was a modest man, but he had a longing in him, and at last he blurted out, "O

great and wonder-working *Rebbe*, if my life and
service are pleasing to you, grant me the secret of
the language of the animals."

Above the *Rebbe*'s tufted gray eyebrows his forehead crinkled like aluminum foil, and his eyes
went like a sword point right through to the farmer's heart, and what he read there pleased his own
heart, because it was a great, great love for all
God's creatures.

So "Yes, my son," he said, slowly and solemnly.
"But you must understand one thing. This is a
grave and dangerous secret, one first imparted
by Solomon the King, and guarded with strict or-
dinances. If you ever tell this secret to anyone, on
that identical exact same day, you will die."

The Zwierzyniec *Rebbe* then blessed the farmer,
whose name was Adam, and the farmer returned
home. Imagine how happy he was as he strolled
around his farmstead, looking as usual, but this
time listening as well! He heard swarms of orange
butterflies rejoicing in the abundance of milkweed
blossoms. He heard two pale-green caterpillars
locked in an argument of whispers, confronting
each other on a one-way twig. He heard baby
sparrows grumbling over the mealiness of their
noonday worms, and a fat grackle utter a benediction before washing its wings with dust. A mother
cat's precise instructions to her striped kitten on
how to stalk a juicy spider he heard, and the murmured courting of two earthworms, their heads
(or maybe it was tails) entwined, waving in the
warm sunshine. He heard the love song of the
jeweled rooster to his plump and clucking concu-
bines. All this he heard, and more, and everything

that he heard he understood, and he laughed aloud for happiness.

His wife was passing by, and as she heard him laugh out loud, she stopped in her tracks and eyed him suspiciously.

"What's so funny?" she demanded. "My petticoat is showing, maybe? Is there smut on my nose? You think I walk funny? Tell me. You heard gossip about me in the town, perhaps. Or, I know, dirty stories you men were trading. Tell me. You spent your time hearing dirty stories. Or maybe . . ."

"No, no, none of these things, Eve, my good wife, my heart's love," he said soothingly. "It's just such a beautiful day, I laughed in praise of God."

She looked him up and down, from top to foot, then went on her way to feed the chickens and the ducks.

The next morning when the farmer came to his barn, he gave the ox some hay, but he noticed that the donkey's coat was dull and his brown eyes droopy, so he didn't give him any food, but left him to rest in his stall. The ox he yoked up and took him out into the field.

When they came back, the farmer led the ox back into his stall, and then he went around a corner to examine some harnesses hanging on a wall. As he stood there quietly, he overheard the ox address the donkey.

"Hey, donkey, how do you feel?"

"Not too bad now," said the donkey. "How about you?"

"I've got a complaint," said the ox. "You spent a nice day resting in your stall, but I worked and toiled for long hours, and when do *I* get *my* rest?"

"Nothing simpler!" said the donkey. "You listen to me, I'll tell you what to do, it'll put you right in the driver's box. When the farmer brings you your hay tonight, don't eat it. The next day he'll see you didn't eat, he'll think you're sick, and he'll let you sleep the livelong day in your stall."

So the ox followed the donkey's advice, and left his hay untouched and curled up and went to sleep on the straw in the far corner of his stall. But the farmer lingered, after forking out the hay, to see what would happen. So he saw the donkey —who, after all, had fasted the livelong day and was very hungry—stretch out a long neck and guzzle up all the ox's hay, and he was tickled at the trick the wily donkey had played on the ox.

That night he was lying in bed, his wife drowsing beside him, when he thought again of the donkey's trick, and he laughed aloud.

"What's that!" exclaimed his wife.

"Nothing, my good wife, my heart's love, nothing. Go back to sleep. It was only my dream."

"A dream!" she said, and sat up straight. She laid her hand on her husband's forehead. "Dreams come of eating too much, I told you not to have so much of the stew, and smoking too much, those filthy cigars, and drinking hot tea the last thing before going to bed, and lying on your full stomach.

"Look at you," she scolded. "You're flushed like a drunkard, your eyes are too bright, you're probably sickening for a fever or a grippe, I told you you should have worn a sweater when you went traipsing off to see the *Rebbe*, you never told me what you did there. Come, I'll fix a nice purge for you, that'll clear you out."

And "No," he said. "I'm fine," he said. But on and on she went, and the long and the short of it was, he had to drink a filthy-tasting purge, which drove everything out of him before midnight.

"I knew when you laughed for nothing this afternoon that something was up," she said. "Now don't you feel better? Admit it, you feel better, don't you feel better?" And she tucked the down quilt tightly around him.

"What would I do without you, my good wife, my heart's love," he murmured weakly, and with that she was satisfied, and smiled, and went back to sleep.

The next morning the farmer went out to the barn and he saw the ox, lying on his straw, sulking, and the donkey was peering with malice over at him to see what would happen.

"My poor ox!" crooned the farmer. "You need a rest, my fine fellow. And extra rations, too. Your comrade here can do his own work and do yours as well." So he led out the donkey, who was furious, talking to himself of what he would like to do to the ox, and to the farmer, and to himself for being such an ass. And the farmer was so tickled at the donkey's speech that he laughed out loud.

As bad fortune would have it, just at that moment his wife passed by. She dropped the full milk pail she was carrying, and while the white pool spread about her and lapped at her shoes, she let her husband have it.

"Okay, where's the joke?" she began. "Once, a nice day. Twice, a dream. But three times is too many. You're hiding something from me, I know

it, I can tell. What's so funny? You're laughing at
me," she said, and burst into tears.

The farmer tried to comfort her. "Of course I'm not laughing at you, my good wife, my heart's love. It's nothing at all to do with you. But it is a secret and I cannot tell." And he patted her shoulder.

His wife threw his arm away from her. And "Don't touch me!" she cried. "Don't you come near me! You keep secrets from me, you don't trust me, your own wife you don't trust. Don't you come near me until you tell me, not by day or by night come near me, not a finger lay on me, until you tell me."

The farmer was very upset. He tried to explain to her that of course he would tell if he could, but he couldn't, because if he told her, it would be the death of him. "On the very day," he said, "the identical same exact day if I ever tell the secret, I will die."

But listen she would not.

"I'll die if you don't tell me the secret," she wailed. "Not a morsel of food or drink will pass my lips, I swear a vow, I'll starve and dwindle to a skeleton, my ribs will show and my hair will fall out, and I'll die, and my death will be on your head, because you didn't tell me." And on and on she went, while the milk seeped into the ground, and the farmer's heart went flipflop like a stranded fish, and his eyes glazed and his ears drooped, and the long and the short of it was that finally he agreed to tell her, because, he thought to himself, it is better that she should be the death of me, than I should be the death of her.

"But you must wait a day or two," he said

wearily, "until I write my will and settle my affairs, because on the very day that I tell you, on that exact identical same day, on that day I will die."

So the farmer went to the notary and drew up his will, and he went to the tradesmen and settled his accounts, and it came to be the morning of the day when he promised to tell his wife the secret. He went out to say goodbye to his animals, and as he was passing the chickens, he overheard his faithful dog barking at the rooster.

"How can you sing like that, so happily, when our mistress by her nagging has driven our master to his doom, and today he must die?"

"Well, what is that to me," retorted the rooster, "if our mistress is a nag and our master is a fool?"

"What do you mean, our master is a fool?" said the dog.

"Well, and so he is," said the rooster. "It takes two to tangle," he said, "and the mistress could nag all she pleased, the master needn't pay her any mind. God intended man to be master in his own home, but our master is no master, he is a coward and a fool, and he gives way where he should not.

"Now look at me," said the rooster, preening his feathers and crowing softly. "I have ten wives, and do they ever bother me? They do not! And why? They know their place, and they know if they overstep it, why, a good blow on the beak or a kick to the wing, and they'll hurry right back into place. And I have ten wives, yet I am master, while your master has only one, and he cannot master even her."

"And what then should he do?" asked the dog.

"Why, if he did as I did, and if his wife began to nag he just gave her a good smack or two, he'd find that before he knew it he'd have as sweet and loving a wife as any of my ten. Yes, sir, show her who's boss, that's all, he'd come out of this smelling like a bandit," concluded the rooster, and he cock-a-doodle-dooed to reach the skies.

"But it's too late," mourned the dog, and he laid his head down on his paws, and he howled.

The farmer stood there, thunderstruck. Just then his wife came bustling out of the farmhouse. She came over to her husband and she began to cluck at him. "Now you'll tell me, now you'll tell me, now . . ."

But the farmer, grabbing the bull by both ears, turned his wife over his knees and administered the rooster's advice, right on the spot. So the secret stayed a secret, the farmer didn't die, and from that morning to the very end of their days together, the farmer and his good wife lived in peace and harmony and happiness forever.

THE MERCHANT: THE TIN SWORD

As soon as he'd finished his story, the Husband of the Interfaith Chairperson retired into his customary silence beside his wife. There was a lot of laughing and hooting and elbow-nudging among the gentlemen. Even the Art Dealer had a little smile playing around his mouth. The Cabdriver especially, he laughed uproariously at the Chairperson's Husband's story, slapping his knee, his bull neck stretching his collar as he threw his head back and roared. He poked

his wife and started laughing again, but she
turned in her seat, she was only pocket-size next
to him, but she gave him a look and said, "Forget
it, Sam. Forget it now, or you'll remember it tonight. In bed. Alone."

And he stopped laughing and began coughing
instead. And all around raged a whole storm, it
was hard for me to sort out the voices. It was like
a whirling cloud, and from it darted forth phrases,
like lightning flashes.

"Bone of my bones . . ."

"What about Lilith then?"

". . . and flesh of my flesh!"

"Look at Samson and Delilah, will you?"

"My wife, my first wife—"

"Jezebel."

"She was a wonderful woman."

"What about Eve?"

"Therefore a man shall leave his father and his
mother and cleave to his wife . . ."

"For heaven's sake, *Eve* ate the apple first!"

". . . and they shall be one flesh."

Just then, at the height of the storm, in the middle distance there appeared an Arab in his sheik's
headdress, swaying atop his slowly stepping camel,
while a woman, black-gowned and veiled, carrying a pitcher on her head, trudged along like a
shadow behind him.

"Isn't it a treat to see a woman who knows her
place?"

It was the Merchant who spoke, the retired one
from Harrisburg, Pennsylvania, and Florida and
New York. He was a nice-looking older man, but
he always looked like he was smelling something

nasty. And he never smiled. He seemed to be in some sort of no-smiling contest with the Caterer to see who could make the longest face and hold it longest. One time, one time only, I remember, he didn't actually smile, but his face softened and the corners of his mouth curved up, and that was in Safed. I had lingered behind the others, and I was hurrying to catch up when I came upon the Merchant, all by himself, looking into the tiny courtyard garden of a tiny house of that mystic mountain town, looking at the roses glowing in clay pots among the vines and shrubs. And he confided to me (I was really surprised) that he loved gardening and growing flowers, especially roses. That when he still lived in Harrisburg, Pennsylvania, he and his wife, his first wife, they had a greenhouse, and his yellow Kaiser Wilhelms (or maybe it was Queen Beatrix, I don't know much about roses, anyway, some royalty) used to win prizes every year at the County Fair. And when she died, he retired and moved to Florida, and he had had pots of roses on his terrace, but now he lived in New York and he had no space for a greenhouse and no terrace for pots or roses, and she, his second wife, roses gave her hay fever anyway. But normally, as I said, he never smiled. And what he did now wasn't really a smile either. He bared his teeth like a dog about to seize a bone, and if you want to call that a smile, then be my guest. Anyway, I had noticed this morning that, when the Widow was telling the beautiful Bible love story of Ruth and Boaz and Naomi, he'd been sniffing and wrinkling his nose all through. So I wasn't surprised when he came back to her story.

"Boaz didn't know when he was well off," he said. "It's not for nothing that every Jewish man every morning is supposed to recite, Blessed art Thou, O Lord, our God, King of the Universe, who has not made me a woman. And the sages said, Woe to the father whose children are girls."

"And the husband whose wife is a woman, I suppose," I said. I couldn't stop myself.

The Adult Bookstore Owner giggled.

"Woe to the husband altogether," replied the Merchant. "Any husband. I know why there's no devil in our Bible. Because women are the very devil, and who needs more?"

"Shame, shame!" said the Chairperson of the Massachusetts, Connecticut, and Rhode Island Tri-State Area of Interfaith Councils. "It is also in our Bible, Who can find a virtuous woman, for her price is far above rubies."

"Only because they're so rare!" he retorted with a bitter smile. "That virtuous woman stuff, they're always reading it at funerals, you'd think only female saints ever died. No, no matter how you slice it, it's still salami."

The Adult Bookstore Owner spoke up in a pleasant voice. "I know a cute story that explains what women are like and why. It starts with God. He was about to create Eve, you know, out of Adam, and he couldn't decide what part of Adam's, you know, body to use. So He said, 'I won't make her from Adam's head, because that might make her arrogant and proud. I won't make her from his eye, because she might have a roving eye. I won't make her from his ear, because she might be an eavesdropper; or from his neck, because she'd be insolent; or from his mouth, because she'd tattle and gossip; or from his heart, because she'd be envious; or from his hand, because she'd meddle; or from his foot, because she'd wander where she shouldn't. I must make her from a pure part of the body!' And He didn't have, you know, much left to work with, so He took a rib and He created Eve, and, as he made each part of her He'd say, 'Be pure! Be pure!' "

"From your mouth into God's ear," interrupted the Merchant.

The Adult Bookstore Owner smiled at him and continued, "But what happened after all God's careful planning? Just what you'd expect! The daughters of Zion, it says, were arrogant and proud; they walked insolently and with roving eyes; Sarah was an eavesdropper in her own tent when, you know, the angel spoke to Abraham; Miriam tattled on Moses; Rachel envied her sister Leah; Eve put out her hand to the forbidden fruit; and Dinah wandered around and got into, you know, *trouble*. So that just shows you, even God couldn't handle women!"

"Amen," said the Merchant. "I have heard it said, If you marry an unfitting wife, it's as if you plowed the whole world and sowed it with salt, barren, bitter and barren."

"I don't know," mused the Mashgiach comfortably. "Mostly it seems to be the men who fool around who have wives who fool around in return. But I think what's worse is the jealous man."

Unexpectedly, in his bell-like voice, the Hasid chimed in. "Set me as a seal, a seal upon thine heart, as a seal upon thine arm, for love is strong as death, and jealousy as cruel, cruel as the grave."

The Mashgiach said, "Yes, sir, the jealous man,

he's in trouble. Of course, sometimes he has reason." He said to the Merchant, "You're from Miami Beach, aren't you?"

The Merchant said shortly, "Not any more."

The Mashgiach said, "I thought you were.
I heard a funny story from Miami Beach, maybe
you know it. It seems there was this man, a nice
retired Jewish man, and he had a nice-looking
wife, his second wife, younger than he was, and
they lived in a condominium in a retirement community. Well, one night they went together to a
show at the clubhouse, and the wife said she
wasn't feeling too good, she had a headache, she'd
go back to the apartment and lie down. But he
should stay there and watch the show. Enjoy! So
he did, but at the intermission he was worried
how his wife was, so he decided to go home, where
he found her lying down all right, in bed, in the
arms of another man! Well, there was quite a hoo-
hah, and when the smoke cleared, the husband
had broken the other man's arm. He swore his wife
to keep the secret, but somehow word got around,
and for quite a while, every man with a broken
arm, people looked at him cross-eyed. And, believe me, in a retirement community where the
youngsters are sixty, there were plenty of broken
arms and plenty of crossed eyes!"

Harry Bailley was among the heartiest laughers
at the Mashgiach's story. He looked over at the
Merchant sitting stiff and angry in his seat, leaned
across the aisle and slapped him on the back.
"What's the matter, friend? It doesn't cost anything to laugh. And our doctor friend here can tell
you, isn't it true, Doctor? that a merry heart is the

best medicine. God knows, you look like you need cheering up!"

The Merchant didn't give way one bit, but sat just as stiff as before. "You laugh, all of you, but I could care less. Faithfulness is a serious matter, and breaking faith is a serious matter. Some men break their faith, I admit it. More don't. But women! King Solomon said it, 'There isn't a just man on earth that always does good and never sins. One man among a thousand have I found, but a woman among all these I have not found!' And truer words were never spoken. You, Harry Bailley, you want a story from us all. I'll give you a story, like it or not."

THE MERCHANT'S STORY

WHEN KING SOLOMON had said these words to his court, "One man among a thousand have I found, but a woman among all these I have not found," many of them burst into laughter. They called Solomon a cynic, they said he'd had bad luck in the women he'd encountered, in short, take his word they would not, they wanted proof.

So Solomon said, "Seek out the finest man and wife in the city."

The court members went out and searched, selected possible candidates, investigations were carried out by the king's men, and at last the names of one man, good, honest, upstanding, and his wife, good and beautiful, were presented to the king.

"This couple, then, represents the finest man and woman the city has to offer," said King Solomon. The court agreed.

So King Solomon sent for the man, and sat with him in private conference.

"You have been represented to me," he said, "as a man of stability, upstanding virtue, honesty and goodness. Such a man is a rare prize, and I wish to make you my chief counselor and adviser, to help me govern this vast domain."

The man's face lit up.

"But," said King Solomon, and he laughed lightly. "When in life isn't there a *but!* To hold such a high position in the kingdom, second only to me, it seems reasonable to ask you to demonstrate your loyalty and allegiance to me before all else. Therefore I make this request of you. I understand you have a wife. If you will take this sword, go home, slay her and bring her head in token back to me tomorrow, I will make you ruler over all my kingdom and, what is more, give you my eldest daughter in marriage, to console you. What do you say?"

He held out a glittering sword, chased along the blade, its hilt of gold and glimmering with emeralds. The sword dazzled the man's eyes, and the prospects dazzled his mind. He bit his lip for a moment, and then he said, "Yes, yes, I will. To serve you, my King."

So the man returned home, filled with a kind of exaltation, but as he neared his house, his steps began to lag, and when he crossed his own threshold where his beautiful wife waited to greet him, his eyes filled with tears. When she questioned

him, he turned her questions aside and blamed his
low spirits on a bad day in the market. That night
his wife slept sound, and the moon had climbed
far above the horizon when the man crept from
his bed, took out the glittering sword, fixed his
mind on boundless wealth and power, and, stern
with resolution, went toward his wife where she
lay sleeping.

He raised the sword. Just at that moment the
moon's rays pierced the hangings and lay across
his wife's face like a silver sword. The scent of
roses filled the air. Her beauty shone like the moon
itself, and pity welled up in his heart.

"I cannot, I cannot!" he cried to himself, and he
sat down and buried his face in his hands. After
a while, however, the riches and power that Solomon had dangled before him once more took
shape in his mind's eye. "One stroke," he said to
himself, "just one stroke, and I am a made man
forever. I will do it!"

So once more he raised the sword above her
neck. But it remained poised at its upswing, for he
said, "Shall all this beauty perish? This innocence
be quenched? This woman might bear my children, and shall I murder my posterity and my
honor together?" A moment more the sword, like a
snake, stayed poised to strike, and then, slowly,
the man lowered his arm.

The next day the man went to see King Solomon.

"Well, and have you come to demonstrate your
allegiance to me? The robes of state and my
daughter both await you."

The man knelt before the King.

"Twice, O mighty ruler, twice my arm lifted to

do your bidding. And twice it failed. Not for all
the kingdoms of the East could I betray my good
and faithful wife. Now punish me as you choose."

But the king lifted him to his feet, praised him
for his goodness and virtue, and sent him home
to his good and faithful wife loaded down with
golden chains and rings, but he cautioned the man
never to speak to his wife of what had happened.

The moon dwindled once and fattened once,
and now King Solomon sent for the wife, and sat
with her in private conference.

"You have been represented to me," he said, "as
a woman of dazzling beauty, and charm, and virtue. Such a woman I desire as a wife, to wear
robes of gold and sit beside me on my golden
throne in my crystal palace, and to share with me
all the treasures of my kingdom."

The woman's face grew pale and her eyes were
dark pools of longing.

"But," said King Solomon, and he laughed
lightly. "When in life isn't there a *but!* What
stands between you and me is just one thing. Your
husband. Were we rid of him, I would marry you
tomorrow."

Her face grew paler still, and her eyes burned.
King Solomon thought to himself. "This one will
truly kill her husband," so he reached out and
took up a glittering sword, studded with jewels,
but its blade was made of shiny tin.

"Take this sword with you," he said. "Tonight
you will lay its sharp edge against his neck, and in
one stroke you will slay your husband, and tomorrow you will bring his head in token, and on that
same day I will marry you."

The woman took the sword and hurried home.

She made up her face very carefully, put on her finest clothes, had the servants prepare her husband's favorite dishes, and when he returned from the market, she met him at the door cooing like a dove.

She served him with her own white fingers, filled his wine cup again and again and gave him to drink with her own white hand, and smiled and laughed until his senses were drunken with wine and happiness. Then she helped him early to bed, and lay down beside him.

As soon as she thought he slept a deep sleep, she tiptoed from bed and took up the sword that King Solomon had given her. She lay its edge against his neck, as the king had said, and began to cut the flesh. But the sword was tin, and its blade bent and turned aside, so the husband awoke.

"What are you doing?" he shouted. "Tell me at once, or I will take my sword and hack you to pieces."

The wife wept, and told her husband how King Solomon had offered to marry her and set her on his golden throne, if only she would kill him.

The man was about to kill his faithless wife when, once more, pity welled up in his heart, and instead he comforted her and told her that the next day they two would go and see the king.

And the next day the king received them before the whole court. The man told him, "My wife would have slain me were the sword not made of tin, for which I suppose I must give thanks to you. And I was about to slay her, which she well deserved, but pity overcame me, and I held my hand."

King Solomon said, "You have done well, both
in your own deeds, and in the proof of what I have
told this court, for indeed, is it not true, one man
among a thousand have I found, but a woman
among all these I have not found."

And the court laughed and cheered and ap-
plauded the wisdom of Solomon.

But the man went home and put his head in his
hands and he wept, because Solomon's wisdom
was his folly, and even a fool's paradise is better
than none. The roses had withered, love and trust
had flown away with the moonlight, and would
never return to his garden again.

THE COLLEGE DROPOUT: THE POWER OF LOVE

WHEN he'd finished his story, the Merchant sat with his head turned away, stiff and silent. But around us the storm broke out again, with redoubled rage.

Then Harry Bailley stood up and rapped his staff against a Coca-Cola bottle.

"Order in the court!" he boomed out, laughing. "The Lawyer wants to speak."

"Let me suggest to you good people," began the Lawyer, "that what Solomon said, that one man in a thousand had he found, but

not one woman in a thousand, he meant as a compliment." That just set the storm raging again, until he held up his hand. "The wise king didn't
mean to defame women, but to do them a good
turn."

The Chairperson of the Massachusetts, Connecticut, and Rhode Island Tri-State Area of Interfaith Councils bounced up, her cheeks pink, her
lips pursed, her blue eyes round, and even her
fluffy blond hair bristling with indignation.

"A compliment? To speak with contempt of a
whole sex of people as faithless, this is a compliment? To cast aspersions, by which I mean lies,
on an entire group, a compliment? Mr. Lawyer,
a man of good sense and learning should be more
sensitive to relationships, relationships of all kinds,
interfaith, intersex, one must be at all times sensitive to others. I myself pride myself on my sensitivity, so that when you insensitively interpret an
insult as a compliment, to the disparagement of
the whole of my sex, I must protest. A compliment, hah!"

"Certainly it is," said the Lawyer blandly.
"Just think about it. What a disaster for all women
would it have been if Solomon had said there *is*
one good and faithful woman among a thousand.
All men would divorce their wives, and this would
be their train of thought: 'My wife is a nag and a
spendthrift. Maybe if I get rid of her with God's
blessing I will be lucky and find that good and
virtuous woman in a thousand that King Solomon
spoke about!' But as it is, a man looks at his wife:
'This woman, another woman, what's the difference? None of them are any good anyway, so I

might as well stick to the one I have.' And he doesn't divorce his wife. Now, isn't it fortunate for women that Solomon wrote as he did?"

"Fortunate, my Aunt Fanny," said the Interfaith Lieutenant rudely.

But instead of her remark touching off the storm again, among the women a calm and a silence followed, and it gradually descended on the bus. It was a big silence, a chilly silence, and little by little it settled and froze any laughter or conversation, and turned the gentlemen to pillars of ice, all except the College Dropout.

His cheeks were flaming like the flowers on his shirt and his halo of hair, and he burst out passionately, "Gross me out! All of this stuff, especially what *you* said" (and here he looked directly at the Lawyer, who retreated behind his aviator sunglasses) "all this stuff is, like, irrelevant! What is it lawyers say? Incompetent, imma—whatever, but for sure it's irrelevant! You say, you know, all those things about men and women, husbands and wives, but not once do you say the word *love*. Like, I don't believe you all! Not even to mention it, such a beautiful word, *love*—"

"A four-letter word, that's a no-no," said the Adult Bookstore Owner, and he waggled a playful finger at the angry young man.

The Dropout just looked at him scornfully and went on. "Not to even mention *love*. Why, love is, love is, like, you know, LOVE is . . ."

"A many-splendored thing," said the Philanthropist.

"Where you find it," said the Fundraiser.

"What makes the world go round," said the English Professor.

"Blind," said the Merchant.

The Dropout looked like he was ready to cry. His beautiful word, and here were these old men just kicking it around like an old tin can.

The Widow rushed to man his barricades. "Listen to the boy! He's closer to what he's talking about than the whole bunch of you. And better suited for it too. Just look at him!"

Obediently everybody turned to look at him.

Well, if it were me, I would have sunk right through my seat from embarrassment. But he's from the Now generation, the Cool generation, the Let-it-all-hang-out generation, such things wouldn't faze him like they did my Nothing-at-all generation. So you can imagine how surprised I was to see him blushing like a girl, his face the color of beet soup, and trying to find someplace to put his eyes.

"Now, now," said the Executive Director. "Now, now, son. I suspect you could tell us quite a story, we should understand the power of love."

The Dropout silently shook his head.

Now the Dropout, when he spoke, was always very pleasant and polite, but he didn't very often speak. Come to think of it, the one time I remember seeing him lively and really involved in a discussion was when all the rest of us, his father and his mother and the other grownups had gone to see some antiquity or other, and he and the Gentile girl had stayed behind. You remember her, the blonde from Arizona, the terrific horsewoman, very pretty, who was traveling with the English Professor. "And she's half his age, the *shiksa*," the Interfaith Chairperson had almost hissed at me through clenched teeth, *"on top of everything else."* When I asked her what was *everything else,* she just said darkly, *"You* know," so I let it go at that. Anyway, I had come back to the bus for a guidebook, very good, very detailed, it told you almost more about antiquities than you really wanted to know, like the little girl's review for school of a book about penguins. You probably remember it, the little girl wrote, "This is a very good book, but it told me more about penguins than I wanted to know." Well, I had come back to the bus, and there were the two young people chattering away, the red hair and the blond close together, it did my heart good to see them. But that was the only time I know of, and otherwise the Dropout was very pleasant and polite, but very, very quiet.

"Now, now, son," repeated the Executive Director, "a young fellow like you, you can teach us a lot about what we've forgotten." (And here he looked for some reason, at the Philanthropist, the Fundraiser, the Professor, and the Merchant.) "Or maybe what we never knew. So what do you say, son? Give us a story. And if you can't say it all, why, you'll sing the rest."

At that the Dropout's face brightened. He reached for his guitar, hung it around him from its broad flower-embroidered strap, plucked a few strings and fingered a few chords with his long white fingers, then he strummed a couple of times, softly, very pleasant to hear, and he began.

THE COLLEGE DROPOUT'S STORY

ONCE UPON a time there was a wise and good and intelligent king, just possibly the best king in the world, who established justice and did mercy, the whole thing, just as he should. He was a father to his people. But the father had no son, and so he had nothing, that was how he saw it.

And then one day, like a miracle, the queen conceived and bore a son, and his name was called David. He was a wonder child. From the day he was born, the boy had everything, the world, like a balloon on a string, and love, like a flood of balloons, but always with strings attached, strings like reflecting honor on your parents, and assuming your proper responsibilities, and taking life seriously.

Somehow, though, as he grew up, he grew up without any strings attached, free-floating, unattached to parents, friends, duty, responsibility. He wasn't interested in being a son or a prince or a philosopher, or even much of anything besides being whatever he felt like right then. So, as the years went by, instead of being the joy and the blessing the king, his father, had prayed for, he was a sorrow and a heartache.

The wisest and the best teachers, philosophers, scientists, doctors, mathematicians, military generals, his father brought them all in to teach him. No way. He ran away from them, hid the books, played tricks on them. But the sky was always blue, the sun was always shining, and the waves on the pebbles on the seashore were always calling, and the leaves on the trees of the forest were always singing. And so what could he do? He didn't *want* to hurt his father, but he had to be true to what was moving around inside him, didn't he? And so he broke his father's heart.

(A minstrel once offered to teach the boy, and the boy was even interested, well, at least a little, but his father thought such instruction wasn't *serious*, it was irrelevant, and the minstrel was sent away.)

The way his father saw it, his son was lazy, thoughtless, selfish, reckless, ignorant, a good-for-nothing loafer and a bum. Where the boy saw the sky and the sun and the waves and the leaves and nothing else, and he would sing all day, his father saw downtrodden people and a ruined kingdom and a throne that might as well be empty, and he wept all night.

And that was the way things were in the kingdom until one day, it was a Friday afternoon before the coming of the Sabbath, the boy was out riding and he saw a girl. But not just a girl like any other. He'd seen plenty of girls. This one was special. Her name was Esther, which is Star, and that's what she was like, a star shining in a sapphire sky to mark the coming of the Sabbath. The Sabbath is a woman, a queen and a bride, and that's how the king's son saw Esther, as a queen and a bride.

She was on the balcony of her father's house, behind the high brick wall with the round moon gates, her face unveiled and turned up to the setting sun.

The boy was bewitched.

He took his lute, and evening after evening, he
would serenade her. He would sing to her:

> *As roses love sunshine*
> *And violets love dew*
> *The angels in heaven*
> *Know I love you.*

And he would sing:

> *Come to me, quietly,*
> *Do not do me injury,*
> *Gently, Esther, my darling-O.*

It was all for nothing. Esther would close the
shutters, and if his music reached her ears, it never
reached her heart. Never did she send a sign or
token to him, and the only time he even saw her
was going to market, and then it was only her dark
eyes above a silken veil.

He kept on singing to her until one day her
maid appeared before him and handed him a note,
asking him to meet Esther that evening by the
trellis where the yellow roses climbed. For an hour
that boy bit into the apple of happiness, and
licked the sweetness from every minute till they
met.

And then, while the perfume of the yellow roses
climbed like a mist around them, the girl told the
boy to go away forever, to stop bothering her.

He couldn't understand that, this king's son, this
wonder child with the world on a string. "I am a
prince," he said. "You dare not refuse me." He
thought all he had to do was hold out his hand,
and candy would drop into it, by right of birth.

She looked at him and laughed with scorn. "You

are the son of a king, perhaps. But you are not a prince. The meanest peasant has a more princely heart than you do. In your heart you are a silly and selfish and ignorant and useless and spoiled little boy. Listen to me. Only a true prince can win my heart. When your heart has become a prince's heart, you may return to me, and not before."

And she slipped back into her father's house and the carved doors closed behind her.

Well, that was the first time that boy had learned anything, and he learned two lessons at the one time. He learned that there was something he wanted he couldn't have just for the wanting. And he learned that his words and his deeds weren't just written on the wind, like he'd thought they were, but were etched in stone for the world to see—and to judge.

First he couldn't believe such a thing had happened to him. And then he thought it wouldn't make any difference, he'd just forget about her. And then he found out that he couldn't, she was in his heart, and his heart was sick with love.

Then he thought maybe he'd make her sorry, and then she'd change her mind, like his mother always did. So he went and sang at her window:

Oh, dig my grave both wide and deep,
wide and deep,
Put tombstones at my head and feet,
head and feet,
And on my breast you can carve a turtle dove,
To signify I died for love.

When the maid came out to him, his heart leaped like a fish to his throat. But what she handed him was some money, and she said, "You

have touched my mistress' heart. She sends you
this to help pay for the turtledove." She laughed,
and went back into the house. And then his heart
sank like a stone in the depths of the sea, for he
knew this time he had to play by somebody else's
rules.

So he sang to himself:

> *Oh, sinner man, where you gonna run to?*
> *Oh, sinner man, where you gonna run to?*
> *Oh, sinner man, where you gonna run to?*
> *All on that day.*

And he answered himself:

> *Run to the rock, the rock was a-melting*
> *Run to the sea, the sea was a-boiling*
> *Run to the moon, the moon was a-bleeding*
> *All on that day.*

He wandered all around the city, and at last, on
the pebbles of the shore of the sea, he sat down
and he *thought.* (He'd never done that before.) He thought of who he was, and what he
wanted, and what he'd have to give up to get it.
(He had never known you had to give up to get.)
He'd always figured the world was his, that everybody else was there with his permission. Now he
found out that everybody has a world, and you
need permission to walk in anybody else's world.
He looked into his own emptiness that day, and
he knew what he had to do.

That day, the king's son disappeared.

The king was upset, but his heart was already
broken, so it couldn't break again. And the people
of the kingdom, they put on their long faces, but

their sorrow was short and sweet. In a while, the boy was pretty well forgotten, and life went on without him like it does.

Meanwhile, in a cabin at the back of the woods, the boy had sent for the minstrel, the Hebrew minstrel who'd once offered to teach him irrelevant things. Together they spent the livelong day under the trees, singing together, the hymn of creation, the song of Moses, the war cry of Joshua, the psalms of David, the lament of Jeremiah. But especially they sang the Song of Songs, which is Solomon's, and was now this David's.

It was on a Friday in September that he'd vanished, just before the New Year, and the months had unrolled and the seasons faded until it was spring again, and he stole into the town one evening with a coarse robe around him and a hood pulled over his face. He didn't know that no one would recognize him anyway, with his full new beard, and the steady light in his eyes and the new lines in his face. He rode up to Esther's house, and he began to play and sing a new song, very low:

> Rise up, my love, my fair one,
> And come away.
> For, lo, the winter is past,
> The rain is over and gone;
> The flowers appear on the earth;
> The time of the singing of birds is come,
> And the voice of the turtle is heard in our land.

Drawn by the strange new sounds came Esther to the doorway. When he saw her, his heart turned over, and he sang:

Your lips, O my bride
Drop honey
Honey and milk
Are under your tongue.

She came down to him, and he went to stand with her where the yellow roses had scented the air long ago, where the new buds peeped yellow from tight green cocoons, and they stood and they talked. She questioned him of this and that, of war and peace, love and hate, good and evil, of what is right to do and what is not, what is owed to the world and what is owed to oneself, and her heart danced within her to his new songs, songs that could only be written in blood from the heart of a true prince.

So when he sang:

> *A garden enclosed*
> *Is my sister, my bride;*
> *A spring shut up*
> *A fountain sealed.*
> *A fountain of gardens*
> *A well of living waters.*

And he sang:

> *Awake, O north wind*
> *And come, you south*
> *Blow upon my garden*
> *That the spices thereof may come out.*

Then she whispered to the roses:

> *Let my beloved come into his garden,*
> *And eat his precious fruits.*

And you may think that we've come to the happy ending, when they all live joyously ever after. But a garden is not the world, and two lovers not all the people in it.

There was another young man, who'd been courting Esther all that time since the fall. The walls of her heart had been shut up before him, but she was *his* castle and *his* siege, no one else's. Well, he saw what he saw, and he told her father of the stranger from the woods in the garden with his daughter. So they were trapped, and bound, and brought before the king for—let's just call it consorting. Or a feast of precious fruits.

They pulled off the robe and the hood of the stranger before the king; then the shoe pinched the other foot. Beard and eyes and lines and all, the father's heart saw right through them, and he recognized his son. In his heart, tears of happiness warred with tears of rage, but on his face not a muscle moved.

The boy and the girl, they took hands, and they approached the king with fear and trembling, for who can tell the way of a father and a son in love? They began to speak, first the girl, that she had refused the king's son with a beggarly heart, and then the boy, how after that he had gone off to the woods, and he'd studied. And as he spoke, the minstrel appeared and handed him his lute, and then the prince sang. He sang of compassion, of justice and mercy, of the debt of a king to his people, of the debt of all people to heaven, of the small things in life (but important) like war and commerce and fishing and politics, and of the big things in life, like love and beauty and music. For

hours and hours he sang, but every song comes
to an end.

The sound of the lute trembled and stilled. The
air didn't stir, not a breath was drawn. The king
was going to speak.

"Great and wonderful is the power of love, which took away a wastrel son from me and returned to me a worthy prince."

The tears of rage dried up in his heart and the tears of joy fell hot and fast as he clasped his son within his arms, and the people whistled and cheered.

To the girl he gave his son, and to the minstrel he gave purses of gold, in reward for their true teaching.

And before the whole court, the prince pledged himself to his wife, and he sang:

> Set me as a seal upon thy heart,
> As a seal upon thine arm:
> For love is strong as death,
> For love is strong as death;
> Its flashes are flashes of fire,
> A very flame of the Lord.

THE LAWYER: TABLE AND TABLECLOTH

THE last strains of the guitar died away, and there out of the desert loomed Beersheba, frying like an egg on a sand-colored skillet, and we went to our hotel for the night. The next day, the Bedouin market was in full swing. Men wearing white head-dresses bound with cords just like Rudolph Valentino in the old movies wandered slowly through the crowds. Some wore swords dangling from sword belts. They seemed to be mostly buying

or selling tobacco, heaped like piles of dry grass
on cloths on the ground.

Bedouin women, swathed in black from head to
toe, faces veiled, eyes glancing sideways, gold
coins tinkling from their headdresses, squatted in
the dust to sell their exotic wares. You could buy
jewelry from them, and ducks, and plastic water
bottles, and wrinkled handkerchiefs.

Before we left the bus, Harry Bailley had
warned us that Arab manners and customs are not
Western manners and customs.

"On one trip of teen-agers," he said, "two American boys were joking to some Arabs about putting
their companion, a fat, fair girl with big blue eyes,
up for sale. She was bid for right away, and it got
a little ugly when the boys said they were only
kidding. Arabs don't kid about their women. So
don't you."

He spoke seriously, but there was the usual twin-
kle in his eyes, so I didn't know if he was kidding
or not. I must have looked a little nervous getting
off the bus, because he took me by the elbow and
said to me, very solemnly, "*You* don't need to
worry." He tipped his cowboy hat and strolled off,
brandishing his staff, before I realized that maybe
I'd rather be nervous!

Well, the market was very interesting and exotic, but it was also very hot there on the edge of
the Negev.

Very hot.

That's about as appropriate as saying, The fires
of hell are very hot.

What is it Shakespeare says? "O for a muse of
fire!" That's what I'd need to tell you just how hot

it was. Even the Coca-Cola tasted warm. So it was with a big sigh of relief when we boarded the bus that I relaxed to enjoy the cool air lapping like waves around me, and I think I even dozed off for a while. When I woke, the Lawyer was talking.

This Lawyer was the soul of what the kids call "cool," but even he could be stirred to passion, generally by a Pentax or a Leica or a Nikon. He was almost never seen without his camera on his chest, and generally a lens or two dangled beside, and he was festooned with rolls of film like the cartridges on a rifleman's belt, and it seems to me that most of the sights that the rest of us viewed with our selective, imperfect human lenses, he saw only through an impersonal camera eye.

"Yesterday," he began, "we heard several divergent views on the nature and status of the female sex. Now it behooves us to judiciously consider the sources of these views, and the evidence offered for them, in order properly to evaluate them." His voice was pleasantly lazy, but cutting, too, and with a sarcastic aftertaste.

"Otherwise," he continued, "we will never be able to arrive at a true verdict concerning the matter of the second most important sex in the world. After all, we are enjoined by the Bible, Justice, justice shalt thou pursue." And in a flash he was off and pursuing, leaving the rest of us barefaced and flatfooted at the starting gate.

"Now I spent last night doing some research on the subject and, if it please the bus, I will offer myself as an *amicus curiae*, a friend of the court, holding a watching brief, purely as a neutral observer. If you good ladies and gentlemen will constitute yourselves a jury, I will set out before you on the table, as it were, solid evidence. Consider it as exhibits A through as much of the alphabet as you should deem necessary, leaving out only such material as is patently incompetent, immaterial" (here he cast a significant look at the Dropout, who retaliated with a loud and rude discordance on his guitar) "and irrelevant, and then you, the members of the jury, can come to an objective, prudent, and unbiased verdict. I might add, to reassure you of my own impartiality and objectivity, that I am a married man, but that my wife is not accompanying me on this trip, so I have no personal ax to grind. I am interested only in the facts, chapter and verse. Is that agreeable? If so, let me offer for your consideration the female of our species as she appears in the pages of the *Shulchan Aruch*, the definitive code of Jewish law."

Now I have to tell you right here and now that I strongly object to hearing women called "females," the "female" this and the "female" that. Female what? Gorillas? Cockroaches? Mosquitoes? Female is a gender, not a person. "Women," I think that's terrific. "Ladies" doesn't bother me. "Girls" I will tolerate, although I know some who won't, mostly younger than I am. But *female*. It's so clinical! "Anatomy is destiny, and don't you females forget it!" I can just hear Freud now, that pompous, overbearing, self-important Jewish father. . . . But all I wanted to do was to let you know that I disclaim all responsibility for the whole story that follows here, and I am acting strictly as a reporter. The opinions, therefore, reflected below and following, are purely those of the Lawyer, and do not carry the endorsement of the management of this book.

So, the Lawyer was explaining about the *Shulchan Aruch*, that it was compiled and codified by Joseph Karo, "K–A–R–O," he spelled. (Which is an unusual name, and I wondered if he was from the same family that made the syrup, but naturally I didn't like to interrupt.) He explained that *Shulchan Aruch* means "The Prepared Table," that it is a code of laws to prepare anyone for all the vicissitudes of life. (Vicissitudes is his word, not mine.)

"Incidentally," he said, "Karo wrote the *Shulchan Aruch* in Safed, after he had come there from Europe, so the thin, clear air of Safed would seem to encourage legal as well as mystical reasoning." He made a slight bow in the direction of the advocate and critic of pure reason, the English Professor, who chose to ignore it.

"As we know it, the code of Jewish law consists of Joseph Karo's Prepared Table with, spread over it, the Tablecloth, which is the commentary of Rabbi Moses Isserles of Cracow. Now I would like to offer in evidence from this leading legal document and authority the following observations on the role, duties, obligations and prohibitions concerning men and females."

THE LAWYER'S STORY

IT IS HEREWITH written, stated, devised, and laid down:

One, that a man should marry to fulfill the precept of propagation, but even after he has done so,

he should be married and if possible to a female
who is prolific, unless he himself is sterile, in which
case it is preferable to marry a nonprolific female.
The precept assumes obligatory status on a man
at the age of eighteen, and an absolute obligation
by the end of the twentieth year. Only if he is
engaged in the study of Torah with extreme dili-
gence, and is concerned lest the obligations of
marriage interfere with those studies, may he de-
lay marriage, provided he is not of a passionate
nature.

Two, that a woman whose former two husbands
have died should not marry a third one without
consulting a sage.

Three, that the ideal in marriage for a man is to
take to wife a respectable female from a respectable family, and the three attributes testifying to
this respectability are modesty, mercy, and the
practice of charity. In other words, gorgeous
doesn't count.

Four, that if one marries a virgin, he must be
prepared to cohabit with her for the first seven
days inclusive. If one marries a widow or a di-
vorcee, the requirement for cohabitation is three
days; although some authorities hold that if the
groom has been a bachelor, even in the latter case
the requirement for cohabitation is then seven
days, although in the latter case, the woman may
relinquish her right to service.

Five, that a husband shall not diminish the duty
of marriage of his wife, and that therefore the performance of marital duties is strictly prescribed
by occupation of the husband. That strong,
healthy men, merchants or middle class, regularly

employed, perform their marital duties nightly. Laborers who are employed in the city where they reside, twice a week; but if they must travel to another city, once a week. Traveling salesmen whose territory is confined to a small radius, once a week. Businessmen who travel by air over long distances, once every thirty days. Learned men and Talmud scholars must satisfy their wives only from Sabbath eve to Sabbath eve.

That, furthermore, if a wife makes a special effort in her clothes, manner, appearance, and behavior, he is then obliged to visit her even if it is not the prescribed time for the performance of his marital duty. But if the female makes a verbal overture, this is considered brazen, lewd, and lascivious, and he may not go into her.

Six, that as we have so rightly been told, intercourse should not be performed for personal gratification, but to fulfill one's obligation toward his marital duty and the command of God to be fruitful and multiply, and therefore it is not fitting for a man to regard the female at that time.

Seven, that all such prescriptions apply only to the clean period of the female. A female's menstrual period renders her unclean, and she must count seven clean days and take the ritual bath of immersion before she is clean again. He who cohabits with her in this period of uncleanness shall be cut off from his people. One cannot come near such a woman in any manner, neither in laughter nor in casual conversation, nor in contact, even with her little finger. Neither should her husband hand anything to her nor receive anything from her hand, nor eat at the same table, nor drink from her cup, nor sleep in the same bed with her, nor sit on a glider together, nor travel in the same car unless it is on business. She cannot make the bed in his presence, nor pour water for him.

The establishment of the menses by equal intermittent diurnal symptoms or intermittent diurnal symptoms or bodily symptoms I will pass over; as I will over the rule of threes and the laws regulating women whose menstrual cycle is irregular, or whose regular cycle suffers a change. And the laws of the purifying immersion are too numerous for me to reiterate. Let me simply cite three final observations.

Eight, that after childbirth the female is considered unclean, for seven days if she has borne a male child, and fourteen days' uncleanness for bearing a female child.

Nine, that a man is forbidden to put on even one female garment, nor can he pluck out even one gray hair from among the black, or dye one gray hair into black, as these are improvements for females only.

Ten, and last, that a mourner is forbidden to do any work of any kind, except that domestic occupations are not included in forbidden work, and therefore a female in mourning may bake and cook and clean the house.

Ladies and gentlemen, the case rests.

There came an outraged hubbub from most of the women and some of the men. The Lawyer pretended to duck the onslaught.

"Why are you attacking me?" he asked plaintively. "I am a friend to the female sex." And he grinned.

"With such friends," said the Rabbi's Wife, her

words dipped in vinegar, "we don't need enemies. Anyway, you are a pervert."

That shocked us all into silence.

And the Lawyer—it was the very first time I saw
him trade his habitual cool for hot around the
collar, but his voice was icy. "My good woman,
do you realize that is slander?"

The Rabbi, who'd been looking troubled, spoke.
"My wife did not mean 'pervert' in the sense normally given to it. She meant you are perverting a
doctrine, am I right, Sarah? And I too am worried,
because I also think you are perverting a doctrine,
but it is hard to prove it from your words, which
are true.

"And yet *not* true, at the same time. Karo intended, in the *Shulchan Aruch*, as earlier sages
had done, to build a hedge around the wall of the
Torah, so that not only might one not infringe,
heaven forbid! any of the prohibitions, but one
does not infringe even unwittingly, because one
is held at arm's length from doing so by a *second*
prohibition protecting the first. That is confusing.
I wish I could explain better."

The Widow, her red head tipped to one side,
considered. "A hedge? A hedge? It sounds more
like a barbed-wire fence, with a big sign posted,
WOMEN KEEP OUT."

"Or," I offered, "like it used to be for the Irish
in Boston, Females Need Not Apply."

The Rabbi was shaking his head sadly, mur-
muring, "No, no," when who should speak up, of
all people, but the Gentile girl, the blonde from
Arizona who was traveling with the English Professor, formerly a Cohen, now a Priest. She was
such a fine horsewoman that she even managed

to look graceful riding a camel, on which everybody looks ridiculous, even a Bedouin. But she
had never spoken out like this in public before.

"Excuse me," she said politely to the Lawyer in
her relaxed, Western drawl, "but that can't be
right, what you said."

"Oh," said the Lawyer ironically. "And what,
my Portia, have I misquoted? To what do you take
exception?"

She flushed, but continued firmly, "All of it. I
mean, all of it is wrong. That can't be the Jewish
attitude toward women, because that's not the
way Jewish men treat women, first of all. Why do
you think so many of us like to date Jewish men?
Because they treat us so nicely, like ladies, not like
mere—mere *sex objects*. You know what I think?"

"No," murmured the Lawyer. "Have we established that you do, in fact, think?"

She gave him *her* look, the one I can't describe,
but you wouldn't want anyone to look at you like
that. And she said, "I think you're talking from
only one book, and there are lots of other books,
but you've only chosen that one, and I think even
from that book you're picking and choosing to
make your point, and there are other things even
in that book."

So. The charge was quoting out of context and
relying on a single authority. That's how the Lawyer or the Professor might have put it, although
they both neglected to do so.

And this time it was the Lawyer's turn to flush,
although you couldn't read anything in his eyes,
because they were hidden, as usual, behind his
gold-rimmed aviator's sunglasses.

The girl went on. "Even if not, even if that was

the only Jewish book that talked about women, and those were the only things it said, then it would be a bad book, and you should know that, I mean, to put down a whole group of people for a biological—a biological *function*—which, if you had more understanding and less education, you might know is a *privilege*, to be able to have a baby, which men can't and never will be able to do. And where do you think you came from anyway? From a—a *womb* that *bled*.

"I mean, Jesus Christ was born without a father, without an earthly father, but even He, who was God and the Son of God, had to have a *mother*. I guess that doesn't cut much ice with you, of course, being that you're Jewish and all. But all your great people, Moses and David and even that precious rabbi of yours, the one you're quoting, none of them would have lived without the monthly stream of blood that you think you're so clever calling *unclean*, I mean, making out that women are unclean, only animals. Our church isn't always any better than your book, either, so it isn't that I'm anti-Jewish or anything. I just can't stand that kind of preaching and judging when *anybody* can see that it's wrong! And if you can't, then you really have a problem, because I don't see why you have to have a *book* to know what's right and wrong, it should be written in your *heart*. I mean, if you can't read what's written there, then you're—you're *illiterate*, no matter how many college degrees you have. So there."

And she stopped, blushing.

The Interfaith Lieutenant got right up out of her seat and she went over and she hugged that girl.

Not a muscle in the Lawyer's face moved, but you could tell from the tendons standing out in his neck that he was mad.

But the Rabbi spoke up in his rich, warm voice.

"Hear, hear!" he said. "There speaks a true daughter of Zelophechad."

Well, the Gentile girl was no more baffled than the rest of us Jews. Who was the daughter of Zelophechad, and what was she, and should I as a woman be glad or sad that this outspoken child was one? Something in the Rabbi's voice seemed to reassure her, though, and she subsided happily in her seat.

The Scribe, now—well, I don't mean to be unkind, but it was funny to watch him. You know how, in a comic strip, when a character gets an idea, the cartoonist will draw in a lighted electric bulb above their head? He was clearly thinking as hard as he could to find the reference, so hard that the electric bulb was almost visible above his head. But the bulb refused to turn on! And his young face fell, and he sat there, baffled, like the rest of us, but unlike the rest of us, he suffered.

The Hasid was the only one who seemed to understand, but instead of smiling, like the girl, a tiny frown clouded his brow and he turned his head aside to gaze out the window, tugging fretfully at his beard, as the rest of us, like good little students, turned to gaze at the Rabbi.

"And the Lord said to Moses, the daughters of Zelophechad speak right." The Rabbi paused and looked around. He smiled good-naturedly and said, "The Book of Numbers is not perhaps the most popular book of the Bible, so in case you've forgotten, I will remind you of what happened.

Zelophechad, a man of the tribe of Joseph, died. He had no sons, so the kinfolk of his tribe claimed his inheritance, but his daughters protested. The leaders of the tribe, the princes, could not find a clear law to govern the case, so they went to Moses. And the kinfolk claimed the inheritance through male descent, but the daughters said, 'Why should the name of our father be done away from among his family just because he had no son?' And the Bible says, 'And Moses brought their cause before the Lord, and the Lord spoke unto Moses, saying, 'The daughters of Zelophechad speak right, they shall surely inherit from their father, and thou shalt speak unto the children of Israel, saying, 'If a man die, and have no son, then ye shall cause his inheritance to pass unto his daughter.' Which is surely establishing a precedent, am I right, Counselor? for the inheritance rights of women. But, of course, if this were just a dry account of a petty legal controversy, it wouldn't be of much interest or importance. No, the words of the Torah are like icebergs. One meaning is on the surface only, but seven-eighths of their significance is hidden underneath, and the hidden parts are called *derashot*.

"So here we have a *derash*—one *derash*, many *derashot*—on the matter. The rabbis commented on the phrase 'Moses brought their cause before the Lord.' But why should Moses, the wisest of the Jews, the leader, the lawgiver, need assistance on a point of law? Well, they said, even the wisest men can fall into evil and boast of an understanding beyond earthly powers. And, the rabbis said, in his pride, Moses had said—just like you, Counselor—to the leaders of the tribes, If the case is simple, judge it yourselves. But if it is a hard case, then bring it to me, and I will solve it. But in this case, when the question of the ownership of the caper fields, I think they were, of Zelophechad was brought to Moses, he could not give an answer, and he had to go to the only supreme source of wisdom, to the Lord.

"And when the Lord had heard the case, the rabbis said, the Lord spoke to Moses saying, 'Did you not say that the law which is too difficult, that should be brought to you? But this law which you are unacquainted with has been cited by the women. Whatever she says, that is what it is. The daughters of Zelophechad speak right.' It's up to you to decide if this *derash* is intended to rebuke the arrogance of Moses or to compliment the wisdom of the daughters. But I can tell you, whichever way you decide, you will find plenty of rabbis to agree with you. And as for me, I plead no contest, except to say that I can recognize a daughter of Zelophechad when I hear one."

THE HOUSEWIFE: THE STORY OF JUDITH

I T WAS early afternoon, and we had been to Hebron and gone. The legend goes that it was to Hebron that Adam and Eve went when they were expelled from the Garden of Eden for disobedience, and it was in Hebron that they died and were buried, although those are probably the only two graves in all of Israel that are not marked and displayed as gospel. But what a shock the rocky hills of Hebron must have been after the effortless green growth and temperate, per-

fumed breezes of Paradise! Here, just as the Bible
threatens, things grow only by the sweat of man's
brow. Here the tragedy of Cain and Abel, brother
slaying brother, reenacts itself regularly in fact
and in imagination. And it was here, at Hebron,
that Absalom, David's well-beloved son, raised the
standard of rebellion against his father. The stares
of the Arab villagers in the market struck cold at
our backs even through the hot sunshine, and
Harry Bailley, serious for once, warned us all to
stay together and not to wander out of sight of his
staff.

The Mosque of Abraham is a holy Moslem shrine
built over the Cave of the Machpelah, a holy Jewish shrine, burial place of the three patriarchs and
three of the four matriarchs. Inside, the Moslem
women, shoeless, gowned and veiled, stretched
out to Mecca on their prayer rugs, knocking their
heads against the floor and ululating in Arabic,
were no more strange or alien to me than the
long-sleeved, black-stockinged Jewish women,
their heads wrapped in cloths, rocking violently
back and forth, weeping and wailing in Hebrew
before the sacred tombs.

My sisters, I do not know you, I thought. I am
a stranger in a strange land.

I guess I was just tired, after so much touring.
On the way back to the bus, someone in a knot
of lounging Arab boys spat elaborately as we
walked by, and as the bus hurried through small
villages on its headlong flight to Bethlehem, a
stone struck one window, which shivered, but
held fast.

At least, I was congratulating myself, I have escaped the fate of my fellow pilgrims, when the well-known hearty laugh boomed out.

"So, my lambs!" said Harry Bailley, beaming. "Most of us have done our part in sending the miles speeding past. Just a few more to go, and Bethlehem and the end of our trip will be in sight. We'll be in Jerusalem before sundown.

"But," he added, "those few of us who owe a story, prepare to pay your debts."

And he sent a stern look around, a shepherd counting his flock and checking for strays. Then it was my direction he was looking in. His eyes crinkled at the corners, and he smiled.

My heart sank.

Do any of you remember taking piano lessons, and hating to practice, and there'd be company, and all through the special dinner you'd know that awful moment was coming when your parents would turn to you and say, "Play for the company, darling. Play the new piece." And you didn't want to play, and the company didn't want to listen, but that made absolutely no difference. You played, and they listened.

"Do you believe, ladies and gentlemen," he began, "that we have here in our assembled midst a real-life, genuine, bona fide celebrity author, and modestly she sits back and lets the rest of us go first? Do you believe that? Well, it's true. I refer, ladies and gentlemen, to our very own El Al slogan contest winner here, 'Promise her anything, but give her Israel'—beautiful! Tell us a story, darling."

Play for the company, darling.

"Author, author!" he boomed. From here and there came a halfhearted "Author, author."

Play the new piece.

"I don't know about author, author," I began, "b-but if you want a story from me, I'll do my b-best," and, taking a deep breath to try and blow away the childhood stammer that had suddenly leapt at me across the years, I began.

THE HOUSEWIFE'S STORY

WITH ONE angry sweep of her arm Allison cleared all the cosmetics, the powders, the lotions, the creams, the bottles, off the bathroom shelf and onto the flowered ceramic floor. Mirrored tiles reflected her to herself, long blond hair disheveled, lips pressed together determinedly, brown eyes blazing, no longer young but ripened, ready.

She stormed out of that feminine bathroom, cocoon for a concubine, a woman's womb she sometimes called it, and strode through the litter of skirts, slips, and bras flung on the floor over to the suitcase yawning open on the bed, half-filled with slacks, blue jeans, sweaters, clothes to face a world in, a *real* world. Then she zipped the suitcase shut with sharp, angry zips, picked it up and strode toward the bedroom door.

Reluctantly she stopped and turned. Her eyes were pulled to the row of pictures lined up in their conventional silver frames on the rosewood desk. There they were, her life, her identity, in their silver frames, her husband, the seven children, the dogs, the cat, the parakeet. For a moment the blaze died down in the brown eyes, and then it flamed up again.

"Goodbye to all that," she said defiantly. "And hello world!" She strode toward the front door of the West Side brownstone, whistling.

She was free, at last.

"What a pack of nonsense!" interrupted the Rabbi's Wife. "It's a *shandah*, a shame, for a Jewish daughter to behave like that, and to boast about it is even worse! Mamma always said—"

But I didn't think I could handle what Mamma always said right at this moment, so I interrupted her in my turn.

"To tell the truth," I said, "that really isn't my style. I've tried and I've tried, but nobody seems to like any of my stories that have a modern heroine and a modern plot like that. Look, forgive me my trespass, and I'll start all over again, a more conventional story this time, with a more orthodox heroine, someone I'm more at home with. I'll tell you about Judith."

Saul—you remember, King Saul in the Bible, David was a little shepherd boy and he played the harp for him to soothe his savage headaches—Saul was angry because the people chanted, "Saul has slain his thousands, but David has slain tens of thousands." But he forgot that quantity is not always the measure of an achievement. Now Judith slew only one, but that death was an important death, worth tens of thousands, because the one she slew, Holofernes, would have slain tens of thousands of Jews. But maybe I ought to begin at the beginning, at the siege of Bethulia, in the eigh-

teenth year of the reign of Nebuchadnezzar, King
of the Assyrians, who went mad and ate grass, but
that was much later. At this time he was still the
splendid and terrible king, and his highest officer,
commander-in-chief of his army, Holofernes, was
encamped on a plain with chariots and cavalry
and infantry and a motley host like a swarm of
locusts. They were laying siege to Bethulia, high
above them in hilly country just like this we're riding through. And only Bethulia stood between
them and Jerusalem.

Up above, the men of Bethulia had closed the
passes, put on sackcloth and ashes, prayed to the
Lord, and prepared for war. The town itself,
perched on a mountain top, was impregnable. But
the Assyrians had seized the springs at the approach to the town, so the people of Bethulia were
forced to rely for water on the supplies in their
cisterns.

Thirty-four days came and went, and God Himself seemed to be on the side of the Assyrians, because each day the sun shone hot and bright as
brass, and no rain fell. Household supplies of water ran dry, the cisterns ran dry. Drinking water
was rationed. Babies whimpered and died, women
and children fainted in the streets.

And at last the people of Bethulia came to their
chief magistrate, Ozias, to ask him to come to
terms with the Assyrians. Some pleaded with him,
some shouted at him, some begged him, and some
threatened him.

At last they wore him down. Ozias promised the
people that if the rain did not fall, or help did
not arrive from Jerusalem within five days, on the

fifth day he would surrender the city to the Assyrians. And the people returned to their homes.

News of Ozias' promise reached Judith, the widow of Manassas, who had died at the time of the barley harvest from sunstroke three years and four months before. She still wore full mourning for him and fasted a good part of the year. She was very beautiful, slim and tall, and a devout woman, who used most of the great fortune her husband had left her to do good works among the poor.

Judith sent for Ozias and the elders, and when they arrived, she rebuked them with hot and angry words.

"Who are you, men of Bethulia, to test God? To set terms for Him, to relieve us in five days *or else?* For shame! It is not up to you to set conditions for God. He will help us if He wills, He will desert us if He wills. We are here to keep faith, and He is testing us for steadfastness, as He tested Abraham, Isaac, and Jacob. We must keep faith even until death, although, please God, it won't come to that."

Ozias would have said one thing, but Judith was a *very* wealthy widow, so he said another. He said, "We have given our pledge to the people, and we cannot break our pledge."

Judith interrupted, "And your pledge to God? What is that, nothing?"

Ozias went on smoothly, "You are a devout woman, Judith. Serve us as befits a devout woman, and pray to the Lord for rain."

"Listen to me, Ozias," said Judith. "You know that God prefers to help those that help them-

selves. I have a plan for us to conquer the Assyrians by our own wit and courage. Tonight I shall
leave the gates with my maid, and the day before
you have promised to surrender the town, the
Lord will deliver Israel by my hand."

Ozias listened with a face like thunder, and
when she had finished, the storm broke. "You will
not go anywhere, tonight or any other night. You
will stay right here in this house, young woman!
The nerve of you, to tell the elders of this town
how to run their affairs. Do not meddle in men's
business, Judith, or think you can escape our common fate by stealing away and selling your body.
Stick to your own affairs, and if God will still listen to you after such a speech, pray to him for
rain."

And out went the elders in an indignant body,
some of them even muttering "Traitress" and "Har-
lot" and "Whore" under their breath.

When they had gone, Judith dropped to her
knees and prayed to the Lord, and this was her
prayer.

"O Lord, our God, King of the Universe, before
You strut and prance the Assyrians, proud and
strong, boasting of their infantry, of their multitudes of horses and riders, and vowing their faith
in shield and javelin, bow and sling. We, O Lord,
who are your faithful servants, who boast and
vow only of You, will fight to worship You, and
to prevent the Assyrians from desecrating Your
sanctuary, polluting Your holy places, striking
Your sacred altar with their swords. We will fight
to the death for you. We will never surrender.

"O Lord, then pour out the vials of your wrath

upon the Assyrians. Let your fires rain upon their heads, and give me, woman as I am, the strength to achieve my end. Let their pride be shattered by a woman's hand, and then every nation will know that You alone are the Lord God, ruler of the universe, creator of heaven and earth, king of all creation, that unto You alone every knee must bend and every tongue swear loyalty. From my mouth into God's ear!"

And she remained on her knees, praying for the rest of the day.

As the fierce sun began to sink behind the mountains, Judith rose stiffly from her knees. She called her maid to her. Then she washed and dried herself, put on fragrant perfumes of rose and jasmine. She did her hair in intricate coils and loops, and put on her most beautiful clothes, the bright silks and satins threaded with gold and silver that she hadn't worn since her husband died. She put on sandals of gilded leather. Then she put on all of her golden ornaments, her anklets, bracelets, rings and earrings.

She gave to her maid a basket containing a skin of wine, a flask of oil, roasted grain, cakes of dried figs, pungent cheeses, and fine white bread.

Then each of the women put on a long hooded black robe and slipped out, black shadows in the black night, through the lines of the guards of Bethulia.

When the women reached the outposts of the Assyrians, black cutouts against the bonfires, the guards stopped them and questioned them with hard questions. Judith threw back her hood, and they fell back before her dark and glittering eyes,

her skin like the pale and glimmering moon, her
dark and glossy hair, the roseleaf of her lips. But
only for a moment. Then all the men were on their
feet, laughing, whistling between their teeth, cat-
calling, commenting on the women in the Assyrian equivalent of Anglo-Saxon four-letter words.

But Judith spoke up in icy tones.

"Stop playing the barnyard, and take me to
Holofernes. Bethulia is doomed, and I have come
to show him a secret passage to take the town."

That squelched the merriment. Two of the
guards escorted Judith and her maid right into
the center of the camp, to the tent of Holofernes.
He came out, the commander-in-chief of the Assyrian forces, tall and strong as an oak tree, as
powerful in his person as in his office. He towered
over the two women, and his armor gleamed in
the firelight.

"I am only a woman," whispered Judith, "but
perhaps I can be of help to the brave Assyrians.
My people are dying of thirst and hunger." As
she went on, her voice became stronger. "Soon,"
she said, "they will be reduced to eating prohib-
ited food, and even the offerings of grain and the
tithes of wine and oil which belong only to God
through His priests. And then will they doom
themselves! For our God is a jealous God, and He
will send forth His thunders upon them, and He
will shake His spears at them, and He will stretch
out His hand to aid you in destroying this sinful
people. And then you shall attack, and you shall
conquer without losing one Assyrian life, for our
Lord will ride with you. But I do not wish to perish
with them."

Holofernes stood there, towering in the firelight, and he listened to her words, and he watched the shadows flickering across her face, and her perfume scented the night air.

"What you say pleases me, woman of Bethulia," he said.

"My name is Judith."

"Come into my tent, Judith."

She followed the commander into his tent and looked around at the furniture of ebony and teakwood, at the hangings of purple gauze woven with gold and emeralds, all lit by silver lamps, and at the bed hung round with a curtain made of golden net, thin and fine, so closely woven that the eye could not see through.

"You will stay here with me, Judith," said Holofernes. "And after I attack, I will bring back the heads of Bethulia's leaders, and lay them at your feet, in tribute for your information—and for other things."

Judith's heart thudded within her, but her voice was calm.

"That cannot be yet, my lord," she said. "For the evil time has not yet come. And I must stay pure before the Lord until then, apart, only with my maid, eating only our clean food, and each night I will sneak through the lines and return to tell you when the moment has come. And then you will lead in your army, and the people of Bethulia will follow like sheep whose shepherd is lost, and not even a dog will growl at you. But not before then, my lord, lest my Lord God turn his spears and arrows of destruction and shower them against you instead."

"A pleasure deferred is a pleasure enhanced,"
said the gallant commander, and Judith's heart
sighed with relief. But outwardly she smiled
boldly and whispered, "Indeed, my lord."

So each night for the next three nights, Judith, accompanied by her maid, went by official orders through the sentry line of the Assyrian soldiers, until they paid her no particular heed, and she returned before morning.

On the fourth day, Judith sent word to Holofernes that she thought tonight might be the fatal night. The commander sent back his messenger inviting her to a banquet that evening. Holofernes, anticipating victory on two battlefronts, ordered double rations of food and wine for all his soldiers. By the time Judith reached his tent, most of the army were snoring in drunken slumber.

But not their commander. He had changed his armor for a soft woolen robe, his leather boots for silk sandals. And if he was on fire, it was hardly from wine. Judith was shown in by the steward, who was then ordered to leave and not reappear until sent for.

All the finery Judith had taken with her from Bethulia she wore this night. As she slowly slipped off her black outer robe, the commander made a rush at her.

"No, no, my lord," she protested, smiling. "Where is the banquet you promised me? Surely you are a man of your word!"

Holofernes smiled in return. "We will take our fences slowly then. All right. Come, taste my food." And he pointed to the gold trays set in a corner, surrounded by fat pillows.

"First, my lord, taste mine," said Judith. And she took out the pungent cheese that she had brought from Bethulia. Holofernes had never tasted such fine cheese, and soon he had finished it. But cheese rouses thirst, and soon Judith was pouring goblet after goblet for him of the strong wine she had brought with her. And then she fed him some of the dried figs, and dried figs demand more wine to refresh them, so Judith helped him over to his bed, and parted the golden net and poured him wine, more and more, and soon his fires were all quenched by wine, and Holofernes lay dead drunk upon his bed.

And then Judith took the great sword of Holofernes, and she kneeled down and she prayed to God.

"O Lord, look with favor upon Your servant, and upon what I am about to do to bring glory to Jerusalem." She went to the bed, she parted the curtains, she prayed once more. "Now give me strength, O Lord God of Israel," and she grasped his hair, and she struck. At the first blow he groaned, his neck half cut through, and at the second blow she cut off his head.

She gagged at the sight and the smell of the blood. Her eyes misted, and she clung to the golden curtain. But the Lord cleared her eyes and her mind, and swiftly she rolled the body off the bed, and under it. Then she took the head by the hair and dropped it into the skin that had held the wine. Then she and her maid, as they had done for the three nights before, slipped through the Assyrian lines, and no one spared a second glance for them.

Up to the gates of Bethulia they went, the two
women. When they were almost there, Judith sang
out exultantly, "Lift up your heads, O you gates!
God has delivered us!"

The soldiers looked with astonishment at the
two women.

"Send for Ozias!" called one, and another ran
off.

"Don't you understand? We are saved!" said
Judith impatiently, but the soldiers looked suspiciously at her. "Why aren't you at home?" asked
one. "What have you been up to, out in the night?"
asked another.

"We have been in the Assyrian camp," began
Judith.

"I knew it!" thundered Ozias, approaching with
his pack of elders. "All that talk was just an excuse
to go and play the whore with the enemy. And
then you think they'll spare you. Well, *we* won't.
Harlots! Traitresses! Arrest them!"

And the soldiers carried the women away struggling and protesting.

Ozias sat at the judgment bench, with the elders arrayed on either side of him. Judith stood
before him, still holding the skin bag.

"What have you to say for yourself, before we
pronounce sentence of death by stoning?" said
Ozias.

Judith looked up and down the row of Bethulian
leaders, then shook her head in disgust.

"Only this," she said, and pulled out by the hair
from the skin bag the bloody head of Holofernes.

If it had been the head of Medusa, the results
could not have been more dramatic. There was

silence in the hall. The judges sat turned to stone. Ozias' mouth was frozen half-open.

Then Judith walked up and down before them, swinging the head by the hair, and as she walked she said, "Praise God! For He has struck down Holofernes, the commander-in-chief of the Assyrians. And for His instrument He used the hand of a woman, and He strengthened it when I struck with the sword. And I swear to you by the name of the Lord that although my face made him lose his head, he did not sin with me, and my honor is unspotted. Then praise God in thanksgiving!"

Slowly, Ozias and the elders slid down on their knees and began to pray.

And high time, too, thought Judith, but she held her tongue.

When they had risen, and had trouble deciding where to put their eyes, Judith sat down and began to talk to them.

"Now listen to me, Ozias—I assume that now you *will* listen to me. This is what we shall do. Take this head and hang it on the battlements. At dawn, when the sun rises, take up your weapons and let yourselves be seen preparing to attack, but do not go down.

"The Assyrian sentries will run for their camp to call their generals, who will then run to call Holofernes. But they will not find him. With God's help, I have seen to that. And then, while they are beset by panic and flee from you, then set your swords at sharp edge and go down to pursue them, and you will cut them down as they run."

And without any argument, with no "buts" or "maybes," they went to do as Judith said.

The men of Bethulia appeared on the walls,
their swords and shields shining. The Assyrian
sentries ran to call their general, who ran to call
Holofernes. His steward didn't want to wake him,
because he thought the great commander was war-
ring on his bed with Judith. But at last he entered, and the tent was empty. He tore aside the
golden net and there was nothing there, but
great gouts of blood splattered the bed. And at
last he rolled out from under the bed the body
of Holofernes, and then might he call in vain, but
the headless body would never again answer any
summons.

The steward wailed and tore his clothes. Then
he rushed out to find Judith in her tent, but she
was gone and the tent was empty. So he raised the
alarm, and he cried aloud, "One Hebrew woman,
one small Hebrew woman, and she has brought
shame on Nebuchadnezzar's kingdom. Behold!
Holofernes lies on the ground in his tent, and
his head is gone!"

And all happened as Judith had foretold. Shouts
and cries, dismay, panic, and terror. The Assyrian soldiers scattered, panicked, by every path
across the plain, like ants pouring out of a ruined
anthill.

And then, high above on the mountain, Judith
saw the ants spill forth this way and that, and she
gave the signal.

Then the host of the Hebrews came down from
the hills upon the Assyrians like wolves upon a
sheepfold, and they cut down the soldiers as they
ran, they put their old enemies to sleep with
swords. And then the men from Jerusalem and

Gilead and Galilee, arriving to help lift the siege, outflanked the Assyrians as they fled, and cut them off on their flanks.

And then there was rejoicing in Bethulia.

"Glory to God!" cried the people.

"Glory to God!" sang Judith, and the women crowned her with olive leaves, and they sang and danced before the gates, and Judith led the women in the dance.

"Hail, woman of valor," cried out Joachim, the high priest of Jerusalem, who had just arrived with his men. And "Hail, woman of valor," echoed Ozias and the elders and the people of Bethulia.

Then the soldiers went down and despoiled the camp of the Assyrians, bringing back the flocks and the herds, the gold and the silver. The tent of Holofernes, with its silver and gold, its couches and bowls and furniture, they brought to Judith for her share.

But Judith gave all her spoils of war to the poor, saying, "After all, I'm only a woman. What was so wonderful that I did? It was the Lord working through me."

And, rather to Ozias' relief, Judith returned to her estate, where she lived quietly for the rest of her life. She had many suitors, but she chose none of them, and remained unmarried all her days. And during her lifetime, and for many years after her death, no one dared to threaten the Israelites again.

I finished, and there was a gratifying murmur of appreciation.

"Wow!" said the Gentile girl, tossing her blond ponytail. "That was *super!*"

"Thank you," I said. "But I don't know what opportunities there are for Judiths nowadays. Can you imagine any of us doing such a thing?"

"*I* can," said the Gentile girl, but very softly.

"Well," said the Interfaith Chairperson, "first Judith would probably form a committee . . ."

"No, no!" interrupted the Cabdriver's wife. (She turned out to be as forthright and overwhelming as her husband.) "She'd go into politics, she'd walk the streets, shake hands, campaign, she'd get elected, and then she'd get action. Like Bella Abzug!" Her eyes were shining.

"I love her hats," sighed the Widow.

"One thing's for sure," said the Interfaith Lieutenant firmly. "She gets no help from the Bible. All that's in there, well, almost, is a man's world."

"You're right," agreed the Widow. "Why couldn't one of those Bible writers, just one of them, have been a woman?"

"No," said the Art Dealer's wife, which startled us a little, since she generally spoke only to her husband. "We need some changes, but they'll have to come from somewhere else. Not from the Bible. But politics, I don't know." And she shook her sleek black head dubiously.

"What we need are leaders!" exclaimed the Interfaith Chairperson, her cheeks glowing. She was obviously ready to woman the barricades.

"Yes," agreed the Philanthropist's wife, with a large sweep of her arm, which accidentally jostled the English Professor and made him drop his pipe. "Who will lead us?"

"Let's see," I said. "We have a tennis player available. And a big television personality. Or— I know—how about Miss America? Will she do?"

Up spoke Harry Bailley, with a chivalrous flourish of his cowboy hat. "I'll be happy to lead you, girls."

There was a brief silence.

Then the Widow said, slowly and with dignity, "Sorry, Mr. Bailley. You're a very nice man. But you're not eligible."

And "Nothing personal!" piped up the Cabdriver's wife in an uncanny mimicry of the Caterer. (None of us suspected she had such a talent.)

Then, most unexpectedly of all, the Rabbi's Wife said severely, but with a little half-smile playing at the corners of her mouth, "Father, please, I'd rather do it myself."

We all looked at her with surprise and admiration. And then she went on resolutely, "We won't despair. We'll have faith in God—"

"And She will provide!" I concluded the old joke in a loud, clear voice, and all the women united in laughter and applause as the bus roared into Bethlehem.

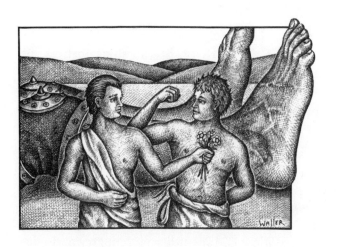

THE ADULT BOOKSTORE OWNER: BROTHERLY LOVE

BETHLEHEM itself was a surprise and even something of a disappointment. It was hot and dusty. Manger Square was a parking lot, and the town was crammed with tourists, and the Arabs here were shopkeepers who put trade before politics. Their hands stretched out toward us and their voices followed us along the narrow, steep streets, imploring, wheedling, whining, Buy, buy, buy.

We had gone our ways according to our inclinations.

Some of us followed Harry Bailley to the Church of the Nativity, a grim stone fortress, lit inside by ornate brass chandeliers burning oil and still decked this April afternoon with huge shiny Christmas balls.

Some of us went with the Interfaith Lieutenant back to Rachel's tomb, where the matriarch lies weeping for her children, and barren women circle around and around, weaving webs of thread, hoping to conceive children they can then weep for.

The Widow had spent her morning trying to determine exactly which of the half-parched fields had once been the lush green paradise in which Ruth met Boaz. (She never did.)

So it was a tired and dispirited bunch that gathered to wait for the bus. As I was about to step aboard, the Adult Bookstore Owner spoke to me for the very first time on the trip.

"Is it accurate to talk about, you know, a *castrating woman* if it's the *head* she cuts off?" he asked spitefully, and nudged his companion, the pretty young boy, and they giggled together like schoolgirls as they pushed on the bus ahead of me.

I know what my mother would have said to him. She would have said, "You could have waited a hundred years before saying that." But I'm a slow reactor, and I only think of the right remark at the wrong moment, too late, when the other driver is far ahead in the distance, or the person who shoved me is already in the next subway car. Some of you may know what I mean. It's a double burden, because besides being angry at the other person, you end up being angry at yourself. Maybe *angrier* at yourself.

By the time I thought through all of this, they
were already sitting down, heads together, toward
the front of the bus. So I decided just to sit down
myself and forget it. But my temper was a little
frayed, I'll admit it. And judging from what happened just a little later, other people's tempers
were frayed too.

We received gratefully the juicy oranges that
Harry Bailley had for us, and were eating them
while he tried to console the Widow for her failure
to locate Ruth's field. He explained that the field,
however unidentifiable, was nonetheless terribly
important.

"You see," he said, "that grain field really gave
the town its name, because Bethlehem is in the
Hebrew *Bet-Lechem*, House of Bread, you get it?"

"House of Bread, ha!" said the Merchant, and
he laughed a short, sharp bark of a laugh, like
Prussian officers were supposed to (I read that
somewhere). "It should be House of Bed! That's
where women buy and sell, in bed."

"Oh, yes," spoke up the Adult Bookstore Owner.
He seemed to be in a chatty mood. "A sage, a
disciple of Rabbi Akiba, or one of those rabbis,
anyway, he said that a woman is disgusting and
smells disgusting, and that refraining from women
assures, you know, a *crown* in the world to come."

The Cabdriver turned white and then red. He
swelled like a turkey-cock, and rose up in his
seat, gripping the hand bar in front of him till his
knuckles were white. Then he lowered his head
and bulled down the aisle to where the Adult
Bookstore Owner was sitting. He reached down
and jerked him up by his velour pullover.

"You smell disgusting, and you *are* disgusting,"

spat the Cabdriver. "I don't like you, and I don't like any of your kind, and if you don't apologize right this minute to my wife and the other ladies on this bus, I'm gonna throw you out of the window!"

I have to say this for the Adult Bookstore Owner. The Cabdriver was twice as broad as he was, and he held a fistful of his shirt. He was sizzling like he was going to explode. But the Adult Bookstore Owner spoke right up to him.

"What, you know, *kind* am I?" he said.

"You know, you know," mimicked the Cabdriver. "*You know* what kind you are. A *faygeleh*, a fairy, a queer."

"Doesn't anybody want a chocolate bar?" asked the Philanthropist plaintively. But the combatants paid no attention.

"I'm the same kind as you are," said the Adult Bookstore Owner, and he picked the Cabdriver's hand off him and he smoothed his pullover. "I am a *person*."

The Dropout was on his feet, holding high his guitar. "He's right, he's right. There's only one kind, that's *humankind*."

Now that, of course, is a lovely sentiment, and right and proper from a fine young boy, especially one who's just setting out to see the world. But quite honestly, looking at the Cabdriver and the Adult Bookstore Owner as they were now, nose to nose, they did seem to belong to different species. The Cabdriver was a huge bull of a man, while the Adult Bookstore Owner, I don't know, he kind of minced when he walked, and he wore gold bracelets and neck chains so he tinkled as

he moved, and he and his pretty young boy companion would slap each other's wrists playfully,
and then giggle together. No, they seemed to be
different all right, like the Cabdriver had said. But
of course they were both human beings, like the
Dropout had said.

Then I had to laugh at myself. I was like the
rabbi in the old story, you probably remember it.
A man and his wife are arguing, arguing all the
time. So they come to the rabbi, he should decide
which of them is right and which is wrong.

The husband goes first. He presents his griev-
ances, the rabbi strokes his beard and he says,
"You're right."

Then comes the turn of the wife, and when she
finishes the rabbi strokes his beard and he says,
"You're right."

Well, the rabbi's disciple is there, and he can't
bear it any more. He jumps up and he says, "Rabbi!
You just told him he's right and you told her she's
right. That's impossible! They can't both be right!"

The rabbi listens to him, strokes his beard, and
he says, "You're right too!"

What was happening to me in this strange land?
Clearly I was losing my grip.

Anyway, the Adult Bookstore Owner looked
gratefully at the Dropout. Then he tossed his head,
making the sparse curls wag, and he said to the
Cabdriver, "You have your way and I have my
way, and my way is just as good as yours."

"That it is not!" said the Rabbi sharply. Which
surprised the rest of us, because we'd never heard
him raise his voice like that before. "It is your
way," said the Rabbi, "and you are free to follow

it. But it is not a good way, and you are not free to
preach it to others."

The Adult Bookstore Owner started to say something, but then he stopped and seemed to think
for a bit. The Cabdriver moved off down the aisle
back to his own seat, muttering words I tried
my best not to hear as he went. The Adult Bookstore Owner smiled, a sweet smile but a little secret, maybe *inward* is what I mean. And then he
said, "I will be a good little boy, and tell a story,
and no one will be upset by poor little me, because my story comes right from the Bible, and it
will be about heroes, the kind you all like, real,
you know, *he-man* heroes, and about love of a
highly moral kind. It will be about brotherly love.

"And when I'm finished—" here he looked spitefully across to the Cabdriver—"we'll see what kind
of love God sanctifies and calls *good* and *natural*."

THE ADULT BOOKSTORE OWNER'S STORY

KING SAUL, you've already heard about King Saul,
King Saul was being tormented by an evil spirit
from God, which manifested itself as terrible mi-
graine headaches. So his servants suggested he
hire a musician, someone to pluck the strings of
the lyre and make sweet sounds to drive away the
evil spirit. So they went out and found a young
shepherd boy, ready for some excitement after the
long nights up in the hills with nothing but a
bunch of sheep to, you know, entertain himself
with. His name was David, the son of Jesse, and

he's described very fully in the Bible. He was
young, tender-eyed, peach-skinned, handsome, and
a very talented musician.

Saul fell in love with him at first sight. It says
so, "And Saul loved him greatly," and he made
David his armor-bearer, and he sent a messenger
to Jesse, the father, saying, "Let David remain
forever in my service, for he has found favor in my
sight." Whenever Saul had those really *foul* headaches, David would play upon his, you know,
lyre, and Saul was refreshed.

Now Saul had a son about David's age. The son
was named Jonathan, another handsome young
man, and he'd been away for some months with a
young friend. They said they were fighting
against the Philistines. Jonathan returned home
just in time for that really thrilling scene when
young David, ruddy and comely in appearance,
takes out his teensy little slingshot and kills Goliath, the Philistines' gross giant-fighter. And it says
in the Bible, "When David had finished, the soul of
Jonathan was knit to the soul of David, and
Jonathan loved him as his own soul." Just like his
father before him, Jonathan loved David at first
sight.

Furthermore, Jonathan made a covenant with
David. He stripped off his own robe and gave it
to David, and his sword and his bow and arrows.
You have to remember, though, that Saul also
loved David, in fact he loved him first, and he had
taken him home that day and wouldn't let him return to his father's house.

But Saul was jealous, too, because when they
returned to the palace after David's battle with

that nasty Goliath, the women of Israel came forth jumping around, singing and dancing, and they sang in their shrill voices:

Saul has slain his thousands,
And David his tens of thousands.

So Saul was still attracted to David, but he was also suspicious of him because of public opinion. And besides, he was jealous because there was clearly a thing going on between Jonathan and David. To break it up, Saul gave David his daughter Michal in marriage. But it didn't help. Saul's paranoia grew.

Here was David, so attractive and beautiful to listen to and to look at. He'd alienated Saul's son and daughter from him, and worse, he seemed to have dropped Saul, who was going gray and just the teensiest bit paunchy. So Saul's anger and jealousy and suspicion and frustration built up until, one day, he blew. He gave orders to Jonathan, his son, and to all his servants, to kill David on sight.

But Jonathan delighted in David, that's the Bible's word, *delighted* in him, so he told David what Saul was planning, and David went and hid.

Then Jonathan tried to talk Saul out of killing David, and after he talked till his mouth was dry and he was spitting cotton, he succeeded. So, for the time being, the two, Saul and David, were reconciled.

But then that evil spirit—remember it?—came upon Saul (right after another fabulous victory of David's, it just happened) and Saul threw a spear at him without warning. But he missed, and David escaped.

He came to Jonathan and he said, "What have I done? What is my guilt? What is my sin before your father, that he wants to kill me?"

Jonathan said, "Not *again*. We just went through all that. Look, if my father had changed his mind and wanted to kill you again, I'd know about it. He tells me everything, absolutely everything."

But David said, "Don't be naïve. Your father knows perfectly well that I have found favor in your eyes, so he's *afraid* to tell you. But I know, as I live and breathe, there's just a step between me and death."

And Jonathan said, "Look, what do you want me to do? Because I'll do anything you want, whatever you say, always."

The two of them made up a plan so they could find out what Saul was up to. Then they went out together into the field for a while, and Jonathan and David swore to their love for each other, as great as the love of their own souls. Those are the words of the Bible.

When Jonathan sounded out Saul on the subject at dinner, Saul flew into a rage, and he said, "You son of a perverse, rebellious woman, I know that you have chosen the son of Jesse before *me* to your own shame, and to the shame of your mother's nakedness. That son of Jesse, that David, must die."

Jonathan got up from the table, absolutely furious, and he hurried to warn David to get out of town. And they kissed one another, it says so, they fell on one another's neck and they kissed one another, and they wept with one another, and then the lovers were torn apart by the jealous hatred of a third.

So David went off into the wilderness, an outlaw, and he had many adventures. Meanwhile, back home, Jonathan was grieving for him until all his old spirit had gone out of him. He wanted to find David and rejoin him, but David seemed to have vanished into the desert. So Jonathan pined away for love, and Saul grieved to see it, but his son would no longer respond to his father's overtures. So the two of them, father and son, found no comfort, but they were sick with love and longing, and cared not one bit whether they lived or died.

When the Philistines came up against Saul's army, the men of Israel, demoralized, fled and were killed on Mount Gilboa, and Saul's son Jonathan, the apple of his eye, the flower of his heart, was killed among them, and Saul was wounded. Saul clung to Jonathan's dead body, and he kissed him and he wept, because he had lost everything, his son, and his David, and his army, and his own self-respect. Then he said to his armor-bearer, "Draw your sword and kill me with it." But the armor-bearer, who was hardly more than a little boy, was afraid to, so Saul drew his own sword, and he fell on it.

When the Philistines came to strip the dead bodies, they found Saul and Jonathan fallen on Mount Gilboa. They cut off their heads and stripped off their armor and sent messengers throughout the land to carry the good news to the Philistines.

At last the news traveled to David, by a soldier
who'd escaped from the camp of Israel. When
David heard of the death of his first protector, and
the death of his best-beloved, he fell down in a
swoon, and then he tore his clothes and heaped
ashes on his head. He mourned, and wept, and
fasted, and he took up his lyre, and he sang this
bitter lament:

> *The beauty of Israel is slain upon thy high*
> *   places:*
> *How are the mighty fallen!*

> *Tell it not in Gath,*
> *Publish it not in the streets of Askelon*
> *Lest the daughters of the Philistines rejoice,*
> *Lest the daughters of the uncircumcised*
> *   triumph. . . .*

> *Saul and Jonathan were lovely and pleasant in*
> *   their lives,*
> *And in their death they were not divided:*
> *They were swifter than eagles,*
> *They were stronger than lions. . . .*

> *How are the mighty fallen*
> *In the midst of the battle!*

> *I am distressed for thee, my brother Jonathan*
> *Very pleasant hast thou been unto me:*
> *Thy love to me was wonderful,*
> *Passing the love of women.*

"Yes," repeated the Adult Bookstore Owner, and
his face was exalted and his tongue relished the
words, "Thy love to me was wonderful, passing the
love of women."

"No!" cried the Rabbi. "Distortion, perversion, blasphemy! You want to turn the Torah itself into the kind of filth you peddle in your store. Woe unto them that call evil good, and good evil."

"Well, I like that!" said the Adult Bookstore Owner. "What is evil in my story? It is a beautiful love story, a tragedy, and it comes from the Bible, just like the stories of Ruth and Boaz, and Jacob and Rachel. Only those people who are narrow and self-righteous close their eyes and pick and choose. *My* story stands with the others."

The Rabbi half-rose to his feet, trembling.

"What is *evil*, Rabbi?" said the Adult Bookstore Owner primly. "What is evil is the *yetzer hara*, the evil inclination, the belief that you are closer to God than anyone else. See, I have studied a little, too. The *yetzer hara* is the vanity of the 'good' man, the same vanity as belongs to criminals."

"God forbid," said the Rabbi, "that I should think that way of myself, that I am closer to God than another. Or that I should speak with the *lashon hara*, the evil tongue, the tongue that is so arrogant that it believes it can speak about another."

"Then don't be so quick to condemn, Rabbi," retorted the Adult Bookstore Owner. "From your own mouth you have said it."

"You twist and turn," said the Rabbi, as he subsided into his seat. "But the lips of falsehood will grow dumb, says the Psalmist, that David whom you have slandered, when they speak in arrogance against the righteous. The Gentiles have a saying, 'Even the devil can quote Scripture.'"

"Are you calling me a devil?"

"Yes, but not for the reason that you may think. Not for what you are, but because you do the devil's work. You pervert the truth, and preach the gospel of evil as if it were good. You lay mines for the unwary, and dig pits for the innocent."

The English Professor spoke up in his most reasonable tones. "Surely, Rabbi, you are behind the times. In the Renaissance, among the Greeks, such practices were accepted commonplaces. And today, modern society says—"

"Society!" spat the Rabbi. "If only one man speaks the truth, his voice must silence multitudes who lie. If thousands, even millions, were to say murder is right, or adultery, or idolatry, does that make them right? No, no, NO!"

The Rabbi had risen again to his feet, flushed with anger and breathing heavily. His wife laid her hand over his hand gripping the armrest, and she smoothed it as one would a child's because, although there were no outward signs yet in his face, she and he both knew that his cancer was terminal, and he had chosen, as the Bible enjoins, to die and be gathered to his fathers in Jerusalem.

The Rabbi slumped down again in his seat, beads of sweat pearling his now pale forehead. The atmosphere in the bus was electric.

Too many people, I thought, too close together, too long.

"Well, well," said Harry Bailley comfortably. "Life is too short to waste it arguing. The Lord made us all different, and we know He moves in mysterious ways His wonders to perform, so who knows? We must all serve *some* purpose or other."

He looked at the Adult Bookstore Owner and his companion and smiled a little. "Some of His ways are just a little more mysterious than others, that's all."

"I have to tell you," said the Mashgiach, raising his bushy eyebrows comically, "that certainly was a different story from what I remember from Sunday School. But we live and learn, live and learn."

Harry Bailley gratefully seized his opportunity. "And we have all lived together these past few days, and we have learned from each other.

"Your stories have been wonderful," he said, "all of them. And are there any more? If so be it that the urge to talk should strike one of you who has up to now stayed silent, speak quickly or forever hold your peace, for we are almost coming to Jerusalem."

Each one craned to look at a neighbor, but no one spoke.

"So," said Harry Bailley. "We are finished. And did I not fulfill my promise to you, that the miles would disappear and you would be entertained all the way to Jerusalem?"

He looked around for applause, but what he got was a timid question from the Dropout.

"Please—who won?"

And then came a hail, a shower, a downpour of questions from everyone. "Who won?" "Who?" "Who?"

"Ah, yes," said Harry Bailley, and he nodded wisely. "There must always be a winner. So who won? Let me answer your question in the Jewish manner, with a question. My question is, 'Who lost?'"

I guess everyone was as taken aback as I was, because a deep quiet fell over the bus. We looked at each other and then at our guide.

"That is the right answer," he cried triumphantly. "*No one* lost!" His white teeth shone in his full black beard and his cowboy hat was cocked at a rakish angle and he radiated energy and vitality, enough to bathe us all in his rays. "You are winners one and all, and for reward—you will each treat each other to the finest dinner the King David Hotel can provide to welcome the Sabbath in Jerusalem."

His enthusiasm was infectious, and we were all applauding the cleverness of this Harry Bailley, this Solomon, this judge in Israel, when the Caterer broke in.

"And you," he said. "While we provide the dinners for our own prizes, what will *you* do for us?"

Harry Bailley smiled, a slow broad smile like the rising of the sun. "Me? I will sing for you *zemirot*, after-dinner songs, happy songs, songs of praise, as is our tradition. And you will join me in our songs, in Jerusalem."

And everyone seemed happy, and everyone seemed satisfied.

All but me.

If you put it like that—who lost?—then I had to agree with Harry Bailley. No one lost. Every story (of course I liked some better than others, that's only natural), but every story had the ring of truth about it. And yet they seemed removed from my life. I tried to imagine King David and Jonathan, the son of Saul, as homosexuals. I couldn't. I thought back to that other story of brotherly love, the Executive Director's, and I tried to imagine any of us on that bus meeting in a field, our arms heaped with love offerings. But I couldn't. I wondered how many of us would sacrifice our children for our faith, or take a life for our people, or survive in Hell. I wondered how much compassion we would show for the stranger among us, especially if that stranger bore an uncouth shape.

What do I think of miracles? I wondered. If one happened to occur, would I recognize it? Or was all that the rankest primitive superstition?

And then I wondered, Is God all-knowing, great, and merciful, or cruel, jealous, and unfeeling? Are men brave and noble, or weak and cowardly? Does love sustain and exalt, or deceive and debase? I tried to put all these stories together, to reconcile them, to make them come together in one statement:

This is a hero.

This is what charity is.

This is the meaning of love, and marriage, and men and women.

But for every truth we had heard, there was an opposite, and the opposite was also true.

Then what good is truth, when truth itself is false?

And these thoughts whirled around inside my mind, big black ideas swollen like thunderheads, small thin wisps of hints of explanations, a fiery comet here and inky blackness beyond it. Our trip, all of us, these stories, my own mind, all was *tohuvavohu*, chaos, like the universe before God touched it, and very uncomfortable it was.

And then a great wave of sadness swept over

me. What was happening to me in this strange
land? Not creation, as I had hoped and dreamed,
but its opposite.

The road has been long, the bus is bumpy,
spears of sunlight dazzle my eyes. I hear my
neighbors speak and the more I hear, the less I
understand. We are a holy people in a holy land,
but little I have heard seems holy. All of us have
come with questions on this pilgrimage. But who
of us has received any answers? The way we
came here, that's the way we seem still to be. And
when we return, will we still be the same? Then
for what did we come?

I peer out the tinted windows of the bus and see
through a glass, darkly. When shall I see directly,
face to face? Before I know it, we will be in Jerusalem, and if nothing happens, how will I bear it?

The end of the journey.

Jerusalem.

Just another city.

Please, God.

I remember the story of Rabbi Haninya, the
martyr. The Romans wrapped him in a parchment
scroll of the Torah, and then set him on fire. His
students called out to him, "Master, what do you
see?" He answered, "The parchment is burning,
but the letters are flying to the heavens!" And he
died.

I am not fit to touch the hem of a Rabbi
Haninya. I am afraid of a spider. The mere imagin-
ing of a bomb on a bus fills me with terror. The
courage to stand fast in the flames to hallow the
Holy Name I am afraid is far beyond me. I had
thought in my vanity that in this air, if God should

choose to smile, perhaps these stories—twenty-two of them, like the twenty-two letters in the *Alef Bet*—poor limping creatures as they are, might take wing and fly toward the heavens.

I don't know. There is a saying I once read: Of making many books there is no end, and much study is a weariness of the flesh. I am tired, and there is no end in sight.

It is a long way since morning.

And then the Rabbi, with his ugly features and his beautiful voice like music, began to speak.

THE RABBI: IN MY END IS MY BEGINNING

JERUSALEM lies thirty-one degrees, forty-seven minutes north latitude, and thirty-five degrees fourteen minutes east of Greenwich, forty miles from the Mediterranean coast, centrally located between Eilat in the south and Metullah in the north. It can, however, be located as accurately in the soul as it can on the map, because it is not only a physical state, but a condition of mind in a state of being.

Jerusalem is a city of stones and dreams, the spir- 307

itual True North of Judaism—and a lot of other
people's religions, too. But I am Jewish, therefore
my sermon will be about what I know, about
Judaism. And if a sermon doesn't exactly light
your fire, well, you can close your eyes and take
a little nap, and I'll ask a neighbor to nudge you
when I am almost finished.

So. About Judaism. One important thing about it
is that it is a very practical religion. It does not,
for example, tell you to love your neighbor as
yourself because love, love is a very big word. We
toss it around a lot. We love this one and that, we
love our dog, our cat, our new car, music, fishing,
jelly beans. To love, really to love, is difficult above
all. It is hard enough to love our wives, our husbands. It may be harder still to love our parents
or our children. It is surely hardest of all to love
ourselves. Then, too, who knows that what *I* love,
you will love? I love going to museums, you hate
it.

So what Judaism teaches is, That which is hate-
ful to you, don't do that to your neighbor. After
all, it's easy enough to know what we *don't* like,
and maybe it's even possible to refrain from doing
it to the next person.

Judaism recognizes that people are only people,
and therefore human, not divine, and therefore
fallible. For instance, here is a sample of rabbinic
reasoning. You may not like it. You may find it
oversubtle, or picky. But listen anyway.

Twice in the Torah you are enjoined about
your parents.

In Deuteronomy 5.16 you are told to honor thy
father and thy mother, that thy days may be long
upon the land.

Leviticus 19.3 says, You shall fear every man his mother and his father, and you shall keep my Sabbaths.

The rabbis noticed, like you noticed right now, that the order is reversed in those two commands. That is, when it comes to honor, father comes first. And when it comes to fear, mother comes first.

Why should this be?

Rabbi Judah Ha-Nasi, Judah the Prince, says it is because each command goes *contrary* to a person's natural inclinations (to follow which, one doesn't need commands).

A child already honors the mother more, because it is she who is closest to the child, who is with the child all the time, swaying him with her words. And a child already fears the father more, because he is less familiar, remote, off doing deeds in the unknown world, and because it is the father who teaches the child the Torah.

Therefore the child is commanded to *honor* the father whom he already fears, and to *fear* the mother whom he already honors.

Now please, don't get all aggravated and psychological about that word "fear." It means a healthy respect and awe, and we could do with a little more of it in our world. Natural reverence, maybe you could call it. It's what is meant in the saying, The fear of the Lord is the beginning of wisdom.

You don't walk up to God and clap him on the back, good buddy.

But I was talking about Judaism as a practical religion, recognizing the frailty of humanity. It is, and it does, so much so that sometimes we forget another side of Judaism. In that other side, our human limitations do not excuse us from our spiritual obligation, which is to live up to that spark of the divine which is within each and every one of us in this world. In short, to be Godlike, as we are made like God, in His image.

That, of course, is impossible.

A dilemma.

The rabbis saw that the only escape is between the horns of that dilemma into paradox. So Rabbi Tarfon says, It is not incumbent upon you to complete the task, yet you are not free to desist from it. To do the impossible while recognizing that it *is* impossible, that is what we are called upon to do.

If you take it seriously, it certainly keeps you awake and on your tiptoes!

Jews have another peculiarity that people comment on a lot. They always answer a question with a question. Well, why not? It reflects a special insight of our people, the knowledge that in this life there are no answers. All there are are questions. Two questions above all, and they are the same two that we ask always on this bus. Where have we come from? Where are we going?

There is a geographic answer to such questions, like the location of Jerusalem in degrees of latitude and longitude. But otherwise, no answers. The problem is that we don't allow "I don't know" as an answer. Nor even "I don't know now, but someday I will." That's not enough for us. We have to *know* everything.

But where is it written that a man—or a woman —must know everything? We know next to noth-

ing! When we get out of bed in the morning, we
don't even know if we will return to it that night.

We want to know, to know, always to know. We
are *scientists*. This is Latin, *scio*, *scire*, the active
verb, active, you notice, to know. We look everywhere for answers that we assume exist. We look
to science, history, philosophy, psychology, soci-
ology, even (as a last resort, maybe?) to theol-
ogy. All of them have answers, generally different
answers, and all are narrow, partial, and limited.

For that matter, how do we *know* the planet
Mars isn't carried around by an angel?

What do we choose to do when we're forced to
admit, as we are sooner or later, that we don't
know? Well, we can sit in a corner all day with a
shawl over our heads, wailing and moaning,
afraid to do anything. Or we can sit and end-
lessly discuss the philosophical implications of our
limited knowledge. Or we can curse whatever we
can think of to curse because of what befalls us
that we cannot foresee or control.

I'll tell you one thing we *can't* do. We can't take
this bus and storm the gates of heaven with it!

But we keep on with our questions, to which
there are no answers. Why does evil exist? All
right. Why do earthquakes and tornadoes
and plagues and droughts and floods exist? Evil is
an earthquake and a tornado and a plague and a
drought and a flood taking place in a human
soul.

I don't know why any of them exists. It is
enough for me to know that they are *evil things*.

Why Auschwitz? You think you will catch me
there. If there is a God, you say, He couldn't per-

mit Auschwitz. But I say to you, how could He prevent it? Auschwitz happened because of an earthquake of evil in the hearts of those who committed
the atrocities, and because of an evil drought in
the hearts of those who saw and turned away.

We can't blame God for what men have chosen
to do. We are not automata, robots, little mechanical men to run about when someone turns a key,
puppets to dance to another's strings. We are *men*.

If God were to interfere, that would make us
nothing but children all our lives, and so we are,
all His children. But we are grownup children.
Ours is the power to make decisions, and ours is
the necessity to suffer consequences.

But with limited knowledge—never forget that.
We can only know what our eyes can see, our
ears can hear, our mouths can taste, our bodies
can touch, our hearts can feel, our heads can
comprehend. How perfect is that?

There is a lovely parable about truth. God's
truth. Once it existed as a beautiful crystal. But
when God handed it to man, man dropped it, and
the crystal of truth shattered to bits. And all we
can do now is go about to find and collect the
glittering fragments, each one beautiful, but only
one small sliver of the glorious whole, which can
never be collected by any one person in a human
lifetime.

Let me ask you a question. Did you ever try to
look at the world the other way around? From
God's perspective? Here we all are, looking up at
the heavens, always asking God for something,
nagging Him, cursing Him, pleading with Him,
bargaining with Him. You think things are easy
for Him? And we have each other. God has no one.

There is a legend that says, After Adam had 313
finished naming all the animals, he came to God ———
downcast.

"What's the matter?" God asked him. "Is something wrong with my garden?"

"No, everything is perfect. It's just that all the
animals have another of their kind, but I am alone,
and lonely."

And God said, "It is not good for man to be
alone." So God gave Adam Eve. But for God,
there is no one. An American President once
said, "This is the loneliest job in the world."
But he was wrong. God has the loneliest job in the
world. That's why He created man. But man, although a pretty good creation, is not His equal, so
God is still alone, and lonely.

And He is also in pain. He is a God who suffers.
He shares in all men's sorrows. Each of us only has
to bear his own pain. But God feels everyone's
pain. Someone among you will say, "Then why
doesn't He make everyone happy?" But only the
person who hands over his daily life to God can
even ask that question. What I mean is, when
people said an earthquake or a plague or a bank-
ruptcy or a sickness was *caused* by God, or a marriage or a rainbow or great riches or a flower was
caused by God, then they might blame Him, because they were also prepared to thank Him.
But we no longer do this. We know the *natural
cause* of everything. God, for us, if He exists for
us at all, is the First Cause that began all the other
causes, and after that, He doesn't mix in. That's
all right with me. (With God probably it's all
right too.) But then we can't go around blaming
Him for everything, either. Certainly not for wars,

or Hitlers, or the evils that men do to other men, for the spite and the malice and the jealousy, or for our being mortal, which means someday, no matter what else happens to us, someday we will die.

Everything that is born will die. Everything that grows must wither. Everything that begins must end. That is the first and only important fact of life. And so we suffer, being born.

All of that suffering God feels, millions upon millions of tragedies, numberless as the stars in the heavens or the grains of sand on the shore, from the world's first day to the end of eternity.

Our air is filled with music and pictures and chatter, with radio waves and TV and CB and I don't know what else. The heavenly air is filled with wails and groans and shrieks and terrible, terrible silences. So, God is a suffering God. And what about the joys, you ask? What about the *simchas?* Of course He feels those too! Otherwise even God would not be able to bear the burden of this world, and it would have to be destroyed for His own protection.

And anyway, even if He were to mix in and suspend the laws of the universe and create havoc in His own created world, what kind of *chutzpah,* what kind of arrogance is it to expect Him to do so for *me?*

"God didn't answer my prayer, so I won't believe in Him." That is a child speaking. Not a grownup.

Of course, there is grownup and grownup. When I was a young boy I used to think that there was a condition of "being grownup," and in this

condition one would know everything. One
would be certain of right and wrong, of what to
do at any time and in any situation. One wouldn't,
in this blissful condition of "being grownup," any
longer be shy, or afraid, or jealous, or fearful, or
helpless, or perplexed.

I am now within sight of threescore and ten
years, and do you know something? I have never
arrived at such a condition. I am beginning to
think it may not exist! For to be fully grownup,
I think, is to be God, or to be one with God, and
there is only one door to the dwelling place of God,
and that is through the grave.

And here is something foolish about me that I
must tell you. I know that death is the doorway to
God's dwelling, which is where I have always
wanted to be. And now I stand before the door,
and it is beginning to open, and I am afraid!

Like people say about New York, God's dwelling
is a nice place to visit, but I am not ready to live
there.

We come to this inn, the world, and we find it
comfortably furnished with all the provisions and
utensils we need for a pleasant stay, and if we are
wise, when the time comes we are ready to leave
willingly and gladly, with grateful thanks. But I
find I am of the foolish folk who mistake the inn for
a permanent dwelling place and are shocked and
horrified to find that it is not, that we must leave.

And I should know better! It is my business, my
profession to know better, to know that we get up
in the morning of our life, and we know nothing
of what will happen to us by nightfall.

The rabbis said, Why do people rejoice and

cheer when a ship leaves port? Who knows where it is going, and what it will encounter on its way? When we should cheer is when the ship, having survived storms and winds and battering waves, arrives safely back in port.

So then should we rejoice when a soul, having survived the storms of a lifetime, comes safe home. Better is the end of a thing than its beginning, and the day of death than the day of one's birth.

There is a funny English nursery rhyme mothers tell to their children, bouncing them on their knees. "To market, to market, to buy a fat pig" (not to eat, of course, when Jewish mothers are concerned), "Home again, home again, jiggety-jig." We are sojourners, all of us, going to market, going to school, going to business, going through Israel on this bus, all sojourners, going somewhere. In the Torah, what is said two times is truer than true. So now I tell you, when market is over, at the end of everything, the end of the road, of the journey, of this trip, of our lives, at the end we go home again, home again. All of us, home again, home again.

And now, if your neighbor is sleeping, wake him up, because at last we have reached the benediction.

O Lord, bless this bus and all who travel in it. May their eyes be opened to each other and to You, and everything that lies between may they see for what it really is, clearly and unveiled. Grant us the courage to say "I don't know" without being ashamed or losing faith. May the Lord bless us, and keep us. May He make His face shine upon us, and be gracious unto us. May He lift up his countenance upon us, and give us peace.

You have blessed us in our comings, may You bless us in our goings.

And now, I pray, may the words of my mouth and the meditations of my heart be acceptable unto Thee, O Lord, my Rock and my Redeemer, from generation to generation, world without end, Amen.

The last words of the Rabbi dripped like honey into a silence that had swelled to fill the tour bus. Then the silence was cut by the click of the intercom and the metallic rasp of an electronic voice, Harry Bailley's voice.

"Ladies and gentlemen, friends, if you look out the right-hand windows of the bus, you will see something well worth seeing."

The sun slanted its evening rays from the west. There before us and above stood the spires and towers, towers and domes of Jerusalem, the setting sun gilding them all until the stones of Jerusalem shone like gold, the stones of Paradise, the golden city, *Yerushalayim shel Zahav*, Jerusalem the Golden, gleaming at sunset, floating above us.

In that golden light there came a white light, and the golden light was in the bus and all around us, but the white light burned within me. And in that flash of light, suddenly I saw.

Lines of pilgrims, on horseback, plodding toward Canterbury. On foot, trudging toward Mecca. On wheels of every size and material, riding toward Jerusalem. Over the miles, over the years, parallel lines of pilgrims, all of us, marching separately toward that Place where parallels meet and all contraries are reconciled.

Even as that white light flashed, it faded and

was gone. But the golden light remained there in the bus, enfolding us all, lighting us the way home, the golden light, the peace of Jerusalem.

How filled with awe is this place, and I did not know it!

A dip in the road, the bus genuflected and then accelerated toward the waiting City.

I have been many places, and I have done many things, and I have followed other ways and studied other teachings. And in the end I have returned.

If I forget thee, O Jerusalem,
Let my right hand forget her cunning.
Let my tongue cleave to the roof of my mouth;
If I do not remember thee,
If I do not set Jerusalem above my highest joy.